EARTH BELOW US

R.V. TYSON

Book I

Spirit Life Sci-Fi Adventure Series

Trending to #1 in Amazon rankings
for Christian Futuristic Fiction!

Earth Below Us is a work of fiction. Names, characters,
places, and incidents either are the product of the author's
imagination or are used fictitiously.

ISBN 978-0-692-09277-4 (Paperback)

Cover Photo Credits:
National Aeronautics and Space Administration
United States of America

Books in the Spirit Life Sci-Fi Adventure Series:
Earth Below Us
Heaven Above Us

Dedicated to my beloved wife Gladys and our family
for their encouragement and insight
which have enriched my life!

Alpha ~ Omega

PART ONE

THE END AND THE BEGINNING

Chapter 1

Earth Below Us

International Space Station, 2037 A.D.

The United States Congress is in session. The President is meeting with his cabinet. Ivan, a rare category 5 hurricane, is barreling down on Cocoa Beach, Florida.

High up in orbit, circling the Earth on the International Space Station (ISS), the Beatle's song "Here Comes the Sun" begins to softly play signaling the start of a new day. Of course, the sun rises 16 times in 24 hours over the space station as the ISS circles the Earth every 92 minutes at nearly 28,000 km/hour. But there must be an official start to the busy workday schedules - and this is it.

Commander Edward M. Foster lays still, strapped in and floating in his bunk. *It is not the gravity, it's the free fall,* he says to himself, savoring the moment and meditating on it. *The most peaceful time of the day. It's all uphill from here,* he thinks. Out of the corner of his eye, he catches a glimpse of an object floating down the center aisle. *Not a good start!*

He slowly unstraps from the bunk, grabs a railing, and angles his body out into the center aisle of Module 6. He reaches out and grabs the aimless floating metal washer, tossing it into his front jersey pocket, then zips it up. Any errant floating objects must be corralled quickly and made secure to reduce the sense of chaos that always lies just below the surface at the International Space Station.

Foster always starts his daily rounds at one end of the station and progresses slowly to the other end, methodically checking equipment, acknowledging personnel on duty, and checking supplies as he goes. Anything out of the ordinary is noticed and logged on a note pad located in his other front jersey pocket; pen attached.

He has kept a daily log, on paper, for the last 20 years, and has the records to prove it. Not that he can't navigate the digital world, he completed his PhD in astrophysics only seven years ago, at the age of 32. There is something about the slow path that keeps him grounded and focused on the tasks at hand.

Slowly Foster makes his way back up the central corridor after his first round is completed, ending in the Cupola, a polygonal observation dome attached to Node-3.

And there she is ... again, he muses. His heart begins to beat faster, the blood pressure increasing steadily, butterflies fluttering in his stomach. *I haven't had these signs since those nighttime combat missions in the desert,* he remembers.

Claire McAlpin arrived on the space station 21 days ago. She was the child movie star everyone loved, until she grew up and did not embrace the Hollywood culture. She preferred her modest upbringing in the mid-west, which did not sit well with the producers and directors, who preferred the wildings.

Claire was naturally beautiful. Her thick, jet-black hair slowly flowed out behind her face in the micro-gravity. She seldom wore makeup since her large eyes and high cheek bones naturally accentuated her features. Her great-great grandmother had been a Sioux Indian, daughter of a chief, who had married a local rancher.

After Claire became an adult, a long 10 years went by without a starring role, only minor supporting roles. She decided to take a chance on this space tourist reality role and the publicity it would undoubtedly bring, hoping it would help jump start her career again.

The Russians have been helping to finance their portion of the space station by offering multimillion dollar two-month rides in their "Hotel Module," much more spacious and accommodating than the cramped crew quarters. It was an unusual and smart move for a country that only recently embraced their version of capitalism.

The second 'vacationer,' as Commander Foster liked to refer to them, was Dolph Bjelke, the 26-year-old Danish graduate school engineering student. His credentials were suitable for a stint on the ISS. He had won the prestigious International Engineering Association's ISS Contest, the reward being a two-month stay in the Russian hotel module. Dolph was tall, broad shouldered and slender at the waist, with blue eyes and a square jaw, which made him appear more serious than he was when you got to know him.

Commander Foster had placed the vacationers in charge of the space debris detail, responsible for scanning their flight path for foreign objects that could hit the space station.

Any solid object has the potential to severely damage the ISS if not managed properly by maneuvering out of the way or quickly sealing off areas that are hit, until repairs can be made. Spacewalk repairs are dangerous and time consuming.

Satellite tracking was also an integral part of their assignment, along with pinpointing space debris, and always sobered up the newbies. It made them much more serious with the knowledge that at any moment they could die from orbiting space junk striking the station if they were not serious about their jobs. It usually kept them out of the crew's hair and on task.

"Did you see anything unusual on your duty station Claire?" Commander Foster inquired as he looked down through the windows of the Cupola at the blue and white shrouded Earth below.

"Nothing much," she replied, "although Dolph thought he saw something strange on the horizon moving like a satellite, but we did not have any records of it, so assumed it may be a new Chinese or Russian launch. Dolph says they often delay announcements or even keep completely silent if it's a military payload."

"Dolph's right on that account," Foster replied.

Foster knew today was going to be different from their normal routine but was having trouble getting his head into the game with Claire so close by. Instead of the usual quiet, peaceful planet below, they would be helping to monitor one of the largest category 5 hurricanes on record in the Atlantic.

These hurricanes were especially catastrophic with sustained winds of over 150 mph. Hurricane San Felipe had killed an estimated 2,500 people around Lake Okeechobee in Florida during the horrendous 1928 hurricane season. An exact count of the dead was impossible to make, as many went missing and unaccounted for. Hurricane Andrew destroyed 25,000 homes in 1992, some with just their concrete floor slabs remaining, when it made landfall in Homestead, Florida.

Foster gazed out the Cupola windows and watched the approaching storm from space. The most recent weather reports were forecasting the hurricane would make landfall near the central Florida coast at Cape Canaveral. He stared intently at the hurricane's huge pinwheel of swirling white clouds below and took a double take, rubbing his eyes to clear them. He could not believe what he was witnessing.

To his astonishment, puffs of storm-like mushrooms began appearing in synchronous rows down the east coast of the United States, beginning with several enormous bursts over the Washington, DC area.

My mind must be playing tricks on me, he thought incredulously. As crazy as it seemed, there was only one explanation - *nuclear explosions!*

"Claire … return to your duty station … Now!" he said in a slow determined drawl.

"I just got off …" she began, and then stopped when she looked up at the set of his jaw. *He has never spoken to me like that before,* she wonders. *It must be serious.*

"Yes sir," she replies and immediately pushes down and then out of the cupola.

Drifting in the micro-gravity for a moment, Foster reaches over his uniform to the shoulder patch and grips the edge of the International Space Station insignia, angrily ripping it off and tossing it across the turret. He keys his shoulder intercom speaker for an announcement to the crew.

"All assigned crewmembers to the observation deck - all crew to the observation deck!"

Foster drifted closer to the cupola windows and studied the picture unfolding on the North American continent below. It began to take shape as he tried to categorize the fiery mushroom-like eruptions by location: Washington, D.C., *multiple eruptions*, New York City (and the United Nations headquarters), military ports and Air Force bases all along the east coast.

He peered westward to the developing mushroom cloud over Houston, Texas. *Darn, took astronaut training there*, he fumed dejectedly. He looked further west to El Paso. *Took that first wild solo flight in an F-16 at Ft. Bliss*, he remembered; s*hifted to a vertical takeoff at the end of the runway, creating a mini sandstorm blasting a ton of desert sand back on the runway*. That is about what he felt right now, on the verge of being out of control. This was going to be a long day and require some serious anger management to navigate through it without alarming the crew.

The duck! Remember the calm duck! He forced himself to envision in his mind's eye a beautiful mallard duck serenely moving across a still pond; all the while, if one looked below the surface, the duck's feet were moving like the wheels of a speeding freight train.

Remember the duck, a soft ripple in a still pond. They will only see the duck, not its feet! he repeated to himself.

Chapter 2

Treason in High Places

Commander Foster's ISS insignia patch floated slowly past the cupola's windows, the only viewing station of Earth on the International Space Station. The Earth shined bright blue and white in the background.

Foster pushed back from the windows as Tokugawa Shikibu, the Japan Aerospace Agency crewmember, swung into the dome headfirst. He was the first crewmember to respond to Foster's command to gather in the cupola. Next to arrive was Franz Moser, from the European Space Agency. Jamila Smith-Owens, the NASA engineer, was the next to swing in as she followed everyone's stunned gaze out the cupola's windows.

The observation dome was crowded with nearly the entire astronaut crew present, but no one complained about the cramped quarters. Their eyes were fixed on the blue planet below and the implications of the ghostly mushroom-like eruptions emerging into the atmosphere.

"Where are the Russians?" Foster shouted.

"Saw Alexei in the galley," Jamila quickly replied. "He didn't seem to be in any great hurry to get here."

"Manny, go to the GIMAP panel and try to track these explosions. I want to know exactly what is being targeted and see if you can get a directional in-coming trail. Try and pinpoint where the attacks are coming from." Foster was clearly restraining a desire to strike something.

Manny was the Commander's nickname for Tokugawa. No one wanted to say it out loud; it was a full-scale nuclear war, World War III, or ARMAGEDDON, depending on your world view!

"Aye, sir," Tokugawa said as he swung his legs around to the deck's opening and pushed off down the passageway.

"We should call home … I mean mission control, right away," Jamila said.

"I'm on that," Foster said. "I'll let the whole crew know something as soon as possible," *that is, if there is any mission control left,* he thought.

"Jamila, right now I need you to do something extremely important. Check the crew return vehicle and make sure it is ready, then go do a quick inventory of the food and water. I want to know exactly how much we have on board just in case we don't get a resupply anytime soon."

"I'm on it, commander," Jamila said.

NASA never quite worked out the science of escape pods. Instead, they rely on a Soyuz-TMA spacecraft always attached to the space station, in standby mode. This serves as the crew return vehicle. However, it only holds three astronauts. Commander Foster already knew who would occupy that vehicle should the time come to evacuate -

Claire and Dolph, the space tourists, and Jamila the engineer, with a husband and young child to return to.

Resupply and cycling astronauts to and from the ISS was always a crap shoot even in the best of times. The lack of funding for the space station and irregular resupply flights had already made many essential tasks iffy. Just two weeks ago they had to start rationing water due to the explosion of a Russian Soyuz rocket resupply mission.

NASA was considering evacuating the crew later this year if further resupply missions experienced difficulties. If that happened, it would be the end of the space program after trillions of dollars and years of work, not to mention the lives lost in this worthy effort. The new private resupply consortiums were working but had limited payloads and were subject to unexpected explosions which increased costs and reduced reliability.

As Jamila pushed off down the tube, Alexei Sokolov, from the Russian Federal Space Agency arrived at the circular entrance to the Cupola. Foster looked sternly into the eyes of the Russian crewmember.

"Alexei, are you aware of what's going on below … back home?"

"I met Manny in the rush to get over here and he briefed me," he said. "I can't believe it!"

"Have you seen Lysenko?" Foster asked. Cheka Lysenko was the wiry Russian biologist in charge of all the agricultural related experiments.

"No, not recently," Alexei replied.

"Would you go check on our passengers, Claire and Dolph, and make sure they don't panic?"

Russia was one of two possible suspects for this size atomic attack (China being the other), and Commander Foster did not want to give Alexei any critical systems assignments at this point. Alexei lifted his head, a blank expression on his face.

"Yes sir," he said, then pushed off.

Awfully formal, Foster thought.

The third world war everyone had been speculating about for the last 75 years was finally unleashing below them. He relied on Moser, the middle-aged methodical engineer who was on his third tour at the space station, to help him make difficult decisions.

Foster thought about the space station program and the fact that it was really on its last legs. It was scheduled to be de-orbited in 2028 and would have been, except for intense negotiations at the last minute, which pushed all sides to agree to operations through 2038. Even so, funds were drying up, dwindling every year along with the economies of the partnering agencies. Since then, repairs and resupply had been a patchwork at best, duct tape and bailing wire, or so it seemed.

The only country in the world that was thriving was China. Cheap labor and lax environmental laws had allowed a huge production cost advantage for the Chinese. For years, Western nations had been moving their manufacturing and industrial base to China, transferring their technology along with it, giving China a huge advantage over other nations.

This new superpower, flush with capital, decided to go its own way in space; it established a brand-new rival space station orbiting the Earth on the opposite side of the planet from the International Space Station. Rumors persisted that the Chinese space station was militarized. To compound the imbalance of power, western nations began to unilaterally de-militarize to shift more of their dwindling assets to social programs.

"Franz, what are we seeing down there?" Foster said, not believing his own eyes. It was just too incredible to take in.

Moser said nothing for a while, waiting until their swift orbit brought them within sight of the Russian Caucuses. He scanned the district housing the Baikonur Cosmodrome.

"Looks like the Russians were not attacked, since there are no mushroom clouds in sight over the Cosmodrome," Franz Moser said matter-of-factly. "On the flip side, it could also mean that they are part of the attack."

This was a critical observation since the Russian space program had the most reliable ISS delivery systems available. Oddly, the one atomic blast exploding adjacent to the Kennedy Space Center appeared to be targeting the nearby Patrick Air Force Base, not the space center itself. Whoever launched the nuclear attack wanted to keep the Kennedy Space Center intact and operational. At the same time, they destroyed the nearest military asset available to prevent the takeover of the space center.

Just then, two heads - the vacationers - bobbled up into the well of the Cupola both speaking at once.

"Something is taking out our satellites," shouted Dolph, finally heard over the commotion. "We are seeing evidence of missiles hitting satellites and clearly defined debris fields forming where the satellites were." This significantly heightened the danger to themselves from orbiting debris.

"Can you identify which country the rockets are coming from?" Foster asked. "Someone has some pretty accurate missiles to be able to take out our satellites in space like that."

"That's the strange part, they aren't coming from Earth," Dolph said. "Something is approaching them from space and taking them out."

"Blast it, the Chinese," Moser said. The Chinese space station was the only likely answer since there were no other space platforms orbiting the Earth capable of carrying out such a mission. "The rumors that their space station is militarized are true!"

Just then, a flaming spear-like object flashed by the Cupola's windows, barely missing the evacuation vehicle. It slammed into one of the large solar arrays, exploding on contact and setting off all the emergency alarms. The space station shook like a 7.0 earthquake had struck them.

"Did you see that!" Franz yelled. "It looked like an air to air missile."

"Who the hell brings missiles into space!" Foster shouted. "They've got to be violating a half-dozen treaties."

"I'll be sure and tell them the next time we meet," Moser said sarcastically. "To the winner goes the spoils. If the Chinese expect to be the last one standing, I doubt a piece of paper will get in their way."

"Dolph, did you see Alexei Sokolov?" Foster asked. "I sent him to check on your duty station a few minutes ago."

"No," Dolph replied, "I haven't seen him for a while."

"You and Claire get back to your station and keep us informed."

"Will do," he replied.

"Yes sir," Claire said. The two pushed off down the corridor.

"We just refilled our maneuvering tanks 3 weeks ago," Moser said. "I suggest we begin moving away from the Chinese space station as fast as this tub will go. The thrusters aren't really designed for anything but getting us out of the way of space junk but that seems to be our only alternative right now. It will buy us some time until we can figure this out."

"Do it!" Foster yelled.

"Delay that order," Cheka Lysenko, the Russian crewmember said as he came into view floating in the tube entrance below the cupola. He held a Glock G43 9mm pistol aimed directly at Commander Foster's head. Alexei Sokolov floated up behind him in the corridor with a wry grin on his face.

"I'm afraid we've made a secret security treaty with the Chinese," Lysenko said. "They are moving East, and we are moving West. In a very short period of time, there will only be two superpowers left on Earth, and the United States will not be one of them."

"Hitler and the Japanese had the same idea when they started the second world war." Commander Foster reminded him. "It didn't turn out very well for them."

"Alexei, get on the Com and let our Chinese allies know that Russia is in control of the International Space Station and they may proceed to board us!" Lysenko said.

Chapter 3

The Quaker's Gallows

Boston, Massachusetts Bay Colony, 1660 A.D.

Drums echoed across Boston Common signaling the arrival of the hangman's party at Alder's gate.

Mary Dyer the condemned Quaker missionary, walking tall and plainly dressed, held her head high above her thin frame vainly peering over the crowd to catch a glimpse of friends or family. Kindred spirits yelled encouragement, "Reprieve, Reprieve," which was loudly drowned out by the extra drummers brought in for the occasion.

A large band of soldiers with muskets and halberds flanked the hangman's party to keep the pressing crowd at bay. Captain Oliver ordered "Drums Beat Louder," to drown out the crowd. Nothing would prevent the exercise of his orders from the General Court of Governor Endicott. The cattle, oxen, and horse had been moved off the common to accommodate the expected crowd of about 3,000 - the entire population of Boston in 1660!

14

The previous year two Quaker men, William Robinson and Marmaduke Stevenson, had been hung on the same site for daring to spread the Quaker faith in the Puritan Massachusetts Bay Colony. Mary Dyer stood in the same gallows with those men, one year earlier, watching them hang one by one and expecting the same. Her skirts were tied around her feet, and the rope halter was tight against the side of her neck. At the last moment, a reprieve arrived from Governor Endicott, grudgingly given because of the begging of her 18-year-old son, Will Dyer. Word circulating through the crowd was that there would be no reprieve today.

The hangman's party arrived at the Frog Pond next to the great elm tree and the drums were ordered to stop. The rope was already hanging from a large middle branch of the elm tree. A crude ladder leaning against a lower branch held the noose in place attached to its top rung, waiting to encircle Mary's neck. Mary needed no assistance, slowly climbing up, one step at a time. Reaching the top, she turned to the crowd, unsteady on the ladder. Captain Oliver, sitting atop his horse, leaned over unhooking the rope and secured the noose around her neck.

"Do you have any last words?" Captain Oliver asked loudly so the large gathering could hear. The crowd quickly became silent to listen to the words of the martyr.

"I came hence, in obedience to the will of our Creator," Mary said slowly, "desiring to repeal thy unrighteous laws of banishment on pain of death, to followers of the Way. His will, I will abide, faithful to death. My life not availaeth me in comparison with the liberty of the truth. The truth will surely set us free!" she said in a strong voice.

Captain Oliver waited to be sure these were indeed her last words, then moved the horse up behind the ladder. He pushed out on the frame, then pulled the ladder out from under her - the fall snapping her neck instantly. After an initial gasp and loud murmur from the crowd, not a word could be heard. The wind picked up slowly, rustling the leaves of the large elm tree and Mary Dyer's thin body began to swing ever so slightly.

The noose had been well placed, as her neck broke cleanly. The search for religious freedom in America received its first woman martyr at the hands of fellow Christians who themselves fled Europe to escape their own similar persecution.

Faith Dyer, Mary's 15-year-old daughter, stood in the crowd next to her uncle barely able to contain her despair. She felt her mother's spirit, carried as if on the wind that day, whisper into her ear, *do not despair, the passing of martyrs produces the seeds that fall on fertile ground, yielding abundant fruit!"*

Increase Dyer, the brother of Mary's husband William, stood in the crowd with his family. They were all dumbfounded by the treatment of the "Antinomians" as the new Quaker sect was known in Boston: imprisonment, flogging, cutting ears off, and boring holes in the tongue with a hot iron poker. Then of course, if all that failed to stop the spread of the heresy, death by the hangman's noose followed!

William Dyer's family had long since fled Boston to avoid persecution and helped establish the Rhode Island Charter with other like-minded families. The Charter was the first in America to legalize freedom of religion.

Increase Dyer was a descendant of Sir Richard Dyer, Lord of the manor of Wincarton, Somersetshire. He was a first-born heir and a high member of the Church of England; thus, he and his family were allowed to stay in Boston and were not subject to the "banishment upon pain of death" for the offense of spreading heresy. The Puritan ruling government of the Massachusetts Bay Colony did not want to offend the King of England and take the chance of having their lucrative charter revoked for persecuting high members of England's state church.

"Go bring the cart," Increase whispered to his son Roger, "and take Faith with you." Roger, his eldest son, 17 years of age, was tall with shoulder length hair and as befitted the time, was considered an adult. Faith was Mary Dyer's youngest daughter. At fifteen, she was on the cusp of womanhood with an angelic childlike face and figure, Faith had stayed with her uncle on the insistence of her mother.

Mary knew that making the missionary rounds among the now mostly underground Quaker faithful in the city of Boston, meant risking arrest and imprisonment. After her sentencing, it had been pre-arranged with the authorities for Increase to take Mary's body back to her family in Rhode Island.

The two Charters were connected by an old Indian trail, barely large enough to accommodate cart traffic, winding well outside the outlying areas of what was considered civilization at the time. It was mostly old forest on both sides, with predators, mostly wolves and bears at night, making it the last choice of most travelers. For Quakers though, it was the only choice since boat captains were forbidden to transport Quakers into or out of Boston harbor on pain of losing their transport licenses.

Prior to leaving Boston on the backwoods road to Providence, the Dyer party stopped at Williams Roadhouse, the last stop before embarking into the wilderness. Sympathetic Bostonians had arranged a room for the preparation of Mary's body for her journey home to Newport via Providence. Fellow Quaker families also accompanied the procession fleeing the persecution with high hopes of freedom in Rhode Island.

In the backroom of the roadhouse, Mary's body was cleansed thoroughly, then rubbed with a combination of lime dust and spices and tightly wrapped in white linen to slow the decomposition. For the sake of safety in numbers, they waited several days until a suitable number of backwoods travelers had accumulated at the inn for the trip south.

On the morning of their departure, a combination of fog and smoke shrouded the wild landscape with an eerie wet mist. Mary Dyer's body was gingerly placed in a two-wheel cart barely large enough to accommodate her and a few belongings: cooking and sleeping gear, food, and ale brought for the occasion. A single stout ox pulled the cart and a wooden plank crossed over the front sidewalls where Increase sat, whip in hand. Several Indians with their families led the way expecting food, ale, and a reward of bawdy trinkets for leading the party safely to Providence.

Increase cracked the whip above the ox, signaling it to move out and catch up as the small band started out ahead of him. Backwoodsmen, Quakers, and Indians - it was a motley crew that wound its way out of the last remnants, the outskirts of Boston that day. With death in tow, the cart was relegated to the last in line. Roger had preferred to go in front of the cart, but Faith would not be separated from her mother's body, so he walked with her behind the cart.

They passed several small homesteads encircled with white pine rail fences to keep in livestock. Once past the smoke fires of Boston, with the trail slowly rising, the fog lifted and the old forest - large, dark, and foreboding - towered over the trail like a gothic cathedral. American chestnut and white oak made up the spires of the forest cathedral, with smaller red and sugar maple trees interspersed where they could find a sunny niche below and between the hardwood giants. Scrubby understory plants and shrubs filled in the gaps between the trees, leaving no clear path off the trail.

Chapter 4

The Revenant

All seemed well enough considering the circumstances as the trail narrowed ahead of them. Speckled rays of sunlight pierced the tree canopy in strange patterns of dappled light, creating a surreal, mesmerizingly wild landscape.

The morning chill was fading and the heat and dust from the trail began to drift up from the road to the back of the line. Faith stared at the ground beneath her long skirt as it whisked along the grassy lane at the back of the cart with its creaks and moans interspersed with the occasional crack of the whip when the ox slowed.

She looked up and sitting next to her uncle Increase Dyer was a little girl dressed in a plain grey Quaker vest and bonnet, her skirt extending to her ankles. She was facing backwards on the seat looking directly at Faith with an upturned face and a sweet angelic smile. Faith returned the smile and nodded, assuming the little one was with one of the other Quaker families making the trip.

Faith felt a strong urge to touch her mother and she reached out, taking hold of her tightly wrapped feet. At that moment, the little Quaker girl on the seat next to her uncle disappeared and Faith drifted into a reverie of her martyred mother, reminiscing about the events which had led up to her hanging.

Ten years earlier, Mary Dyer felt a spiritual calling to join the Quaker movement. She left her family in Rhode Island to return to England and learn this new faith that accepted women as equal partners.

She followed George Fox and other itinerant preachers, immersing herself in this new faith with its emphasis that everyone was capable of direct, inward encounters with the Creator. The idea of spiritual equality meant that anyone could speak in assembly when prompted by the spirit. After studying and learning the new faith for seven years, Mary returned to her family in Rhode Island. She became a Quaker missionary holding meetings in the outdoors, which was the way the itinerant preachers in England spread the Way among the people.

Faith, the youngest of Mary Dyer's children, was five years old when Mary sailed by ship to England to join the Quaker movement. Little Faith was devastated and refused to let anyone cut her hair, saying she would cut it once her mother returned, but not before. She imagined herself like a modern-day Samson, gaining strength from her long unshorn hair. In some sense, it did strengthen her, giving her a sense of purpose until her mother's return.

On the night of Mary's return from England, Faith, now 12 years of age, pulled her mother into a private space in their small clapboard house. She removed her bonnet and let her hair fall to her knees. She knelt and handed her mother a pair of scissors.

"Mother, I hath permitted no one to touch my hair since you departed. Now that you are here, only you may cut it." Kneeling in front of her mother, she waited sorrowfully for her strength to be taken from her as she did not need it now. Her mother had returned. Tears began to well up in her eyes and she could hold it in no longer. She cried as she reached out and clutched her mother.

Mary waited patiently for her daughter's sobs to subside, all the while stroking her head and calming her, then moved slowly to stand behind her with scissors in hand. She raised up the beautiful full strawberry blond hair and held it in her hands. As she ran her fingers through the strands of Faith's hair, she felt a shimmer, a feeling came over her, and the story of Samson entered her consciousness.

"Child," she said. "hath thee allowed thy hair to grow for its strength or for the vain pride of its beauty?"

"My hair hath been the strength I needed to keep faithful til your return," she replied.

"Then I endear you to never cut it. I sense a growing faith in you that will lead to many trials. Endeavor to persevere and you will discover many triumphs, as have I." Mary placed the scissors on an end table and left Faith alone on her knees to contemplate her future.

Faith followed her mother everywhere after that, refusing to leave her side, and so, also learned the innermost truths of the Quaker faithful. They spent hours together, Mary and Faith, under a tree studying the new King James Bible and comparing it to the Latin version while waiting for the indentured workers and Indians to finish their labors so that the outdoor assembly could begin.

Faith so wanted to be accepted by her mother that in one month she completely memorized the entire King James Bible. Mary kept this accomplishment hidden as others could think her daughter possessed. Based on the teachings of the Quaker enlightenment, they determined that this talent was from God and nothing to fear except from those in the world keen on persecution of the faithful. Later, this gift would be called photographic memory, but Mary Dyer considered it a miracle and confirmation that the light inside them was indeed growing.

Faith insisted on accompanying her beloved mother on her missionary trip to Boston where the threat of certain death at the hands of the Puritans awaited them. Mary allowed it, provided Faith stayed with her uncle Increase Dyer and did not accompany her on her rounds, secretly meeting the Quaker faithful in the city.

Chapter 5

Into the Wilderness

The day's travel wore on and Faith's remembering was interrupted by Roger, who had grown close to her, his forlorn cousin, during her stay with his family in Boston.

He held her hand from time to time and spoke comforting words to her, only barely imagining the depths of despair she was in. Faith would reply in short sentences. She was never sure exactly what to say. After all, she was only fifteen, and the ways of the world were still a mystery, but her mother's vision was clear to her.

"I miss her so much, but mother knew in her heart that this journey was only temporary," Faith finally said to Roger.

After a short stop for rest and refreshment at noon, the company continued through the hot afternoon. As the looming shadows of late afternoon approached, the party arrived in a clearing in the road which opened into a large meadow. The Indians led the way, circling a crude camp in the thick grass just as dusk began to settle. Firewood was plentiful in the adjacent thick woods and it was not long before campfires sprang up around each family group. Cooking utensils were brought out for hot meals.

When the Indian families circled the meadow to set up camp, they ended up next to the Dyer party and settled down. The two groups began to share food and to communicate in stumbling sign language and the few words each knew in the other's language. Faith was distracted for a while as she began to communicate with the two daughters amongst their new-found companions. One was slightly older, and the other younger than Faith. She even accompanied them into the woods to gather wood and attend to necessities before turning in for the night.

As the wilderness darkness settled in, the backwoodsmen among the company became rowdy after uncorking a small keg of mead. Wolves howled in the distant hills. Everyone tried to settle in for the night. Faith, with her head propped up against baggage by the wagon wheel, could not sleep. She watched as the fathers of the Indian families spoke in low voices and one moved closer to the campfire facing the backwoodsmen's camp. They had apparently considered there was more danger to their daughters from inside the encampment than outside, so were going to take turns on watch.

As the last logs thrown on the campfires became dying embers, the stars in the night sky began to light up. Faith contemplated them for a while, her eyes slowly scanning the sky, sometimes seeing patterns. She wondered what her future would hold now that her beloved mother was dead and gone forever. *"Endeavor to persevere and you will discover many triumphs amid the pain of life ..."* she remembered her mother saying. The sadness she felt was alleviated somewhat by the occasional thrill of watching a string of shooting stars sweep across the dark sky.

Faith began to become sleepy and would have dosed off if she had not noticed in the corner of her eye, a dark cloud in the sky slowly moving over the meadow, blocking out the stars. It hovered for a few moments directly over the encampment and the air began to shimmer.

She felt a heat wave of rushing air move past her cheeks. Then she saw a pinpoint of light begin to glow over the meadow, followed by the sound of a swirling wind. The light became brighter and opened up, no longer a narrow point but now a large swath flowing brightly over the meadow. A loud humming sound grew in intensity until the light was blinding, the wind blasting, and the sound deafening.

The occupants of the camp woke quickly. No one could be heard unless they were close as they shouted at the top of their lungs. Muskets, along with bows, arrows, and knives came out, but since the light was all around them, there were no targets to aim at. Many were temporarily blinded, groping around with their hands outstretched to avoid running into anything.

The light overpowered everything else. Faith rushed to the back of the cart and clung to the body of her mother. At just that moment, she felt herself being lifted up as if by a tornado. Roger ran to her and reached out to try and hold her down but found himself also drawn up into the whirlwind. Faith continued up into the hot air hysterically calling out to Roger and her mother.

Suddenly the wind grew silent and she could make out many others caught up in the tornado's pull, ascending through large open doors into the bottom of a metal boat floating in the sky. Hugh insects, looking like menacing praying mantis, were everywhere. She nearly fainted from panic as the largest one nearest her reached out and grabbed her by the arm with his finger-like talons. In a panic, her flailing free arm dislodged her hair pins and her bonnet fell off. Her long reddish blonde hair fell around her in a swirling mass.

The large soldier insect pulled her roughly through the air to a cylinder, opened the door, and threw her against the back wall of the cryogen tube. Her thick hair flew forward from the backpressure in the tiny cabin and surrounded her body with only her face emerging distraught and panicked.

The soldier insect called another smaller Mantis over to look at her. "She is too young, we must discard her," the soldier clicked in their staccato language.

Pulling an instrument from his belt, the smaller insect technician scanned Faith's body with it and said, "The scan confirms she has just entered her maturity, but you are right, her body appears to be that of a child. We will hold her for last and see what can be done. We must depart now; the slipstream is collapsing. We don't have time to evaluate further - seal her up!"

Faith's eyes flickered up as the door closed and the cryogen tube hissed, filling with gas and frigidly cold air. She was instantly frozen, with tears streaming down her cheeks and her reddish hair frozen in mid-air around her. Her last image through the glass window of the small cylinder was that of two large insects making guttural clicking sounds as they gestured towards her and then everything went black.

Chapter 6

The Third Eye

"Our whole business in life is to restore to health the eye of the heart whereby God may be seen."

~Augustine of Hippo

The large torpedo-like rift flyer carrying the frozen bodies of Faith Dyer and her expatriates exited the slipstream just outside Mantis space, near the planet Gannicus. The flyer entered the planet's atmosphere, hissing as anti-gravity wells activated slowing its descent to the planet's surface.

The cryogen tubes containing Earth's progeny were carefully removed and taken to an underground metallic laboratory in the insect's Citadel. Once out of cold storage and brought back to room temperature, the women would be impregnated with genes the Mantis deemed important for their offspring to have as elite future mercenaries: athletic, 20/20 vision, with a dose of chemically induced strength, quick learning and enhanced healing abilities. The males

28

would be pressed into service for the Mantis Empire as slaves or mercenaries depending on their abilities.

Bodhidharma, Prince of India, was one of the first to be taken by the Mantis from Earth to Gannicus in the year 158 B.C. His entire entourage was taken while on a hunting expedition to the hinterlands of their kingdom. He and his people were well treated by the insects since they understood a cast system (as was the Mantis custom). A similar cast system existed in India. The Mantis treated Bodhidharma as the royalty that he was.

Bodhidharma himself in turn, understood the complex Machiavellian politics the Mantis were playing (as was the custom on Earth), including the use of mercenaries, which was common in his time. He played their game, and his people prospered on Gannicus and Earth, as the spoils of conquest were shared.

Being the leader of his people, he accepted many of the available alien enhancements to his body; in particular, the rare anti-aging technologies which elevated him to God-like status among his people. This was an enviable position to be in, by any standard, on any planet. He built a palace on Gannicus that rivaled the palaces of his home in northern India and was given land where he built a city around him. He even returned to Earth, sometimes for long periods, pursuing the aims of the Mantis as a mercenary and for his own personal ambitions.

Bodhidharma approached the broad double doors of the underground bunker in the insect's Citadel. As was his custom for many years of service, he came to claim his reward from the recent arrivals from Earth - several beautiful women for his harem.

A half cohort of Gurkha warriors, his hand-picked personal bodyguards, accompanied him in all their splendor. Bodhidharma himself was dressed in the regalia of a Gurkha warrior prince typical of the warring princedoms prevalent in northern India after the disintegration of the Mauryan Empire. He was careful in the presence of the Mantis to maintain his princely appearance at all times and with all its trappings. This was a well thought out plan to appear a strong and faithful ally, while at the same time, keeping his options open should there ever be a change of power on Gannicus, or Earth, or the Mantis Empire.

Bodhidharma was a tall lean man with piercing coal-black eyes. His very presence sent a chill down the spines of many of those around him. Just his cold dark stare was often intimidating enough to command obedience. The Mantis respected this authority, since it precluded them having to interact with the humans themselves, just Bodhidharma and the leaders he chose from his men. In his belt was the famous khukuri knife, an 18-inch long curved blade that was never to be drawn from its scabbard without being bloodied before being returned to its proper place. This blade was not like any other though, it was made of pure silver, with precious jewels encased in the handle.

"Prince Bodhidharma," clicked the Mantis at the door entrance, "come and choose your reward." Bodhidharma nodded and ceremoniously entered, followed by the Gurkha Captain of his guard. The remaining warriors took up their places at the inner and outer entrance to the underground bunker.

The physical appearance of the "Mantis" is closest to Earth's praying mantis insect – thus the moniker given to them by the expatriate inhabitants of the planet Gannicus. They are larger than most humans, averaging about seven feet in height. They have triangular shaped heads with equally large almost snake-like eyes at the opposite sides of their wide head tapering down to a pointed mouth. Their societal structure closely resembles that of an ant colony, with clearly delineated roles – Queens, soldiers, and laborers, but in the Mantis's advanced space faring society, scientists and their technicians are part of this hierarchy.

Like all insects, Mantis have six legs. The bottom four are adapted for walking, the two closest to the head, for arms. The head and abdomen stand nearly erect and the head can turn almost 360 degrees. The upper two appendages have armored jagged forearms which can trap and hold prey while the mantis eats the heads of their victims, considered a delicacy. The hands have claw-like opposable thumbs and three fingers, hence their ability to accurately manipulate objects, one of the reasons for their rise in intelligence.

Bodhidharma walked slowly but confidently up and down the rows of cryogen tubes leaking a white mist which skirted around the floor, appearing to scurry off as he approached. He would occasionally stop and appraise one of the captives, some of whom he marked for retrieval later, until he came to Faith Dyer's tube.

He stopped cold. His alien enhancements, especially the ones designed to give him an advantage over a stealthy enemy in a fight to the death, were setting off alarms throughout his body. His hand instinctively went to the handle of his Gurkha knife, which did not go unnoticed by his Captain, who also became immediately tense and alert.

Bodhidharma slowly turned his head without taking his eyes off the cryogen tube and said to his Captain, "Go to the end of this row and let no one come down here!"

"Yes Prince!" The Captain bowed and slowly backed away.

Bodhidharma reached out and brushed away some of the crusted ice on the window of the cryogen tube to get a better look at who was inside. What he saw stunned him. It was a girl, appearing perhaps 14 years of age. She had an angel's face surrounded by thick strawberry red hair which puffed out around her; only her face showed through, nothing else was visible. There were several frozen lines of tears coming out of her eyes, which were still open in obvious agony, eyes that were staring straight into his soul. Her hair contained several leaves and broken twigs sticking out of it, evidence of her rough handling by the Mantis insects.

For the first time in his long life, he was convicted to the depths of his soul, facing the personification of all the wrong he had committed at the behest of the Mantis. He felt crushed of his pride, his wealth, his princedom. He was reduced to staring at the face of innocence. He realized that he held the power to let her drop into the fiery volcanic lava stream that was the insect's universe, or hold her up above the pyre, no matter the cost to himself. It left him bare, naked, like a convicted man standing in the gallows awaiting the death sentence to be carried out, all the while staring at the rope.

Sensing a strong spiritual presence around her, he slowly crouched down, slipping into a familiar lotus position. He took several deep breaths, releasing each slowly before inhaling again, calming his heartbeat. He closed his physical eyes and opened his third inner eye, the one that sees visions, the spirit world, and the many auras that surround all living creatures.

He focused on the bottom of the tube as a white/silver aura appeared laced with pink and brown, pulsing an exceptionally gifted, loving person inside, in the depths of confusion and discouragement. It was pulsing the pure essence of Faith Dyer in her current circumstances. Once again, he was convicted to the depths of his soul - bereft, lost. The odd sensation was unknown to him before today.

His inner eye rose slowly to the center of the cryogen tube and a pair of wings appeared, enveloping the tube. There were long soft white feathers cresting the wings, sparkling in the spirit light. He fought panic to keep control and not revert back to the physical world. Heat began to build up in his body. Forcing his inner eye up, he saw that the wings extended behind the cryogen tube and were attached to an angel. The angel's face was bowed down over the tube in a posture of prayer and protection.

Bodhidharma felt a twinge, the heat in his body rising again, as the angel slowly looked up, its eyes meeting his inner eye. There were tears on the angel's cheeks. The sound of alarm bells went off in Bodhidharma's head, signaling retreat, as the countenance of the angel changed from one of sorrow to righteous wrath. The angel rose, towering over him, and his eyes bored down into the Prince's soul through his third eye. Panicked, Bodhidharma immediately closed his third eye, severing the contact with the spirit world.

This man, who had lived for nearly two millennia, and seen and experienced things that no other human has experienced, knew exactly what he must do. He opened his physical eyes and turned to the Captain of his personal bodyguards at the end of the row. "Bring three gurneys and remove this tube and the other two I have marked - Now!"

The captain motioned to the cohort waiting at the door. They immediately loaded Faith Dyer's tube onto a gurney as well as the others and quickly escorted them out with Bodhidharma leading the way, his hand firmly gripping the Gurkha knife, as were his Gurkha warriors. An innocence protected by a heavenly being meant connection to the heavenly realm, and Bodhidharma was going to find that connection! By bringing all three tubes out at once, it masked the importance of Faith's tube and kept the angel protecting it in play.

The Mantis technicians were beside themselves since this had never happened before. It was an unexpected breach of past protocol. They would always meticulously catalogue the Prince's choices, deliver the tubes to his palace, then revive their occupants in his presence. Bodhidharma could not take the chance that the Mantis would also notice the importance of Faith's tube and replace it with another before delivering it to him. Moving about - click, click, click - as their insect's scampering feet contacted the metal floor, they protested. Meticulous at record keeping, pushed out of the way, they hurried around to record the numbers on the cryogen tubes, gathering what information they could, so a report of the Prince's unusual actions could be made to their superiors.

Chapter 7

The Sentinel

Time meant little to Bodhidharma since his alien biogenetic enhancements provided him a long, nearly immortal life. As a matter of fact, time was his ally. He could take years to master any skill, learn languages, influence a region or country's direction on Earth. But that still made him not a prince, but a servant and he longed to break the yoke of his Mantis overlords.

Now this new opportunity comes into his sphere of influence, an untold hidden treasure; a beautiful girl on the cusp of womanhood who possesses or will do something so important, that she is accompanied and protected by a spiritual being. He had lived long enough to know that this was a rare event.

Bodhidharma knew instinctively that he must protect her to discover the secret, the knowledge that made her so important. He would commune with the angel and position himself to take advantage of every opportunity this nexus between the spiritual and physical realms provided.

Still in their cryogen tubes, Prince Bodhidharma locked Faith and her two female companions up in the most secure chamber deep underground in his palace. He kept them asleep and placed their cryogen tubes upright at the head of the room. Faith was in the center with her companions on each side as if attending her in a royal ceremony.

Bodhidharma's first attempt at communicating with the guardian angel was a disaster. Slowly crouching down about ten feet from the center cryogen tube, he slipped into the familiar lotus position. He took several deep breaths, releasing each slowly before inhaling again, calming his heartbeat. He repeated this process, then closed his physical eyes and slowly opened his inner third eye.

A large warrior angel materialized in front of the cryogen tube. He wore a long white robe which touched the ground and a bright golden breast plate across his chest. Tucked in his waist band was a ram's horn with strange symbols etched into it. In his hands, at the ready in front of him, was a silver European longsword with a handle in the form of a cross.

Bodhidharma could still feel the strong, protective spiritual web the angel wove enveloping the cryogen tube. The warrior angel angrily stepped toward him and shouted, "Stop this now or you will draw dark spiritual forces to this place!" The Prince quickly closed his third eye and the angel disappeared.

Bodhidharma realized this was going to be a long process. He began delegating many of his duties to his many sons as he planned to spend hours in lotus position meditating. He would seek the guidance of the heavenly being since he now knew there were forces at work that he was unaware of. His hope was that once he and the guardian angel came to an understanding that he wished only to protect the girl, the exchange of knowledge would begin.

The best way to protect the girl and gain the trust of the heavenly being for the foreseeable future, he thought, was to keep her out of the crosshairs of the Mantis. Thus, the girls remained in cryogenic sleep under the palace, guarded by the Prince's inner circle of Gurkha warriors. Slowly over time, in long meditative sessions, his entreaties were accepted as real by the angel and the barriers were lifted. He finally felt safe enough to open his third eye and see this spiritual creature once again.

The Prince made a ceremony of their second meeting, decorating the chamber as if for a royal visit. *This will yield far greater results than any meeting with any human dignitary,* he thought. There were magnificent tapestries hung on the walls along with Greek, Roman, and Indian statues positioned about the room. Each corner of the room was fitted with fountains misting gently into the air with exotic colorful flora in bunches around small ponds. Sparkling red, blue, and green rare and precious gemstones were mixed among the smooth white river rocks at the water's edge.

When the day arrived, Bodhidharma positioned his most trusted half cohort of Gurkha warriors in their ceremonial dress about the room. He assumed the lotus position ten feet in front of Faith's cryogen tube and took several slow deep breaths, exhaling each time, bringing his heart to a near standstill. Eyes closed; he allowed his third eye to assume control. As the spiritual realm came into focus, the angel was also sitting in a lotus position, wings folded behind his back, with a wry smile on his face. He wore no weapons or armor.

"You did not have to go to so much trouble Prince of India," the angel said. "Trappings such as these do not impress angels much." He waved his hand across the chamber. "We live in the heavenly realms with their myriad senses and bright colors."

"I wanted to honor you, Great One," he replied.

"A word of warning before we begin," the angel said with a stern expression on his face. "Be careful of your motives when you access the spirit sight. Selfish motives will attract dark spirits that can harm you or those close to you. Keep your motives pure, and you will have nothing to fear!"

"Thank you for the warning, I was not aware of that," Bodhidharma said. "What shall I call you?"

"You may call me Sentinel. You would not call me Great One if you knew the heavenly realms as I do, for I am a lesser angel, below the rank of archangels. I have a singular purpose to protect this martyr's daughter behind me, the girl called Faith. You have shown yourself to be of the same mind."

Bodhidharma looked up, staring at the face of innocence showing through the window of the cryogen tube.

"So that is her name - Faith! Why is she so important that an angel protects her?" he asked.

"The girl's full name is Faith Dyer, daughter of a Christian martyr named Mary Dyer. That fact alone is enough for a Sentinel to be her companion, to watch over her, but I sense a greater purpose here, a purpose which has not yet been revealed to me," the angel said. "I also perceive that my purpose is enhanced by imparting knowledge to you that will give you advantage over these Mantis demons that threaten her, should the time of need arise."

38

The Sentinel explained that he could only interact with the physical realm in a limited way compared to the archangels, who were all powerful. In this physical world he could manage the pain of those he watched over, slow a physical blow to them but not stop it and improve healing as well. "But if any human opened their third eye as you did," he said, "sentinels can be serious adversaries causing untold pain unto death in the spiritual realms."

Bodhidharma suspected as much. "How may I be of service to you in this quest to protect Faith?"

"Tell me of this world, the Mantis, and how they are connected to Earth, as you know it," the angel replied.

"The Mantis take advantage of the rifts in space that appear and disappear creating slip-streams of energy flowing back and forth between the multiverses," Bodhidharma began to explain. "All their technology is geared to detect the signs of impending rift-like connections, then rapidly deploying ships, personnel, and resources to ride the energy flows sweeping back and forth through the cracks in space to exploit any usable resources at the distant end. They are especially keen to exploit underdeveloped water planets – like Earth. I don't understand why they need us. With their abilities, they could rule the entire planet unopposed," Bodhidharma speculated.

"I will tell you why they need you," the angel replied. "In the vast system of galaxies that make up the known universe, Tertiary Developed Species, consisting of the most advanced space faring races, banded together and formed a Consortium Guild regulating trade among members and lesser tiered species. When species progress to permanent self-sustaining colonization of their off world surrounding space, they advance to Secondary Developed status with the Guild. This entitles them to Guild protection but also subjects them to the Guild's strict trade rules.

They established sustainable trading rules that allow resources and trade to be managed in such a way as to keep future generations from running out of the precious resources needed to sustain life. The Guild also prohibits exploitation or interference in the development of Primary Developing Species, underdeveloped worlds and cultures, like Earth."

"So, what the Mantis are doing on Earth is illegal," Bodhidharma replied.

"Quite illegal," the angel said, "and the reason the Mantis are secretly kidnapping, training and reinserting the offspring of your species back onto Earth as mercenaries for their empire. They can work through you to mask their involvement and escape any consequences from the Guild.

Earth is an ideal candidate for such exploitation: an isolated habitable world far off the trade routes and close to a rift in space. The races occupying Earth are also war-like, always fighting for domination and employing mercenaries or surrogates themselves. These characteristics suited the mindset necessary for effective mercenary recruitment. Also, Earth is not advanced enough to effectively detect and repel the Mantis infiltration."

"That makes perfect sense and answers many questions I have had over the centuries," Bodhidharma replied.

"Tell me more about this planet and the makeup of the mercenaries the Mantis are training here?" the angel asked.

"Gannicus has two large continents separated by a world ocean with icy polar regions similar to Earth. The Mantis populated one continent with primarily Indian/Asian stock and called it the Nepali or the Eastern continent. The other continent was populated later with Roman stock and named Valeria or the Western continent. The Mantis have a cruel fascination for organized warfare and the emergence of the Roman empire on Earth compelled them to populate half of Gannicus with legionaries from their remote outposts in Gaul, Germania and the British Isles along with their families over a period of 300 years."

Bodhidharma was making great strides in developing a relationship and gaining much knowledge from the Sentinel when one day the angel appeared and imparted some much-needed intelligence.

"The Tertiary Consortium Guild has a law which allows primary developing worlds to apply for Protectorate status provided they can prove that they are being grossly exploited by more advanced species. You must be prepared to colonize the surrounding off world space of Gannicus within 25 years, or the Protectorate will be lifted."

The angel would be absent from time to time on missions to gain intelligence helpful to the prince, returning with other important updates to his mission. After one especially long absence, the angel returned with an item of immense strategic importance - a path to Earth not controlled by the Mantis.

"There is a very stable rift in the multiverse, unknown to the Mantis, connecting this space with Earth in a remote solar system known as Epictetus. The rift is only visible by entering the ice cloud of the fifth planet which is a gas giant."

The Sentinel was finally satisfied that Faith was safe with Bodhidharma provided she remained in cryogenic stasis. He

41

therefore gave mystical and stealthy knowledge to the Prince so that he could carry on a discovery of the inner workings of the multiverse while the angel departed to assist others. He trained Bodhidharma in the ways of spirit travel and other rare knowledge that would aid him in protecting Faith.

Bodhidharma spent many years perfecting the unique skills imparted to him by the Sentinel. Unfortunately, when the 20th Century dawned on Earth, events on the planet Gannicus took a turn for the worse. The Roman descendants living on the Valerian continent, having become effective mercenary legionaries for the Mantis, finally had enough and revolted against their insect Masters.

Chapter 8

The Roman Revolt

"If one life holds no worth, then worthless all. Make voice, look to Creator and Tech for luminance!"

~Seediq of Gannicus

The blowback down the Karst tunnel was immense! It dissipated somewhat as it reached the side tunnels where the last living members of the 13th Legion waited. It was like a small tornado moving through the camp, picking up pots and pans, clothes, and anything not tied down.

Seediq knew the end was near. He stared across the chamber at the small band of teens waiting to join the fight. Thin, dirty, and stoic, they stared back. Their faces told the story of their short lives. Each held their most precious possessions: weapons, and one or two heirlooms handed down from their deceased relatives. The wailing horn had sounded loud and mournful, signaling the defeat from what could only be the last few remaining warriors holding off the

Mantis warriors in the nearby underground tunnel. The last barricade defending their refuge was breached!

Mal, the leader of the waiting teen cohort, walked over to Seediq and placed the Lorsgun in his hands.

"You, Seediq, of 13th, are now leader! Keep faith and all trust you, let perish none, until all meet in Resurrection City," Mal said as he stared into Seediq's eyes. The transfer was ceremonial, unless Mal and his group did not return, then it was law, based on a long 100-year tradition of war with the Mantis demons on Gannicus.

"I fail not Mal, or 13th, until all meet in Resurrection City," Seediq replied, remembering the exchange from other leaders over his short lifespan.

The ceremony was dimly illuminated by a tiny oil lamp and bio-florescent lichen growing on the walls of the underground tunnels. The lichen are symbiotic organisms in which each benefit from their association with the other and consist of tiny fungus and plants. Both being rare edible species, they and the blind fish that inhabit the underground rivers have kept and sustained the legions from starvation these many years.

Mal pulled the half full bandolier of shotgun shells over his head and placed them on Seediq's shoulders. Seediq could not believe what his eyes were telling him. With this transfer of authority - the leader of the 13th Legion always carried a Lorsgun - he was now in charge. Slowly, each member of the band walked over and gave their most precious possessions to the mostly children who were left alive from what was once a thriving proud legion on the surface of Gannicus. Only a remnant remained. They had not encountered any other legions in months, and for all they

44

knew, they were the last people still alive on the planet. Mal slowly led his team out into the corridor and toward the diminishing noise of battle. Each in turn, paused to look back at their younger brothers and sisters for the last time, the last of their parents were dying in the tunnels ahead of them.

It was a big responsibility leaving a 15-year-old in charge but there was no one else, all others old enough to fight had joined the fray, some as young as sixteen. The attack had come so close to their hideaway, deep in the remote tunnels beneath Gannicus, that there was no choice but to lay it all down for the sake of saving the youngest among them. This was the last major tenant left for them, so that the legion would survive.

Seediq entered the side nursery chamber, pulling back the tattered curtain. "Luna, gather younger boys, girls, and infants; make for main tunnel and go to underground river. Prepare rafts ready, will join you there!"

Seediq had been on a few raids. He mostly knew what was necessary to survive, keenly watching others, as their numbers dwindled from the relentless attacks by the hated insect Mantis. Even so, there was no one else to consult. They had all been trained in survival skills from an early age. And so, they would disappear deeper into the karst tunnels to rebuild, repopulate, and wait until enough of them were old enough to continue the struggle.

Luna, barely fourteen, but the oldest remaining female in the small legion, rounded up everyone that was left, organizing the older to supervise and carry the younger. Deeper they went, into the abyss of tunnels crisscrossing the underworld on Gannicus. They always ended up at the underground rivers. There was no hope of survivors above them, the horn had spoken.

Seediq gathered the remaining boys old enough to offer some resistance and handed them what was left of the weapons including a small but deadly crossbow for skinny Rem, 14 years old. Moro, the 13-year-old, received a short sword. Belk, also thirteen but ill and malnourished, looking no older than 10 years, received a scorpion; a wicked knife with three triangular sharpened edges that could cut from almost any angle. Seediq ruffled the boy's hair as he turned. Belk was delighted, swirling the blade around in his hand, pretending to stab the enemy. Ben, nine years old, received a bow and arrows. He would not last in a physical fight, so the bow made sense – killing from a distance. Ben should have gone with Luna but refused. He was the last remaining descendant of the 13th's once proud leader, the centurion in charge of the remote outpost in Germania when they had been abducted. Ben insisted he would stay with the older boys and fight.

What difference, all will perish most like, Seediq thought as he adjusted the Lorsgun, a short multi-barreled shotgun that was perfect for close fighting in tunnels. He tightened the strap on the bandoleer, half filled with shotgun shells, across his chest from right shoulder to his left hip.

The Roman fighting philosophy on Gannicus was a simple two-part plan. The first was to avoid contact with the Mantis for as long as possible by being very mobile, with the ability to move from camp to camp on a moment's notice. The Mantis were amazed when they would find freshly made food and cook fires still burning but no inhabitants.

The second part of the plan was called *"All In."* When they were cornered and were forced to fight, they would bring every available warrior to the point of attack and get in as close as possible, up in the midst of the Mantis ranks, so that the insect's special weapons and chemicals could not be used without injuring their own. It was hand to hand, savage tunnel fighting. With little space to move and within reach of the insect's long serrated arms, they would drop down to the ground, stabbing and savaging the insects soft unprotected underbellies. By doing this they could often overwhelm their enemy and create enough panic to win the day and allow the legion time to escape.

Seediq positioned his half cohort of six fighters in the narrow breach tunnel carved out above the ceiling of the main tunnel leading to the river, the escape route of his legion. He was determined that no Mantis would get past this point. The floor of the breach was only an inch thick. It was enough to hold the weight of a small group of boys but thin enough to be easily broken, tumbling down on top of the Mantis, should they be bold enough to continue deeper into the tunnels.

Ben, with his bow, took up a position at the entrance to the breach, ready to jump down and let fly a flurry of arrows. Seediq and the rest, further in, readied themselves for the fight, sitting up on the slanting sidewalls of the breach. Seediq loaded the Lorsgun and made ready to discharge all six barrels at once, more than enough to bring the floor of the breach down, which was also the ceiling of the main tunnel, on anyone below.

Loud clicks could be heard along with the scratching of the Mantis's feet on the rock floor of the tunnel as they approached, like armored spiders, toward their prey down the main tunnel. Seediq waited until the lead element of the Mantis patrol was just past his position, to get the maximum effect, then relayed the word down to his cohort, "Yell, life depends on it!"

He turned and fired the shotgun at the floor of the breach as the boys inched up the sides, ready to jump down behind the falling rocks. The impact collapsed the roof and the young fighters leapt right on top of the hated Mantis insects patrolling below.

The boys yelled at the top of their lungs, frightening shrieks, and loud howls, while at the same time coming to ground and maneuvering down under the Mantis. They began slicing with their knives up into the fleshy underbellies of the insects. Wild shrieks, emitted from the clicking jaws of the wounded insects, added to the mayhem.

The loud explosion and cave in of the tunnel roof, combined with the high-pitched human and Mantis screams, echoed up and down the tunnel. The fierceness of the battle was so great that the main body of the insect force coming up behind the scouting squad halted their advance.

As soon as Ben heard the blast of the Lorsgun, he immediately jumped from the breach into the main tunnel. Bow drawn, he turned, facing back to the oncoming Mantis. Only one made it past the collapsing ceiling, snorting and clicking like a crazed animal. Ben let go an arrow, which lodged in the fleshy abdomen of the creature, who shrieked in surprise, stopping for a moment in disbelief. His rage became evident as he barreled headlong toward the boy with maniacal screams, arms raised to the tunnel ceiling. Ben let loose another arrow which bounced off the armored right shoulder of the creature. The third and last arrow lodged in his breast plate.

The insect paused long enough to break the shafts of the two arrows sticking out of his body, and then, looming over the tiny human warrior, he grabbed the boy's shoulders with both clawed hands. He lifted the tiny warrior to head height, jamming his forearm spikes into the boy's chest, and spread his jaw plates preparing to rip the boys head off. He switched to slow motion, savoring the moment when the blast of a Lorsgun shattered the insects head against the cave wall. The explosion shot an involuntary jerk into the forearms of the insect releasing the boy from his grasp, but at the same time sending the serrated edges of his right forearm upwards, slicing through Ben's left cheek, eye, and upper brow as they fell back onto the tunnel floor.

Seediq knelt down, surveying the injuries, and hoping beyond hope that Ben still lived. "Ben," he yelled, shaking the boy's shoulders, "Ben, wake up!" Slowly Ben's right eye cracked open, blurred vision starting to coalesce on Seediq's face.

"Did we win?" Ben croaked.

By this time, the others had formed a circle around their fallen brother, holding their breath. Each one had their own bleeding cuts and scratches from the fight since it was impossible to go *"All in,"* without feeling the wrath of the insect's serrated armored forearms. Seediq's own face was sliced open from just above the right eyebrow to the upper cheekbone, just missing his eye.

Before anyone could move, they all looked at each other at the same time in disbelief. They erupted in a huge shout of joy, raising their arms in triumph as the greenish insect blood they were coated with mixed with their own red blood. Only one seriously wounded, and no one dead - unbelievable good fortune!

"Grab all weapons and Tech and run to the river!" Seediq yelled.

Luna had prepared two of their three rafts, loading them with what supplies they had left. They had lost a third of their small company in less than a day. All three rafts were connected by ropes. The third raft would be used for firewood when they reached their new destination, if they reached it. Wood was a precious commodity now in the underground dwelling places after 100 years of warfare.

She stared at the tunnel entrance straining to see who would exit the tunnel, Seediq and his cohort, or the demon insects. She waited with a hand axe, poised and ready to cut the rope tethering them to the shore and severing the link, sending them down the river.

Suddenly she saw little Belk running out the of tunnel entrance with his greenish bloody hands raised in victory, waving his scorpion knife around like it was a flag. She screamed, dropping the axe, and with it, letting out all the built-up tension of the last several days! She could not imagine a life without Seediq.

Seediq and the rest soon followed, carrying Ben between them, his wounds still oozing blood from the shoulders and face. She could not hold her emotions in any longer and ran to the half cohort screaming her relief, jumping up on Seediq as they twirled around. She was not alone any longer or the oldest left alive, a burden she did not want to bear. The other children followed her and surrounded their brothers, celebrating with them in a wild dance!

They gathered in the small boats and Seediq made sure the ropes were secure between the rafts. They would escape together or die together. Seediq and Rem took the first raft, Luna and the children along with Moro occupied the second, and Ben was carefully loaded onto the third raft accompanied by Belk. They headed down stream, deeper into the underground caverns of Gannicus, further away from the menace. *"All in"* had worked, but barely saving the remnants of the 13th Legion. So, few were alive, but none had been lost while Seediq led the group. The admiration of the survivors was evident in the reverence they showed him.

Chapter 9

Seediq of Gannicus

Gannicun children are encouraged to keep pet cave frogs. Their delicate skin reacts to the toxic chemical weapons released by the Mantis into the tunnels. They began playing with their frogs as the rafts swayed in the river currents. Luna smiled as she watched the children. It was the first time in days she was able to relax.

All was well until the sound of the rushing river water increased. Seediq peered ahead fearful of approaching rapids, or worse yet, waterfalls - both could prove deadly. The walls of the cavern began to narrow, and the water sped up, increasing the speed of the tethered rafts. The cavern began to change from a straight line to curving sides which created undercurrents rushing up under the rafts after every turn, sending their bows skyward and then crashing down. The children began to scream, holding onto their few possessions and the raft for all it was worth!

Seediq could make out a sheer wall ahead where the river split; the left fork narrowing, creating a swifter current, while the right fork widened, slowing the flow. He immediately signaled to the rafts behind him to use their long oars to move right as he did the same. The floating platforms were swiftly approaching the wall and it became clear to him that the rafts on their current trajectory were going to smash right into the face of the massive rock wall, unless ...

Seediq quickly raised his long oar and positioned himself on the rear corner of his raft. Stretching his oar out, he began to push Luna's raft toward the slower river path which had the opposite effect of moving his raft into the river's narrower path. At the very last minute, after one last push, he grabbed a hand axe and swung hard, severing the rope connecting the two rafts. They both narrowly missed colliding head on with the sheer wall face, each glancing off their respective side walls. Luna's two rafts skirted into the slow path of the river, while his raft skittered down into the rapids.

Seediq could hear Luna yelling his name over and over in a sorrowful chant, "Seediq, Seediq ... Seediq!"

He yelled back, "See you in Resurrection City!"

Seediq prayed for relief, holding onto his raft for dear life. He wasn't sure what prayer was at his young age, but the last person that he knew that had actually known a priest, swore to him that prayer brought deliverance – so he prayed - hard.

The sweat began to form on his brow. His hands tightened on the rails of the raft which crashed into the next curved rocky side of the solid stone wall of the cavern. The raft cracked and began taking on water. Just as it seemed that nothing could get worse, the roof of the river cavern began to get closer and the sidewalls narrowed - top, sides, and bottom - creating a vortex which shot them forward. When it seemed that it would close and pin them alive in a death trap, the raft broke apart. Seediq felt the cold water surrounding him completely as he desperately held onto a single log. The tangled mess of logs, rope, and raft parts were spit out a cliff hole joining a waterfall crashing down into an underground lake.

Luna collapsed on her raft, wailing and rocking back and forth. The children gathered around her, but she would not be consoled. The thought of continuing without Seediq, the one thing she dreaded most, was unbearable. He had always been there from her earliest memories, consoling her when her parents died, and she him as well, when his parents fell. When the adults began to disappear from their presence and their memories, it was Seediq who rallied the children to the cause. He encouraged them to have hope and stay alive another day. Now he was gone!

It turns out that the river fork Luna and her fellow refugees were traveling on was an oxbow, slowly curving around and meeting up with the underground lake that had swallowed Seediq's raft. The last remnants of the 13th could just make out a campfire on a nearby rocky outcrop. Lookouts shouted their arrival back to a village whose curious inhabitants gathered on the shore as they approached. Others, already in rafts patrolling the lake, approached and gave them assistance. Their rafts were tied up and everyone proceeded to the main campfire.

The inhabitants had been alerted to the battle upstream by the sounds of fighting; sound travels far echoing in the underground tunnels. They were in a state of agitated preparation just in case they should have to depart their relatively stable village and go further into the depths of Gannicus.

Exhausted, the weary refugees collapsed around the central campfire. The village consisted of two legions, the 9th and the 11th, both having served in the remote hinterlands of the British Isles on Earth. The 9th mostly disappeared from the historical records before 120 A.D., while the 11th was brought in soon after to help build Emperor Hadrian's Wall after the disappearance of the 9th legion.

The two legions had banded together years ago and traveled deep into the interior of Gannicus when it was clear the revolt would end in disaster. Together, they had mapped the gentler river patterns and settled there, calling the place Nain. It was thought to be a place of safety and refuge, a place to regain strength and nourish life, away from the chaos. Their numbers had increased greatly, though most were still young.

The remnants of the 13th Legion gathered around Luna to comfort her as Timoni, the middle-aged leader of the 9th legion approached. He knelt and placed his hand over her shoulder. "Don't cry," he said, "we have rescued more of your people!"

With this, Luna's head popped up. "What?" she asked, hope returning to her distraught mind.

She peered around Timoni and saw a group approaching supporting several limping figures. They were Seediq and Rem. Both were scratched, bruised, and bleeding from being hammered about the tunnel with loose logs on all sides, but otherwise alive, breathing, and in one piece. Seediq was glad when several adults had rescued them from the base of the waterfall. Age was a telling sign of Mantis contact on Gannicus - the younger the age of the legionaries, the more recent the skirmishes with the insects. Seediq's legion arrived with no one over 15 - a troubling prospect for their rescuers.

Timoni ordered first aid to stitch up the wounds of these young legionaries and a hot meal for all. Then he called for a council meeting around the central village fire. Leaders from the three legions and their lieutenants took the forward positions while all other members surrounded them in anticipation.

"Seediq of the 13th Legion, we here have seen no Mantis at village Nain." Timoni began the proceedings. "Please tell us of your journey. We heard sound of battle, you fought the Mantis and escaped - how so?"

"You see our numbers," Seediq gestured around the campfire. "We have just lost one third of what was left of the 13th Legion." The villagers gasped at the implications of what Seediq said. The 13th Legion had been one of the largest on Gannicus. Their most trusted leaders had always come from the 13th.

"Our leaders called 'All In' and lost. The wailing horn blew, and we fled down the tunnel to our rafts." Seediq looked down into the fire trying not to relive the events of the last days, the devastating loss of two cohorts to the Mantis onslaught.

"That's not all," Belk piped in, "after that, Seediq called 'All In' with only a half cohort of us and we ambushed the Mantis and killed them all, not losing one of our own!" A cheer rang out from the crowd.

"And we will do the same if they dare to come this far!" Timoni said enthusiastically. Another cheer rose from the crowd.

"It was scouting party, not the Mantis main force. We caught them unawares from a breech tunnel," Seediq said to damper their enthusiasm. He had seen too many die in his short life to take any move against the Mantis lightly, especially here in the open.

"What's a breach tunnel?" someone asked.

Truly they have been out of the fight for too long if they know not the breach tunnel, Seediq thought.

"The best council I give is leave this place and save all. It is too open to defend. In the tunnels, each side is limited in the number of fighters brought to the point of attack, which evens odds for us. Here they overwhelm you with their numbers and Tech, all is lost," Seediq said.

"I understand you and your council shows wisdom in the fight against the Mantis, but this is our home and we will defend it!" Timoni said as a cheer rose up from the crowd.

"Then we fight with you," Seediq said.

"No," Timoni said raising his hands to quiet the crowd and get everyone's attention. "You have sacrificed all. None are left of proper age to fight. I have more important task for you and your brave young fighters. Lead our families down the river in rafts and await the outcome of the battle. If we win, you will return and join us here. If we are defeated, go as deep as you can and protect our three legions from further harm."

Seediq thought for a moment. "It will be done as you say," he said.

Preparations were made for the departure: rafts were loaded down with food, cooking utensils, remnants of lodge poles, canvas, and bedding. The departure ceremony was brief.

Timoni, representing the two legions at Nain, walked over to Seediq and placed a Lorsgun in his hands. He pulled a full bandolier of shotgun shells over his head and placed them on Seediq's shoulders.

"You, Seediq, of the 13th, are now leader! Keep faith and all trust you, let perish none, until all meet in Resurrection City." Timoni used the words Seediq had heard too often. The transfer was ceremonial, unless Timoni and his brave cohorts did not survive - then it was law, based on their long 100-year tradition of war with the Mantis.

Seediq could not believe that this was happening again in such a short period of time. "I fail not Timoni, or Legions, until all meet in Resurrection City," Seediq replied.

Slowly, each member of the waiting cohorts walked over and gave their most precious possessions to the women and children who were to leave soon for safety away from the Mantis. They were the remnants of three proud legions who once thrived on the surface of Gannicus. The boys of the 13th legion were given weapons, knives, swords, bow and arrows, as well as several more Lorsguns for the older ones. Rem was especially pleased to receive one of those.

Seediq oversaw the final departure preparations, making sure the rafts were secured together, then gave the order to release the ropes holding the rafts to the shore. All eyes were on them as they drifted slowly down the underground river.

Seediq anchored the boats well down stream. He huddled up with Belk and some of the older boys from the other legions who briefed them on the downriver maps they brought with them. Several likely places of refuge were identified. Their discussion was interrupted by the sound of gunfire.

Loud fighting erupted far up the tunnel from the rafts as all eyes and attention focused upstream. Seediq signaled his young teen boys to be ready to raise anchors. Human screams and loud clicking shrieks combined with explosions from larger pulse weapons, echoed off the walls of the underground river. Slowly the noise of battle began to subside until all was silent. That was when the wailing horn blew, echoing down the tunnel signaling defeat, and everyone knew all was lost. The demon Mantis took no prisoners.

Seediq of Gannicus, who as leader of the 13th Legion, had yet to lose one soul to the Mantis, now became leader of three legions. He led them deep into the sanctuary of the underground realm of Gannicus, to rebuild, repopulate, raise, and train more warriors, and continue the fight of his forefathers!

Unknown to them, events on the far away Nepali continent were also about to spiral out of control and change their lives forever.

Chapter 10

The Betrayal

Betrayal comes in many forms. Small betrayals like a wink and a nod or a wry smile behind your back can be over-looked, brushed off or even forgiven, if not repeated. Large betrayals like murder and assassination, must be avenged and atoned for.

As it turned out, the death of Prince Bodhidharma was the latter, committed by trusted sons, eager to place one of their own on the throne. The Mantis had full knowledge of the assassination and encouraged it. They lost confidence in Bodhidharma after his passionate pursuit of the spiritual realm, for the sake of his people's future and the protection of Faith Dyer, the sojourner.

The sudden death of Prince Bodhidharma was a shock to his people after such a long tumultuous and eventful life covering several millennia. During the latter years of his reign, he spent an increasing amount of time in meditation alone in his secure vault under the palace; the room containing the cryogen tubes of Faith Dyer and her companions.

At the same time, the unexpected Roman revolt on the Western continent shifted a much heavier burden onto Bodhidharma's people to satisfy the mercenary needs of the Mantis. This took place at a time on Earth when two great wars occurred – World Wars I & II. Many lives were lost on Earth and among the Gannicun mercenaries. They were tasked with trying to slow down the technological advances of the 20th century which could have resulted in the colonization of Earth's solar system and inclusion into the class of Secondarily Advanced Species. This recognition would have ensured their protection by the Tertiary Guild from exploitation by the Mantis empire.

The reports coming from the successor to Bodhidharma, Harish, the son with the most support among his brothers, indicated the cause of death most likely a malfunction of the ventilation system in the meditation room. This cause was close to the truth, but the malfunction was induced by those wanting a change in power on the Eastern continent. Prince Bodhidharma was found lifeless, in lotus position, in his underground vault. All efforts to revive him were futile.

The ruse would surely have gone undetected had it not been for a serious mistake by the Mantis, a mistake with world changing consequences. They insisted on the return of the cryogen tubes from the underground vault, especially the one that the Prince had spent so many hours meditating before – Faith Dyer's cryogen tube.

The guardian angel, when he appeared to Bodhidharma, made sure that the Prince's Gurkha guards could not see him. To them it appeared that Bodhidharma was communicating and worshiping the form of Faith Dyer occupying the center cryogen tube. He always sat directly facing her.

Even though the inner guard was sworn to secrecy, over the years, word began to circulate about these meditation sessions. A cult had developed, one that added Faith Dyer to the many deities already worshiped on Gannicus' Eastern continent and subsequently in India. Bodhidharma made no efforts to suppress this cult, even secretly cultivating it, especially since it was most prevalent in the warrior class among his people. Surreptitious drawings of her face were circulated among the populous and the Prince pretended to be angry with his guard to deepen the mystery surrounding Faith. Ever the Machiavellian prince, he hoped this ever-growing cult would someday come to the aid of Faith if she ever needed it.

Bodhidharma had allowed the nexus of his power to shift to his most trusted sons in order to fully absorb and experience the teachings of the Sentinel. The angel taught him how to travel in the spirit which opened many opportunities to finally extricate himself from his fealty to the Mantis. He would strike out on his own and protect Faith. It was his undoing.

The exact details of his death are officially unknown, only rumor and innuendo remain. What is certain is that the moment the Mantis brought Faith Dyer's cryogen tube back to their Citadel and opened it, pulling her out of stasis and re-starting her heart, the Sentinel awoke on Gannicus. The result was a swift and heinous retaliation against those responsible for the death of Prince Bodhidharma.

Chapter 11

The Avenging Angel

Bodhidharma's body lay atop the wooden funeral pyre at the head of the large outdoor palace amphitheater dressed in full Gurkha warrior regalia. His silver curved khukuri knife, with the handle studded with precious stones, sparkled in the sunlight. His inner circle of Gurkha guards surrounded the pyre while holding torches at the ready to sink them into the wood, engulfing their master in flames.

Eulogies were being made by the same sons who had betrayed him, praising his extraordinary long life and his great deeds that were recorded for posterity. The mood of his subjects was visibly swaying from mournful sobs to cheers of praise for their leader's courage and foresight. One moment there would be shouts of praise, then silence, followed by screams and sobs!

The Sentinel angel watched the eulogy, invisible and perched on the corner of a tall column. He felt conflicted by the strong urge to enter the body of Bodhidharma and reverse the corruption of the tissue. This would enable him to use

Bodhidharma's skills and warriors to recover Faith from the clutches of the Mantis.

I have been gone so long and don't know the strategies of an assault on the Mantis strongholds. It could make matters worse for Faith, the angel thought. *Worse yet, I would become a dreadful fallen angel, no better than my former brethren Aramos and Tamiel. They will be chained and thrown into the fiery pit with Lucifer.*

The Sentinel's inner soul anguished because of the overwhelming need to protect Faith. He was given a holy charge, *protect the child of the martyr.* But it conflicted with his utter loathing of becoming a fallen angel, failing an even more vital role, *being the righteous angel!*

His mind kept going back to the Mantis claws and the way the insects carelessly rough handled Faith when she came out of stasis. Her body was thrown on a cold metal table in the Citadel's underground laboratory. Frustrated with her long hair, which kept getting in the way of their instruments, he watched in horror as they clutched her head with their scaly hands and began cutting off her beautiful hair with dull clippers that only tore and ripped, leaving her bleeding. His hands covering her head reduced the pain considerably, but she still squirmed and moaned under the rough handling. When it was done, he could not watch anymore and flew directly to Bodhidharma's funeral with this crazy plan, one he had never in his long life contemplated before, *becoming the fallen angel - Faith's only hope!*

Bugles blew mournful sounds echoing about the outdoor amphitheater. The Gurkha torchbearers, honor guard to Bodhidharma in life, solemnly approached the tall funeral pyre and placed their torches into the crevices between the

64

wooden slats. All the Sentinel could visualize at this moment was the anguish of Faith struggling with the physical pain of the Mantis medical devices, carelessly inserted into her body. He tried his best to ease her pain but could only go so far. In Bodhidharma's body he could do so much more, his only hope of rescuing her entirely. Anxiety rose up in him as quickly as the flames rose from the funeral pyre.

Protecting Faith means Fallen ... Condemned! Smoke obscured the body, the flames licking higher: *It is now or never. Perhaps, if I strive to refrain from sin, I could be redeemed - one day,* he reasoned deep in thought. The decision loomed large in the depths of his soul with the body of Bodhidharma about to be consumed forever by the fire.

The Sentinel leaped swiftly up from the pedestal, spreading his wings, and swooped down from his perch, disappearing into the thick smoke. As he entered the body of Bodhidharma, it slowly rose with him through the smoke and flames over the funeral pyre.

The Sentinel struggled with the strange feelings of possessing a human body, unknown to him before today; reigniting the nerve endings to each physical extremity, each finger and toe, firing up the brain synapses to make it possible. The energy of the angel's spirit immediately reconstituted the slowly decaying flesh, reenergizing the tissues, the heartbeat. As the body touched down on the stage, a huge gasp of startled amazement and bewilderment spread throughout the amphitheater. The Sentinel was uncertain what to do next, staring at the throng in front of him, until ...

The spirit of Bodhidharma, which had been lingering about the amphitheater, flew into his reconstituted body, igniting it with a passion for revenge, for retrieving what was stolen from him, recovering Faith, his kingdom, no matter the cost.

"*If you want Faith to live*," Bodhidharma spoke into the spirit of the Sentinel, their minds melding, "*let me take over!*"

"*Take the lead*," the Sentinel replied without hesitation, "*but do not sin!*"

"*What is sin?*" Bodhidharma asked.

Gurkha Hindu warrior tradition held that should a soldier receive less than an honorable death by his enemies, his spirit returns in the form of God's avenging angel and wrecks a terrible havoc upon his slayers. Standing before his subjects now, Bodhidharma was the embodiment of that tradition - come to life. Eyes ablaze, air shimmering around him, he reached down and drew his pure silver, jewel encrusted sword, holding it high above his head, his piercing wide open black eyes showing no mercy. Visible waves of energy emanated from the combined spirits of the Sentinel and Bodhidharma creating a synergistic powerful response. Those closest to them cowered down and away, feeling the heat emanating from their combined spirits.

"We have been betrayed by the Mantis!" Bodhidharma shouted. "Bring my sons to me!"

His personal guard quickly rounded up his sons and brought them before him, pushing them into a kneeling position in front of him.

"The instruments of their betrayal are before you!" he yelled, voice echoing throughout the amphitheater.

He slowly walked from one to the other, lifting the head of each in turn, his coal black eyes piercing into their souls.

Some he spared as innocent. Others, he grabbed the hair on their head and swiftly sliced through their necks with his sword. He tossed their heads into the flames of the funeral pyre, their bodies falling lifeless to the floor. Reaching the end of the line of kneeling figures, drenched in blood, he turned slowly to face his subjects.

"Every one of you take up sword and knife; kill every Mantis you can find - spare none!" he commanded.

The crowd was so moved that everyone obeyed and streamed out of the colosseum, shouting with raised fists as they went. Absolute chaos erupted throughout the city with everyone of like mind - to destroy the Mantis. The chaos swiftly spread to surrounding towns, the people erupting in a pent-up fury against their Mantis overlords!

Chapter 12

The Battle for the Citadel

Bodhidharma planned for almost all possible contingencies, including this attack on the insect's Citadel on Gannicus. He took it slow and deliberate, stretching the time to take advantage of the chaos he was creating.

Mantis warriors were dispersing their ranks to put out fires of rebellion springing up spontaneously across the Prince's realm. The chaos forced them to respond to the ever-increasing uncoordinated attacks from all sides, away from their Citadel, away from Faith. Bodhidharma's fearless patience instilled confidence in his inner Gurkha guard. They would follow him anywhere!

He brought together the palace guard, two cohorts of his best trained Gurkha warriors. Twenty-four men loaded into the transport vessel that had been provided as part of the largesse by the Mantis: their destination - the Citadel, Mantis headquarters on Gannicus.

The fortress contained the underground experimental labs, only a thirty-minute hop from the capital in the cargo flyer.

He had been training his inner guard in the use of all sorts of weapons from Earth and from alien origins. He also trained a select cadre of warriors on how to pilot the cargo flyer that was now making its way to the Citadel. They had often taken this route on previous occasions. The current chaotic riots created the ideal cover for a bold deception.

The body of Bodhidharma lay on a portable platform lined on both sides by his personal guard. The Mantis watched and recognized the approaching cargo flyer of the Prince, keenly aware of Bodhidharma's death. The ship's gravity wells hissed, bringing it down inside the inner courtyard of the fortress. When the rear doors lowered, the Captain of the Gurkha guards walked out and up to the awaiting Mantis military leaders.

"We seek asylum for our leader's body to keep it from being desecrated by the rioters. Will you let us wait here until the unrest is over?" the Captain asked.

Loyalty to one's superiors was a trait admired by the Mantis and since these men were known to them, and the Prince was dead, they sensed no ill intent. They were only armed with swords, useless against the firepower the Mantis possessed. This would also give them the appearance of neutrality in the internal coup d'état instigated secretly by them through Bodhidharma's own sons.

"Come down into the infirmary, you can wait there." The Mantis leader said.

The guardsmen lifted the platform carrying the body of the Prince and solemnly moved out of the ship and into the Citadel. The corridors were wide, and they were ushered into a large infirmary which accommodated over 100 beds. The facility was designed to hold the human kidnapping victims periodically processed from Earth to Gannicus. Today there were only five females occupying the beds.

One was Faith, near death. She had been mishandled, her long hair roughly shorn, which left her head bleeding. She was injected with several experimental Mantis formulas to test the resiliency of a very young female specimen to their latest enhancements. They did not expect her to survive. She lay curled up in a fetal position, barely aware of her surroundings, save for the constant pain that wracked her body. She felt her spirit slipping away into an immense oblivion and welcomed the release from the pain. She let go.

Suddenly, her spirit popped out of her tortured body and the pain stopped immediately. She floated up over her ravaged body, looking down in bewilderment, not believing what she was seeing. Her heart had stopped, and she could see that she was not breathing.

The Prince's spirit had been taking the lead in this scheme to fake death, but as soon as Faith's spirit left her body, she entered the realm of the angel. The Sentinel, lying dormant in the body of Bodhidharma a few beds away from Faith, suddenly awoke. He felt her there and immediately rose up and out of Bodhidharma's body. This caused the Prince's heart to stop beating - it being the spirit of the angel that kept their physical body alive. Bodhidharma's spirit did not have the power to keep those functions active after his death, in the absence of the spirit of the angel possessing it.

The Sentinel sensing Faith's death experience, moved toward her spirit which was still floating above her body staring at it in bewilderment. He knew he only had moments to act and approached Faith in a reverent posture, arms outstretched, touching her shoulder. She was not shocked to see an angel, with large beautiful, outstretched wings floating next to her. She felt peaceful, relaxed, with the pain of her earthly physical life finally over. It was a tremendous relief and she looked forward to seeing her mother again.

"Dear Faith, your time is not yet over, you still have much to accomplish," the Sentinel said.

"It is alright, to die is my gain," she replied. "I am ready, take me into His fold!"

She raised her head to get a better look at this beautiful angel. His hair was golden and sparkling as if the sun was shining on the mythical golden fleece. He was muscular but lean with a silent strength emanating from his core being … and their inner eyes met. The angel, resplendent in a flowing white robe, its wings outstretched, with feathers iridescently sparkling, displayed the reality of the spiritual realm in all its splendor. Faith instinctively knew the angel in its elemental form, its purpose, its reason for being.

"Return now!" he said. "There are many that will depend on you here; there is much to do, much to accomplish, for the Lord's sake, for your mother's sake!"

The angel slowly stretched out his hand, letting it hover above Faith's physical body. He willed his spiritual energy to flow, sending a visible spark of life through her. Faith's spirit immediately sank back into her body, flowing in along with the spiritual energy of the angel. Her body lifted off the bed and a bright light swept out in all directions.

As her body settled back into the bed, she gasped and sat up, screaming as the pain suddenly reappeared. Her female companions, at first startled by the flash of light manifested by the angel's energy surge, circled her bed to give comfort as they saw her cringe in pain. They had been weeping, thinking her dead.

The Sentinel, already back in the body of Bodhidharma, reacted swiftly as did Bodhidharma, sensing the despair he had first felt when he saw the pitiful face of Faith in the cryogen tube centuries before.

The avenging angel, now once again the fused spirits of the Sentinel and Bodhidharma, soared up out of the bed and hovered over Faith. The sight of her writhing in pain, with her hair shorn, head bleeding from gashes in the skin, was excruciating to them both and their rage began to quickly build, heating the air around them. The Sentinel knew what she looked like after her experimental treatment by the Mantis, but Bodhidharma had never seen any vision of her except the one in the cryogen tube before today. Their enraged reaction was swift as the fused spirits swung into action.

Pointing at his inner Gurkha guards, the avenging angel said, "You six, secure this room and let no one in. Protect this woman and her companions from harm on pain of death!" The heat emanating from his body began to move out further causing everyone to back away and distance themselves from it.

Eighteen well trained Gurkha warriors followed the avenging angel out of the ward, quickly eliminating the Mantis guards posted by the infirmary. The armory was also underground, and the avenging angel sent a blast of fiery energy into the Mantis guards at the door, disintegrating them. The weapons they found inside the armory were not dissimilar to the ones they had trained with. Automatic projectile weapons, pulse rifles, even an assortment of

Lorsguns, relics of the Roman revolt. Arming themselves to the teeth and making sure weapons were loaded and ready, they turned to Bodhidharma, his black eyes burning with revenge, and awaited instructions. They were simple.

"Kill every Mantis in this Citadel; open the gates so our people can enter and take over. I will circle from above and prevent any Mantis ships from returning to reinforce them." A war cry erupted from the throng of Gurkhas as they raised their weapons in salute to their once fallen, but now returned leader. Bodhidharma has returned from the dead!

Chapter 13

Mysterium Fidei

Faith's body became transfixed. The energy from the angel's touch combining with the uncertain elements of the Mantis's alien enhancements, made her stiff as a board on the bed.

Shock waves pulsed through her as the chemistries interacted. Synapses were rapidly firing new and revealing recognition into her body and mind. The pain was disappearing again as the tissues healed themselves. This was a welcome relief from the excruciating sudden pain she first felt after re-entering her body from the spirit world. The relief was overwhelming. It was almost as if the pain free spirit world had accompanied her into her physical presence ... *the kingdom of heaven is living within me,* she thought. The bright colors and sheer amazement she felt in the spirit world was absent though.

Fighting to reorient her mind, body, and spirit to the present reality, she sat up and swung her legs over the edge of the bed. She felt better than she had ever felt in her entire short life. Looking around, she was startled to see the huge space with so many beds. This was a far cry from the remote wilderness she had disappeared from on Earth, one of her last living memories. It stunned her when she thought of her small plain wood plank home in the Rhode Island colony that she had grown up in. She recognized one of the girls around her bedside as the older Indian sister, her companion on the wilderness road from Boston to Providence.

"Pray tell, what has befallen us?" she asked.

They spoke at once in whispers, so the Gurkha warriors could not hear them, about the insect demons and how they had molested them with strange metal instruments. They made her promise not to reveal it, lest they all be disgraced. The leader of the Mantis laboratory had told them they would become pregnant soon. Faith remembered waking from her long sleep and being roughly carried to a metal table, but the rest was masked by the angel's touch.

Her head began to tingle, and she raised both hands up, laying them flat on her mostly hairless, scarred scalp. She stroked her hands over her head to the back of her neck. She then felt a rush of heat moving to the top of her head from the center of her body. She stood up and closed her eyes, reveling in the sensation; without thinking, she repeated the motion with her hands over her torn scalp, releasing more heat.

First, there was the shock of being hairless with open wounds on her scalp, then an almost automatic response from inside her to fix it - make it right. *Lord, make it right!* she prayed. The heat spread out over her head. She could not see but felt the wounds closing and the hair beginning to regrow. *Yes, re-grow, restore – now,* she thought. It was her heartfelt wish, her declaration!

75

Her confidence soared; out of the corner of her eyes, she saw her strawberry, reddish-blonde hair flushing out, thicker and longer than she remembered it. An image of her mother stood before her.

"Child, hath thou allowed thy hair to grow for its strength or for the vain pride of its beauty?"

"My hair hath been the strength I needed to keep faithful til your return," Faith said.

"Then I endear you to never cut it. Endeavor to persevere and you will discover many triumphs!"

Her female companions gasped and stood back from her. One screamed, which attracted the attention of the Gurkha guards, who were protecting the entrance door. Several swiftly approached with swords drawn.

Faith opened her eyes, assessing the chaotic situation immediately. She spread her arms out, palms up and open towards the Gurkha guards, a universal sign of peace.

"Fear not!" Faith said. "Blessed have I been with healing and will harm no one."

Recognizing her as the face in the center of the five cryogen tubes from the many sessions the Prince conducted in the underground room, the Gurkha leader and his cohort kneeled in front of her. "We are your servants!" he said. *This can only be the one worshiped by our Prince, who now heals herself*, he thought.

Just then, the rap-rap-rap of pulse rifle blasts and the sound of explosions erupted above them. The sound of battle could be heard throughout the Citadel compound.

"Secure the door!" yelled the Gurkha commander as he stood and returned to guard the entrance.

It was some time before the outside noises of a raging battle subsided to occasional firing and the loud booms of Lorsgun discharges. The Gurkhas were anxious to get out there and see if the avenging angel and their warrior brothers were victorious or dead.

"Let us go," one of the warriors pleaded with their leader. "Either we celebrate with them or die with them. Either way, waiting here is a coward's path."

The cohort leader approached Faith and asked, "How shall we address you?"

"I am called Faith ... Faith Dyer," she replied.

"You are of great importance to our Prince who we have sworn allegiance. Since he is not here, we will live or die by your command." He had witnessed the miracle and had no doubts she was the one with divine powers: the object of their warrior's cult.

"I agree with your companion. Let us not stay here but rather, seek our liberty out there, to live or die the same fate as your Prince and his warriors."

The Gurkha leader smiled ... *she is wise beyond her years.*

"But wait," she said, suddenly aware and embarrassed by her bare uncovered head and her hair cascading down. She turned to the nearest bed and pulled a pillowcase from it. She covered her head with it, holding the ends under her chin with one hand. "Now I am ready," she said as she gestured toward the door with the other hand.

They entered the corridor wary of their surroundings. Chips and black carbon marks on the walls mixed in with Mantis body parts along the floor gave evidence of a fierce battle. They could hear crowd noises as they approached the Citadel buildings' exit. It led to a large square courtyard

77

which normally housed the fleet of small flying craft the Mantis used. A shout went up as they opened the doors.

A large mob of knife and club wielding people of all ages were staring transfixed at the battle scene taking place in the air above the Citadel. The avenging angel had just grabbed the tail end of a Mantis attack craft and flung it into another one that had been pouring pulse cannon blasts in his direction. Each blast had been deflected by a shimmering heat shield that surrounded the angel and his wings. His body was skillfully maneuvering around in the aerial dogfight. The resulting explosion when the two crafts collided was like a firework display which was immediately celebrated by loud shouts and praises by the crowd below.

The human mob, flushed with victory in the city and the surrounding countryside, had followed the Mantis as they retreated to the Citadel. When they arrived, the Gurkha guards had already opened the gates to the compound, and the crowd poured in as the last of the Mantis occupants were being wiped out.

The avenging angel, with the fused spirits of the Sentinel and the Prince, was at the peak of its fighting prowess. He scanned the horizon from left to right looking for more ships, but all had been destroyed. There were no Mantis left on Gannicus. They were either killed or fleeing back to Mantis space.

The tension in his form was clear as he sailed back and forth around the Citadel, then drifted down into the large square. The avenging angel relaxed when he saw Faith restored to her former self and her companions safe, surrounded by the Gurkha guards. Her countenance glowed and the hair flowing out from under her covered head was shining as the rays from the afternoon sun reflected off it. The great white feathered wings flapped as the avenging angel slowed and came to rest yards from Faith. The lingering heat from his body forced those around him to back up, but not Faith. The warmth drew her in.

She moved forward relishing the heat and the divine energy it brought to her senses. It reminded her of the heavenly place she had first met the angel and his divine touch.

Most people in her position would have been overwhelmed by the events of this day, but her Christian upbringing, including the miracles and interventions by angels of old she remembered from the holy book, only reinforced her growing conviction that she was part of a grand divine plan. She pulled herself together, head held high, and approached the avenging angel with her right arm upraised, palm open facing the warrior angel.

"Be calm, angel," she said in a soothing voice as she basked in the heat emanating from him. "The demons are all dead; you may now enter your rest."

The angel bowed his head and the sparkling golden glow emanating from him slowly disappeared, along with his visible wings. He looked up, fixing his gaze on Faith's ocean blue green eyes. The moment seemed to stand still and everything around them in the periphery of their vision faded. They focused solely on each other with a growing awareness, an 'ah ha' connection of their centuries old bond which Faith was just now coming to realize. Then the angel heeded her call and folded his will under Bodhidharma's but staying in the Prince of India's body to keep it alive. The angel's task to protect Faith was fulfilled.

Chapter 14

Resurrection City

Bodhidharma swiftly implemented his plan to resurrect the human population of Gannicus from their bondage by the Mantis. A Guild Protectorate was quickly applied for and approved, thanks to the contacts the angel provided.

A Third Tertiary spaceship was in orbit around the planet populated with historians and archeologist from different species wanting to record every detail about the evolution of the planet, details that Bodhidharma did not want to reveal yet.

Bodhidharma's Machiavellian mind was turning over the various scenarios, the pros and cons of this new relationship. His whole being was working in overdrive. He initially focused the efforts of these new investigators on the Roman revolt and the nearly successful mass genocide which occurred on the Valerian continent. This was a key element in the swift approval of the Gannicun Protectorate status. The Roman legions were only sporadically emerging from their underground lairs, suspicious of a Mantis trick to flush them out of their hidden sanctuaries. They were dismayed by the strange alien visitors they met, who were introduced by Bodhidharma as protectors.

The wreaked aircraft of the Mantis, all space worthy when operable, were gathered and cannibalized to produce new slip stream flyers. Their parts were quickly reverse engineered and copied in new manufacturing facilities springing up around Resurrection City, the new city being built as Valeria's capital.

The moon circling Gannicus became the first off world platform to be colonized using lava tubes as entry points into the underground. It was just a matter of constructing and securing airtight covers over the entrances to the lava tubes with subsequent injection of a nitrogen/oxygen rich air to make large underground areas habitable. Establishing a permanent colony in space with regular resupply using space worthy craft was the first requirement of the new order. This accomplishment extended the protectorate status another 25 years.

Bodhidharma was satisfied that the years of meditation, seeking relationship and knowledge from the Sentinel, paid off handsomely as the planet thrived under these new arrangements. However, his suspicious mind could not help but feel developments were unfolding too easily. There had to be danger in the background he was unaware of, dangers like the one that resulted in his death. He explained to his alien protectors that his apparent death was in fact a deliberate ruse, planned by him to overcome the Mantis overlords, not an actual death, which it was. The mystery surrounding Prince Bodhidharma and the avenging angel only increased as did the admiration of his people for their leader.

Faith and her companions insisted on sanctuary away from the prying eyes of everyone in order to have their precious babies in secret. Her companions were ashamed that they were made pregnant by the hated Mantis insects. Faith was ambivalent, rejecting everything that resulted in the pregnancy, but understanding from her upbringing on Earth that triumph often overcomes tragedy with the proper discernment and faith in the outcome. And so, on orders from the Prince, they were taken to his mountain hideaway on the Nepali continent, an isolated retreat overlooking a waterfall that Bodhidharma often used to get away from the stress of governing.

The young ladies occupied the guest wing of the remote royal grounds. Gurkha guards, sworn to secrecy, were assigned to protect them. Bodhidharma tried to convince Faith to abort the unborn child, explaining that there was no way of knowing what kind of enhancements the Mantis had put into the child's essence, his DNA. She refused, aghast at the thought of taking the innocent life growing inside her.

"They meant it for evil, but God will turn it into good - you'll see!" she said.

Bodhidharma traveled to his hideaway in the mountains often to check on Faith and speak with her about events unfolding on the planet. Her pregnancy was complicated compared to her companions, which were normal and on schedule. They each had babies about nine months and within weeks of each other.

Faith's pregnancy was accelerated, and the rapidly evolving fetus grew at an extraordinary rate. So fast, in fact, that she lost weight as the fetus absorbed her nutrients and calories faster than she could replenish them. The best doctors were brought in; in addition to all the calories she could ingest orally, they began pumping intravenous nutrients into her.

When it came time to give birth, the Sentinel angel assumed control of Bodhidharma's body. He insisted on holding Faith's head in his hands throughout the birthing process, masking the pain, easing the delivery, and ultimately saving Faith's life. She delivered a healthy strong baby boy who she named Trueman Dyer - just five months after conception.

The tertiary investigators spent nearly a year studying the Roman population which were surfacing in larger numbers now from their underground tunnels. They had been decimated to the point that little history of their origins was available, only cryptic references to a mysterious place called Resurrection City.

For this reason, Bodhidharma began the construction of a city near where the largest concentration of Romans were appearing on the surface. He named this new dwelling place Resurrection City. This pleased the Romans and the alien investigators as well.

The historians reported rumors reaching the surface about a man named Seediq, leader of three legions and a legend among his people, who was refusing to come to the surface. They asked Bodhidharma's help in facilitating the re-introduction into society of Seediq and his legions.

Being infatuated with Faith's beauty and intelligent innocence, Bodhidharma slowly began to bring her into his sphere of knowledge. He wanted to test the waters of a potential future together. She gladly accepted all he told her about himself, showing great interest in his bizarre life story. She remembered many unusual stories from the holy book and so thought those experiences were not so terribly different from their current circumstances on this alien world.

She considered Bodhidharma like a benevolent uncle, similar to Increase Dyer, her real uncle on Earth, who had kept her safe in Boston. The difference was that the Prince, despite his old age, remained a young-looking man of about 28 years old due to the alien enhancements in his body.

"We have a problem on the Valerian continent," he told her one day. "Most of the Roman population has surfaced and we are helping rebuild their society, but one group who was nearly wiped out by the relentless Mantis underground attacks has not come to the surface. All attempts to convince them to come up have failed. We have sent Roman emissaries into the tunnels and they have found scouts from these legions who say their leader is a man named Seediq. All efforts to speak to this leader of the remaining under-ground legions are being rebuffed. He apparently considers this a trick by the Mantis."

Faith considered the problem for a moment. She thought about her background and the stories she had memorized from the Bible, trying to apply them to the current situation.

"Consider this," she said earnestly, "have the angel make appearance to this Seediq in a dream and show him a way to the surface, encouraging him to join the other Roman legions in Resurrection City."

Bodhidharma thought for a moment. "Your council is well thought," Bodhidharma said, surprised at her insight. "I will approach the Sentinel" - *can you do this* - his mind shifting to communicating at an inward level deep in the recesses of his mind where the Sentinel dwelled.

It is what we are made for, the angel replied.

"It shall be done," Bodhidharma said turning his focus back to Faith.

Surprised, Faith could see from the expressions on Bodhidharma's face the back and forth that was taking place. This was her first inkling that the "Avenging Angel" was still present in the Prince since the battle of the Citadel where it was obvious to everyone that something miraculous had occurred. She had long since concluded that only the angel could have brought the Prince back from death, it could not have been a ruse, given the results. This opened a whole new perspective of this man in Faith's eyes.

He is not a believer, but the angel is, she thought.

She searched her memories and found many instances where God used unbelievers to fulfill his purposes. This revelation eased her tension around this stern, driven man. She remembered the pure spirit that embodied the angel when their eyes met, floating above her deceased body in the infirmary.

Surely the angel would not allow Bodhidharma to sin while they shared the same physical body, she thought.

She began to see Bodhidharma's actions in a different light, not focused on selfish gain, but rather on efforts to benefit his people, to prosper them and keep them out of alien bondage. With this new revelation, she began to look forward to their meetings with anticipation and the new insights they would bring to her.

Chapter 15

Ghosts of Nain

Seediq, Luna, with their young son between them, lay curled up together under a pole tent on the sandy outcropping in what used to be the underground village of Nain.

Seediq had setup a series of refuges throughout this part of what has become an underground Roman kingdom. It had been two years since the disastrous battle that took place here and no sign of the Mantis.

After first settling deeper underground, they had slowly started reconnoitering back up the river systems reclaiming territory lost to the Mantis, discovering other lost cohorts and small fragments of legions scattered among the tunnels. The current silence of this place sometimes overwhelmed him. He often imagined the terrible battle that took place here and the blood stains that could sometimes still be seen in the sand if one knew where to look.

Seediq's biggest regret was not convincing the elders at Nain to come with him. Their complete destruction here at Nain left a bloody debt on his soul. He was ashamed that he was still alive, and they were not. His warnings should have been more forcefully convincing.

He knew now from observing the scarring and blast holes on the cavernous walls what he had only suspected would happen before; large kinetic weapons had been used here, weapons capable of taking out any defensive position. He had never seen such weapons in use but had heard rumors of them from his elders among the diminishing ranks of the 13th legion. He was told they were too powerful to be used in the smaller tunnels the legions normally resided in for fear of collapsing the walls and trapping everyone, attacker and defender alike, under the rubble.

Seediq would often gravitate back to Nain while traveling up and down the river systems checking on the outposts, wondering when the next Mantis attack would come. Reports from the surface that they had been defeated by some avenging angel seemed far-fetched. He kept his legions on high alert.

The intensity of his short life, the lives lost, this last battle, and then the silence that followed, kept him on edge especially here in Nain. It felt like those times were the real times and this slow silent time - only a fleeting dream.

Seediq listened to the breathing of Luna and their son as he lay beside them. The underground river ran slow and wide at this point near their sandy shelf plateau. The three legions and their families were now spread out among many different temporary settlements to lessen the damage from a renewed attack from above. Nain now housed about thirty people. All was quiet as he lay listening to the rustle of the water soothing his nerves. With his mind concentrating on the river sounds, the breathing of his family, and their tranquil effect, he fell into a deep sleep.

The dream began as usual with the sounds of battle. He could just see the Mantis rounding the last turn in the oxbow section of the river coming into the open lake with pulsing bursts of light coming from the end of large tubes. He ran from one defensive position to the next encouraging the warriors to hold fast. As he left each position, it exploded in a flash of bright light and from the light emerged the ephemeral spirits of the lost warriors. They circled about frantically as the battle continued.

This night as he ran near the shoreline of the large lagoon, Seediq sensed something not seen before; he saw a movement below the surface of the water, followed by a slowly rising golden glow. He stopped, frozen in his tracks, transfixed. He could not move a muscle in his body. The spirits of the dead continued to move frantically back and forth behind him, their ghostly light clearly reflecting off the surface of the water.

The angel broke the surface headfirst with his bright white wings spread out behind him and with hands outstretched. He moved slowly along the surface of the water toward Seediq and the shoreline. Coming down, his feet resting on the sandy shoreline, the Sentinel spoke.

"Seediq, your yearnings have been heard. The God of your fathers has eliminated the Mantis from Gannicus and now is the time for you to return to the surface."

"I do know not this God," Seediq replied.

"You will, but first you must return through the same tunnels you traveled to get here, back to the surface. You will find there a man named Prince Bodhidharma with a woman named Faith Dyer at the surface waiting for you. They will lead you and your people to Resurrection City, and you will find what your people have lost."

Seediq could not believe what he was hearing. "If this be true, show sign and give the spirits behind me their rest. Help them!"

"It will be done as you say." The angel rose up in the air and stretched out his arms. "Be still. It is over," the angel's voice echoed around the cavern. "Follow me to your rest!"

The ghostly spirits circling over the battlefield of Nain all came to a halt at once and focused on the angel. When he had their complete attention, he turned, beckoning them to follow. He slowly drifted over the river. The ghostly spirits followed after him. A flash of his hand created a rift opening in the cavern side wall just above the river line. With the angel leading them, in one fell swoop, they all disappeared into it.

Seediq awoke with a start. The ephemeral ghostly spirits and the angel's glowing presence were gone. The river sounds and the breathing of his family were all that remained.

Chapter 16

Koheleth

I have heard of complications between man and woman relations, Faith thought, facing a dilemma. *It would not be the angel or the warrior prince, it would be the angel and the warrior prince, with an avenging angel revealing itself when events spiral out of control.*

"You seem distracted," Bodhidharma said, seeing her far off look. "Will you marry me or not?"

Bodhidharma was used to getting his way - persuading, cajoling - until the conversation circled around to agreement with his position. Especially now, after the awe-inspiring appearance of the avenging angel and his resurrection from the dead; his status as leader of his people was unquestioned.

"I bring you to the most beautiful spot on Gannicus, express my undying love for you and you have nothing to say!"

"I ... am considering ... your proposal," Faith hesitantly replied, "and have questions."

90

"I expected you would, given everything you've been through," he answered softly, thinking about the trauma of her abduction, the centuries in the cryogen tube and the abuse by the Mantis when they awakened her.

Faith was now 18 years old but her experiences and the contact with the angel energies had given her a level of maturity and insight much older than her years. Bodhidharma, who had lived for millennia, still had the appearance of a healthy 28-year-old man due to the alien enhancements administered to his body early in his sojourn as a mercenary for the Mantis.

They stared out from the mountain villa's private terrace, overlooking the beautiful waterfall flowing into a lush valley. The villa was well hidden in Bodhidharma's secret compound.

He had decided to marry Faith Dyer. It was a decision made in part to help unite the south Asian Indo-Aryans and the Romans on Gannicus. Faith was becoming on the one side, a deity worshiped by many, and on the other side, he sensed that she would become a long-awaited religious leader. He knew that such leaders were common among the Roman population before the revolt and the loss of their way of life.

In the depths of his inner soul though, he had fallen deeply in love with this rare woman. Watching her childlike innocent face with tears frozen in mid-stream for those many years, enamored him toward her; when she awoke, the power and beauty with which she carried herself in every situation, sealed the decision to ask her to marry him. He reached over and held her hand, patiently waiting for her questions.

Faith closed her eyes in contemplation. She wanted to start a real family, missing the close-knit large family life of her upbringing in the Rhode Island colony: sharing a bedroom with her sisters, her mother Mary combing her hair until it shined. But these were all light years away in time and space, creating a disorientation of her thoughts, especially now with Bodhidharma right next to her.

Her son Trueman was growing quickly, too quickly according to the doctors, and she prayed daily for his safety. The evangelical work on Gannicus that she wanted to pursue following in her mother's footsteps was progressing slowly since she had few opportunities to reach out beyond those individuals permanently housed at the retreat complex.

She barely knew the angel but felt exhilarated on those rare occasions when she felt his presence. She especially remembered being drawn into that warm golden glow surrounding him in the courtyard of the Citadel. The Prince himself, on the other hand, was the consummate leader of men, his personality forged during a time of upheaval and warfare. He was tall and lean, with piercing eyes. His very presence could send a chill down the spines of those around him.

He never treated me that way, she thought, *but rather always tender and loving.*

She knew he loved her, would die for her if necessary, but she was determined not to enter a marriage relationship unless she and her partner were equally yoked. Then there were the concubines, hers would be a monogamous marriage relationship - the only kind she would abide. So many questions, and how to broach them.

His kiss caught her off guard, tender and unexpected as it was with her eyes closed contemplating the marriage relationship. Startled, Faith stiffened and moved back slightly, this being her first kiss. He followed her; his lips full against hers. She started to feel the pull, the warmth, begin to manifest itself - *was this the angel's energy?* She wondered as she tentatively returned the kiss. The sensation was pleasurable, which surprised her. They kissed like this for several moments when unexpectedly, his mouth parted slightly, and his tongue began to slowly caress the crease between her lips. She barely opened her mouth and their tongues met.

She felt his arms begin to encircle her, drawing her into his body. He slowly laid her down on the sofa and it was clear that he was aroused. Faith began to panic as he pulled her in closer. They had not worked out her expectations, the yoking between them: the concubines, her evangelical work. She would not give herself up without knowing in her heart that this was the true and right path for her. She sensed that there was no clear opening yet.

She began to struggle, squirming in his arms, working her hands up between them and pressing back against his chest. He didn't yield, holding her tightly, not willing to release her. Suddenly, his body went limp and he stopped breathing.

Faith jumped back, then reached out tentatively and felt his neck for a pulse. There was no heartbeat. She panicked looking frantically around the room for help - and that is when she saw him. The angel perched atop the railing of the terrace; his countenance showed bright against the blue sky beyond. There was no golden glow this time, it was more like a silver light emanating from his body. His arms circled his knees which pressed into his chest. Wearing a simple white covering, he looked like a Greek god with his face upturned looking out and up into the sky, as if seeking guidance. That face was serene and with a calmness to it, but also firm jawed and handsome.

Faith moved tentatively toward him. "Are you, the avenging angel?" she asked.

"Not today," he replied softly.

"Can you help our friend Bodhidharma, he appears to be - he's dead!" she pleaded.

"I will, but there is still time, sit beside me," he motioned with his hand toward a bench next to the railing. "Has Bodhidharma said anything to you about me?"

"Very little," she replied. "We have not spoken at length about any topic of personal importance between us, and yet today, he proposes marriage. I would consider the match, but have too many questions unanswered," she said.

"As it should be," the angel replied. "I know the Prince like no other. His intentions are pure, and he truly loves you, but he is a man, raised in an age when power and domination were virtues. After many years he now knows there are other ways to project strength, through mercy, for instance, or through love. That is why he supports you, loves you, and seeks your hand. He sees the positive affects you have on his people. Did you know that he was born almost 200 years before Christ, in 185 B.C.?"

"That was unknown to me," she replied surprised, "but I did know he is very old, perhaps old enough to live during our Lord's time," she replied. "All this is so daunting; it has not been opened to me yet what my path should be. It is still a mystery. What of me, am I to live a normal life, or is my life to be extended by these alien potions as was his?"

"Your life has been enhanced, not only by the alien influences but by the angel energies I sent flowing through your body. That's what brought you back from the dead at the Citadel."

"I remember. It felt veiled to me then, like a dream. I was outside my body moving where I knew not. Your hair, it was golden - I remember - but brown now?"

"We see things imperfectly here in these physical realms, but in the heavenly places we see with perfect clarity! You deserve to know the truth before moving forward with any marriage. Bodhidharma was murdered by his sons. He was lying on his funeral pyre the same day you were being experimented on by the Mantis monsters.

All martyrs, their children, and all true servants of the almighty have angels accompanying them. They call us Sentinels. We nudge, guide, warn and deflect harm but have limited ability to interact in the physical world without the Lord's blessing. I knew the treatments performed on you would result in your death and I could not abide that. I sinned, failed, and have become a fallen angel, deserving the fiery pit for what I have done."

"Pray tell and heaven forbid, what on earth have you done deserving of the fiery pit?" Faith asked, perplexed.

"I entered the dead body of Bodhidharma and forced its rebirth. I did this because it was the only way I could interact in the physical world and save you. It was a selfish act and I will be condemned to the hell fire for it." The angel's sad blue eyes looked down, forlorn and distant.

"Many lives you have saved on Gannicus since you entered Bodhidharma's body!" she said forcefully. "The genocide on the Valerian continent has stopped. The Mantis monsters departed. A thriving city is being built for survivors of the carnage. From what Bodhidharma tells me, a new energy and purpose thrives in the people. I sense a great opening from the Lord is possible here. Tell me, why do you dwell on this as a selfish act?"

"Because," the Sentinel hesitated, "I love you too!" he replied. His piercing blue eyes, which matched the sky behind, revealed his perplexed confusion.

She gasped and brought her hand to her mouth, covering it, as a path suddenly opened. "As I love you," Faith replied quickly. The disorientation was leaving her, replaced by discernment. It was clear now, the years in the cold cryogen tube with the angel often wrapped around her physical and spiritual bodies, soothing, relaxing her anxiety. She could visualize it now, though she was unconscious of it at the time.

"Bodhidharma's body cannot live unless I live inside him, in the physical realm with him," the angel said. "If I stay out too long, he will surely die again. So far, after the original sin of entering his body, we have not sinned. As the avenging angel, our mission was righteous to protect the innocent against the Mantis threat; thus, a path may yet be open to me to return for good to the heavenly places. If you marry him, I will be unable to refrain from consummating the marriage along with him, the pull will be too strong. I will be damned for sure as a result, the same as the angels of old who came down and took earthly wives, fathering the Nephilim."

"If that is the case, I will surely refuse to marry him, of course!" she said emphatically.

The angel looked down sadly, quietly raising his hands and shoulders in a shrug - the conundrum clearly stated.

"But perhaps … there may be an opening," Faith said after a moment in contemplation. "God is love as you know, the holy book says as much," Faith said confidently. The angel nodded in agreement. "Can it be that such a love will allow us a clear leaning towards His purpose here on Gannicus – and on Earth?"

The angel thought about this new revelation for a moment. "It may be possible. Why don't we seek guidance on the matter together?" He sat down on the bench beside her and reached out his hands, palms up.

This Faith knew only too well how to do, having practiced it often with her mother. Clasping the angel's outstretched hands, she felt a strange almost undetectable current move into her, warming her hands. It was a slow charge, not a golden glow or real heat associated with it.

In an attitude of prayer, they remained in silence for a while as was the custom – the Quaker way. She drifted, wondering if this warmth exuding from the angel was deliberate, or only his normal essence, always present. She determined the latter, since it felt a natural flow, his essence and not forced. The warmth moved slowly up her arms, but not distracting, rather soothing. It went on this way until her whole body from head to toe felt the energy flow from the angel, fully charging her entire body. It felt as if she was relaxing in a warm bath, an unusual rare event where she came from in colonial America. And at that moment, an opening showed itself to them.

Chapter 17

The Deliverance

The next morning arrived with fanfare, this being the day Bodhidharma and the angel had arranged for the meeting with Seediq and his legions at the surface of a large tunnel complex near Resurrection City.

Faith prepared for a lengthy trip and long stay but carried only one bag, as did her two expatriate girlfriends. The ladies all waited patiently lounging in the tropical grassy common area between their guest bungalows and the large main villa. The babies of her girlfriends, nearly a year old now, were laying down on a throw blanket making giggling noises. Trueman went from one to the other making funny faces while tickling them.

Trueman appeared to be about the size and physical strength of a three-year old boy even though he was much younger. This rapid physical development by Trueman did not surprise Bodhidharma, him being familiar in his travels with all sorts of unusual out of the ordinary upgrades and alien enhancements. Being nearly a child herself when

Trueman was born, Faith had few reference points; she just took it all in stride, cherishing every moment with her son.

Gurkha warriors were loading several black cigar shaped craft brought in the night before for the trip to the Valerian continent. Bodhidharma, with a small retinue of attendants, exited the main villa full of energy and headed straight for Faith and her circle of expatriates.

"Faith," he said heartily with outstretched arms, "I trust you are well this beautiful morning!"

"I am indeed sir; your mercy and favor to us cannot be repaid," she replied with heartfelt enthusiasm.

"Have you informed your friends of the importance of our diplomatic mission today?"

"I have indeed, and they are most willing to accompany us. Little did we dream we would have the occasion to serve you in such a worthy and good cause." They all nodded their agreement. "Such deep grief and trouble the Romans have sustained these many years through the enmity of those evil monsters, the Mantis."

"Mount up then!" the Prince said to everyone in a loud boisterous voice.

Trueman waddled behind Faith as best he could, not liking to be carried in the presence of so many adults, especially the serious looking straight backed guards of the Gurkha cohort. Faith wondered about this behavior. *He is surely growing up too fast!* The thought tugged at her heart.

Bodhidharma made a ceremony of placing Faith and Trueman in the place of honor next to him in the pilot's compartment. He pulled the shoulder straps over Faith's head and secured them tightly to her waist harness. She stared into his dark eyes wondering about this enigmatic man who could be a stern ruler one moment, and the next, a compassionate companion. Today, he was outdoing himself, ever attentive to her and Trueman.

He was very proud of the miniature seat he had ordered especially built for Trueman between the pilot and co-pilot seats just for this occasion. Trueman also was very thrilled to be sitting in front where all the action was. While Bodhidharma secured him in his little seat, Trueman stared wide eyed at the array of dials and gadgets along the flight console and then turned to his mother with the biggest smile she had ever seen on him. He reached out and grabbed her hand, holding tight. Turning his head, he held out his other hand to Bodhidharma, who at first looked embarrassed, but after seeing the smiles on their faces, he gladly held on and cherished the moment.

The craft lifted off with a flourish, rising above the secret complex, then moved out over the magnificent waterfall. The day was gorgeous, not a cloud in the tropical sky. After settling in and posting the destination into the console, Bodhidharma placed the craft on automatic pilot and turned to Faith.

"What happened last night," he asked, "did I fall asleep?"

"I'm afraid so," she replied mischievously, "you were very tired."

"I must have been, but there was something important I wanted to discuss with you."

"Oh," she replied, her nerves tensing at the thought of the subject of marriage about to be brought up again.

Not now, it's too soon, the angel nudged Bodhidharma from within his mind, *there is a time for everything, but not this now!*

Are you sure? the Prince nudged back.

I'm, sure. You are making a great impression on her right now. She is young ... there is time.

Perhaps you are right, he nudged back, then turned and gave Faith a big smile. "I suppose it can wait until another day. We have a big responsibility ahead of us today and we don't need too many distractions."

Faith breathed a sigh of relief. She could tell by his facial expressions that there was an intense conversation going on inside his head with the angel and she wished she could have eavesdropped on that discussion.

They arrived outside Resurrection City on the Valerian continent in the early afternoon. The sun's rays were bright against the barren rocky landscape, a stark contrast to the lush tropical nature of the Nepali continent. This place had been ravaged by years of war. The Gurkha guards fanned out in a semi-circle facing a large cavernous opening in the earth that was the closest entrance to the underground tunnels. The city was just over a small ridge behind them, a one hour walk from the cavern.

It was obvious to everyone that advanced guards from the Roman legions were close. Some were hidden behind boulders while others stood upright in plain view; their Lorsguns were propped on their hips and nearly full bandoleers of shotgun shells were strapped across their bodies from shoulder to waist. They were all young, their clothes no more than rags, and all were barefoot, but the look on their faces and the scars many wore on their bodies, showed a life lived in constant struggle.

Faith's heart went out to them. She reached down and picked Trueman up, cradling him on her hip. He struggled at first, but the look on her face made him calm down as he surveyed the serious nature of his surroundings. He somehow understood that at this moment he must let his mother lead the way. Faith's friends were already holding their babies when she slowly began to walk forward, and they followed.

"Faith," Bodhidharma said alarmed at her actions, "what are you doing? Stop!"

She stopped and turned. "We must show our compassion and mercy to them quickly, or this meeting could turn to grief and sadness," she beseeched him.

She speaks the truth, the angel spoke into the mind of Bodhidharma.

"Very well," Bodhidharma acted quickly, "but let me take the lead." He stepped in front of the women and began slowly walking toward the Roman scouts. His hands were clearly visible with palms up, showing no weapons. Faith and the women expatriates, holding their babies, followed behind him.

With this development Seediq, and Luna holding their son, came out of the shadows leading the legionaries and their families. They slowly emerged into the light at the surface of the underground karst tunnels, now behind them for good.

"Diligio vita," Bodhidharma said as they met in the middle of the open ground.

"Diligio vita," Seediq replied, shocked that this obvious outsider from another culture entirely, knew his language.

Faith, standing next to Bodhidharma, turned to him with a shocked expression on her face as well and asked, "How is it you both speak Latin?"

"Do you know it? It is the language of the Romans," he said. "I spoke it for many years, counseling with the legion's leaders, before the rebellion."

"I know it well enough," she replied. "I was a disciple at my mother's feet, and we read a Latin Bible over many times and memorized it."

"Good," he replied, "then I am appointing you to be in charge of settling these new refugees into Resurrection City and seeing to their needs!" He stepped back and offered her the lead position.

"It would be my honor to serve them, and you," she said. So, from then on, they spoke Latin.

Seediq studied her face and gauged her to be young and a real beauty by the standards of Gannicus: well fed with a confident and caring quality about her. She held her head high with sparkling blue eyes staring directly into his. *This is someone I can trust,* he thought.

"We accept you into our presence as equals," she said.

"And we you," he replied.

With that, Bodhidharma, Faith Dyer, and her friends began leading the group toward Resurrection City. Faith and Luna swapped stories of their children as they walked along.

Bodhidharma pulled Seediq aside to get the measure of the man. *Not much older than a boy*, he thought. But Bodhidharma himself had assumed leadership at a very early age and he did not consider that a detriment. The young man already had a reputation among his people. Seediq was tall for a Roman, about six feet, wiry but firm with not an ounce of fat on his body. He carried himself erect, showing no fear, with a confident straightforward calm demeanor.

"Seediq," Bodhidharma said, "you have a reputation as a leader among your people and that is sorely needed here on Gannicus."

"I have heard of your reputation as well: a battle leader, scourge of the Mantis and liberator of our planet Gannicus."

"It's true I led the revolt, but without the people who followed me, it never would have succeeded. The people have to believe in their leaders!"

"That is true," Seediq agreed.

"I am going to need your help in the future if we are to rid our worlds of the Mantis yoke. There has been too much unnecessary innocent blood split!" Bodhidharma said emphatically.

"But I thought they were defeated, and you … and we, were victorious," replied Seediq.

"Here on Gannicus that is true, but I am referring to our home world."

The Roman's history was completely lost to Seediq's people after the total collapse of their society and the nearly successful genocidal war waged by the Mantis.

"Our home world?" he replied bewildered.

"Yes, our home world," Bodhidharma said as he put his hand on Seediq's shoulder, "our home world … Earth!"

PART TWO

GANNICUS PREPARES

I was in sorrows during the time of the first workings the Lord manifested in me. He showed me a vision of my mother - teacher and martyr; then the spiritual discerning came into me, what it was that did veil me and what it was that did open me. The path was clear to declare the truth!

The Journal of Faith Dyer

Chapter 18

The Proposal

Planet Gannicus - 2032 A.D.

Bodhidharma named and began constructing Resurrection City immediately after the Mantis genocidal war ended to accommodate the steady flow of survivors emerging from their underground caves. It was two years later before Seediq and his legions emerged from underground, wary of a trap being set by the Mantis insect warriors.

Bodhidharma built the city using the architecture and city planning that was present before the war with the Mantis. The general style was Earth colonial and fashioned after English General Oglethorpe's plan for the city of Savannah, GA. The Oglethorpe plan was an embodiment of all the major themes of the Enlightenment period on Earth. At the heart of the plan was a vision of social equity and civic virtue with equitable allocation of land outside the city limits to preserve a sustainable agrarian economy there. In keeping with the current needs on the planet, an industrial park was added, with manufacturing facilities replicating the Mantis

106

technology necessary to fuel the space program and keep the Consortium's protection status in place.

The fashion of the clothes was also colonial styling since the technology for making clothes was rudimentary, mostly simple homespun, using materials made from cotton, wool and hemp grown locally outside the city.

Several months after Seediq's legionaries and their families emerged from the underground Karst tunnels, Bodhidharma visited Resurrection City.

The furious pace of rebuilding was continuing. A warehouse complex was constructed near the outskirts of the city to house and feed the recently arrived legionaries from the 9th, 11th, and 13th legions, along with their families. This being the last of the organized underground legions to emerge, keeping them here for the time being allowed ample time for them to transition into Valerian society.

The warehouse cafeteria was bustling with the lunch crowd consisting mostly of mothers with children. Most old enough, and thus eligible to work, ate at the industrial park for lunch. Luna, Seediq's wife, and Faith Dyer, the Quaker expatriate, stood side by side in the serving line ladling out food to a long line of very grateful Romans.

The mood was cheerful and friendly. Having this abundance and variety of food was a luxury for them after so many years underground. Many volunteers from other legions, previously integrated into life in Resurrection City, were also present to help welcome the new arrivals.

Bodhidharma, the Prince of India, dressed in the splendor of a Gurkha warrior prince, entered the cafeteria to visit with Faith, accompanied by a half cohort of his best Gurkha warriors. He was visiting the city to hold planning meetings with Valerian leaders. When he entered, every activity came to a sudden halt and complete silence fell over the entire assembly; all eyes were focused on the oddly dressed newcomers. Keen to make an impression on the new arrivals, Bodhidharma stepped confidently over to where Faith stood in the serving line and ceremoniously invited her out to an open area.

Shocked by his sudden unexpected appearance, Faith removed her apron and walked slowly out from behind the serving console, following his lead. She was dressed rather Quakerish, with a plain brown homespun long-sleeved blouse and a skirt that nearly reached the floor. Her long reddish blonde hair was drawn back and secured in a loose braid that reached down her back to her waist. Her head was covered, except for an inch or two above the brow, by a simple light brown kerchief held secure by a clasp under her neck. Several tiny beads of sweat etched her face and her cheeks glowed pink from the heat of the serving line.

Even though she was now 18 years old, her simple childlike features remained, along with the grace which always surrounded her. Bodhidharma could not help but stare in awe at this rare woman in front of him. Faith, embarrassed by the attention and remembering her 17th century manners, lowered her eyes to the floor and curtseyed respectfully before the Prince.

Accompanying Bodhidharma were the same six Gurkha warriors that were assigned to protect Faith at the battle for the Citadel and had witnessed her death and resurrection. They immediately fell to their knees around her. They would not rise until each one had been blessed by Faith placing her hands on their heads.

Bodhidharma then led Faith to an unoccupied corner table for some privacy. The Gurkha guards stood in a semicircle just far enough away from the couple's table so no one could hear their conversation. They faced out towards the silent crowd in the cafeteria and slowly everyone resumed their normal activities.

"I am here visiting the important leaders of Valeria and I could not leave without speaking with you," Bodhidharma said.

"Lo, you place honor on me with your presence, Prince Bodhidharma," Faith replied.

"Please don't be so formal. I have something of great importance for us to discuss together. The angel revealed to me that we may have the same desires for the future, but that you have more questions."

Faith hesitated on hearing this unexpected news. She looked away, gathering her thoughts together and resting her chin on her clasped hands. *Where to start*, she mused, deep in thought. She closed her eyes for a moment. To speak less formally for her is to revert to the Quaker speech she grew up with, the one her mother and family used. That was her natural way of considering problems in her head and of talking about them. She did not have to think about it.

"You ... refer ... to the marriage proposal," she said as she turned to look back at him.

"I do, and you have questions," he said, looking intently into her eyes.

"Y-Yes, I do," she said quickly, looking away, trying to gather the long list in her head and start with the highest priority. Nervously sitting up straight in the chair, she turned and began with the one overarching question ...

"Pray tell, what stirreth you to avail yourself to me in this way?" she asked. She naturally fell into the Quakerly speech she was most familiar with to try and ease her tension. "From what is told, your life til now sufficed without the need to marry. You hath ample opportunity with concubines that requireth no marriage bond," she said.

"When I first saw you in the cryogen tube deep in the Mantis' Citadel fortress, you were fifteen at the time I believe, but looked much younger, with the face of a child. All I could see of you was that face in anguish, with tears trickling down, frozen for all time on your cheeks. Twigs and leaves were sticking out of your beautiful red hair.

"At that moment, it struck me to the core, how the Mantis had mishandled you and how they likewise spread their terror wherever they go without regard to the pain or suffering they caused; I was a pawn in their schemes. I was determined to rescue you, regardless of the cost to myself.

"When I brought you to the underground sanctuary in my palace, I spent years in meditation, studying every curve and line of your face. It was because of you that I decided to risk everything to throw the Mantis yokes from our backs and give us both our freedoms. To state it plainly Faith, I fell deeply in love with you!"

Faith was taken aback by the depth of this confession and the inner feeling Bodhidharma was able to express for her. She had never experienced anything like this before.

The perfect answer, she thought, *now to discover the true relationship!*

"Since you speak of yokes," she said slowly, "if I marry, my husband and I will be equally yoked, if in relationship one with the other. What is your mind on this?"

"To be honest, I have not given this idea much thought," he replied. "But where you are concerned, I agree, we are equals. Why do you think I allowed my Gurkha guards to kneel before you? Faith Dyer is considered a goddess on the Nepali continent after you were seen by hundreds of my people calming the avenging angel with your words and outstretched hand. You approached him even into the golden glow while others could not get near him for fear of being burned. My people have long thought me a god and now they worship you as a goddess. Therefore, we are equals."

"Perish the thought! That is not at all what I intended by saying we are to be equally yoked!" She cringed back in her seat and her hands went palm up in front of her. "Wo is me if I dare contemplate being a goddess. I wish only as normal a family life as the perils of this world permits."

Bodhidharma thought for a moment, his face was serious, forming a wrinkle in his forehead. He had stopped aging due to alien biotechnology at about the age of 28 years old. He had lived for millennia and never found the need to marry. Faith was 18 years old now, but in reality, she had lived for centuries herself.

"There is no normal life for you and me," he said finally, coming out of his reverie. "You have been touched by the spiritual energy of the Sentinel, brought back from the dead even, as have I. And the alien enhancements the Mantis infused you with to produce your son Trueman, are unique. In that respect, we are also equals, like no others."

Faith began to see his point. Who else could she marry that would have had the same extraordinary experiences as she has had besides Bodhidharma? And then there was the protection and knowledge he could bestow upon her son

Trueman. And last, but certainly not least, there was the angel who lived within Bodhidharma, keeping him alive. He and the Prince came as a package. You could not have one, without the other.

"Know this about the concubines," she said, "I will not abide relations outside the marriage."

"I have laid with no one since the angel entered me. He will not allow it, for fear of becoming a fallen angel," he replied.

She giggled at this, her hand to her mouth. "He won't allow it." She smiled, thinking of what that conversation had been like. "So, have you dismissed them all then?"

"I cannot just throw them out on the street. That would be a disgrace to them and to me."

"I agree when you put it such a way," she said. "Perhaps if you let them marry, many suitors would avail themselves of the opportunity."

"That is a very reasonable solution," he said. "I will make it so when I return to my palace. So, will you marry me now?" he asked forcefully.

"You intimidate me!" she blurted out.

"What?" he replied, taken aback.

"We need to be honest, one with the other, if this union is to come to fruition. You intimidate me!"

"Explain to me your meaning, so that I may understand it," he said slowly, somewhat offended.

"You are royalty, a prince in a line of princes and kings. My origin is simple, a Quaker girl hailing from colonial America. I grew up in a log cabin. You grew up in a palace. Your bearing is so erect and straight. You tower over people and are so stern and proud. How could I possibly please such a man?"

"What you see is the persona I want people to see and respect. Without respect, you cannot rule. I feel different when I'm with you. I feel at ease and, I'm in love with you." he said plainly.

She blushed as he took her hands into his. "I want to be alone with you, so that we can get to know each other better," he said peering seriously into her eyes.

"We cannot be alone again or something like … almost happened before … could happen again," she replied.

"Do you not trust me?" he asked.

"No, I don't. Even be it so, alone with you, I trust not myself either."

He smiled knowingly at that. *She is a true honest soul*, he thought.

"I have more questions," she said quickly to change the subject of the conversation.

"You have really thought this through, haven't you?" he asked.

"It's all I've considered for weeks now, that and aiding Seediq's people to settle into Resurrection City after their long ordeal," she replied.

She considered her next priority carefully. "For the sake of the Life of the Seed here on Gannicus, I wish to continue my mother's teachings. I will stand up in assembly and speak. I will be a bold witness to the people!" she said emphatically and with confidence.

"I would expect nothing less from a goddess," he said, with a wry smile on his face.

"I am no goddess," she replied. Exasperated, she pushed his hands away, "Stop claiming that!"

"I'm only teasing you," he said sheepishly. There was silence between them for a moment.

"One more thing," Faith said slowly, tenderly, "avail me this, if our intimate bonded relationship is to come about; I would call you by a nickname. Bodhidharma is much too formal."

He thought for a moment, then grudgingly replied, "Alright, but only in private, I cannot let my respect fall among the people."

"That is reasonable – Bodhi!" she exclaimed.

"Bodhi!" he said, looking around to see if anyone had heard. "That was the nickname my mother gave me," he whispered. "It is only right that you should use it."

"Perfect," she smiled broadly, her face glowing.

"If we are going thus, we will be chaperoned until our wedding night. And the engagement will be long, just so we are both sure this is the right path for us. Agreed?"

I have waited many years ... centuries even, he thought, *a few more months or years will not matter.*

"Agreed," Bodhidharma said, his eyes nearly tearing up.

Now the last test, she thought with abandon.

"Come with me, Bodhi," she quickly said, standing up and grabbing his hand.

"We are going to buy you some new clothes." She pulled him up in a rush, leading him out of the cafeteria, hand in hand. They were going on their way to the nearest mercantile store to find several simple Valerian outfits for her too proud prince to wear. The Gurkha guards followed, looking around the cafeteria with proud sheepish grins on their faces.

114

Chapter 19

Suo Gan

"Silence restores the ability to hear."

~ George Fox

Trueman's rapid physical growth was exceeded only by his exponential mental capabilities. He absorbed everything from an early age.

Faith was well aware of this as they were thrust into this chaotic uncertain future together, in the fast lane compared to her slow relatively simple existence in colonial America. She encouraged Trueman to keep his abilities a secret as her mother had warned her when she was memorizing the holy book and learning Latin in such a short period of time.

They were life's outliers, savants from two widely separated ages in history. Even so, their bond was inseparable, and they hid nothing from each other. It was almost as if they could read each other's minds, sensing what they were about to say, like twins floating in their mother's womb holding hands.

Faith and Trueman walked the perimeter of Resurrection City, their evening promenade, with dwellings on one side of the dusty road and the countryside stretching out on the other. This was their lone time together, their bonding time. At the end of each day, they caught up on each other's activities. Trueman was in training to be a leader of cohorts and Faith continues serving the needs of the Roman population, once starving, and nearly wiped out underground. They held hands with no shame, for mother and son were well known in the community and respected for their intelligence and foresight.

It was said that Faith had the gifts of the spirit including prophesy, foreknowledge, and yes, even healing, which she denied. Nevertheless, she never turned anyone away, and more times than not, a sickly visitor or stranger left her presence feeling more whole than when they arrived.

Some she felt compelled to visit on their sick bed near certain death and after her touch and earnest prayers they often began to recover. She suspected she may have accumulated some of the angel's healing ability when he resurrected her. When she ate in the cafeteria with the Roman population, glasses that she drank from would disappear and any cloth she touched would vanish and end up being given to someone who had an illness in the family.

Trueman was also considered special, but undefined, like an athlete refusing to compete at their optimum potential, the pent-up qualities waiting to burst forth. Trueman was only nine years old by human standards but appeared to be 17. He was over six feet tall with broad shoulders tapering to a thin waist. His rapid growth was always a topic of discussion in the city, there was no way to hide it, but the Dyers kept their

116

abilities close to the vest. Concerned, Faith begged Bodhidharma to delay the wedding, allowing them to focus their full attention on her son, at least until he reached manhood.

Among humans, only Bodhidharma knew that Trueman was actually an alien enhanced savant, whose abilities were just beginning to reveal themselves, coming to the surface in spurts, unpredictable. He knew Faith, being a martyr's daughter and witness to her mother's death at the hands of Earth's authorities, kept a sense of wariness about her. This was tempered by her insight into how present and future events might unfold. He trusted her instincts and agreed they would focus on Trueman until he became a mature young man.

Faith kept her son grounded by enveloping him in a mother's love. At the same time, she passed on the spiritual teachings of her mother, which she learned from George Fox and other itinerant dissenting preachers who roamed the English countryside in the 17th century. Trueman had the entire knowledge of Faith's short life on Earth engrained in his mind.

Coming upon a quaint garden nestled between two tall buildings, Faith sat down on a bench with scrolled ironwork and guided her son Trueman's head, nestling it in the crook of her neck. They both leaned into each other. In this way, they could speak in whispers without anyone knowing what they were saying. This had become a long-standing habit, starting when he was only a toddler. Trueman was at an age in appearance when most men from 17th century Earth assumed manhood. This brought a heightened sense of foreboding to Faith. She sensed his quest, his testing, was near.

"The Life of the Seed is the Word, a direct revelation to us all," Faith whispered slowly into the ear of Trueman.

"This revelation is available to everyone," he whispered back.

"Let us procure equality in spirit through the priesthood of all believers," she replied.

They waited in silence for a while, pure silence, the emptying out of all worldly things in the mind … bringing divine revelation to the Quakers. With the silence came the unseen noises in the garden making themselves known: the continuously running water cascading down the rocks to the nearby garden pond, the buzzing of flying insect wings, the rustle of leaves in the breeze.

Two foreign mercenaries working for the Mantis stood unobserved in a secure room on the top floor of the nearest building overlooking the garden. They zeroed in on the Dyer's activities using strategically placed sensors.

"This is the queerest part," one said.

"Agreed, how does the silence bring it on?" the other asked.

"That we don't know," the first replied, "perhaps some spirit followed them from Earth."

"That's not possible, you know there is no God, no spirits, and no afterlife," answered the second, giving a stern look to the first.

"Of course," the first replied. "I was only providing an explanation that they would understand." The two turned back to observe the pair in the garden.

After a while, Faith began to shake. A low voice began to speak in a hoarse whisper which seemed to flow from her mouth, shimmering in the air. "Behold, go forth as sheep in the midst of wolves; be ye therefore wise as serpents and harmless as doves."

Trueman began to shake, and a deep whisper emerged from his mouth as well. "I see the new heaven and the new Earth opening up, the lion is lying with the lamb, and the tears are wiped away."

A myriad of sounds, thoughts and feelings flowed from mother to son and back. Telepathy, but they did not know it as such. Faith being very young and a novice in the Way when she was taken by the Mantis, assumed this was a natural part of the Quaker enlightenment.

Even so, Trueman was not all human. The Mantis impregnated his mother with genetic material from other species. The genes that made them special on Earth, the instant recall, combined with the genetic soup the Mantis experimented with, made Trueman truly unique, exceptional, one of a kind.

The angel's special touch on Faith, resurrecting her body from death while Trueman was only a developing embryo, had also added unknown spiritual energies, some expressed, some potential, inside both of them.

"What are your instruments showing?" the first asked.

"There is a definite increase in electromagnetic energy, but it doesn't appear to be at harmful levels; they are worth watching more closely," the second replied. "The Mantis were right about them!"

Minutes later Trueman and Faith both woke as if from a trance. "Remember," she whispered, holding his face with both hands, staring intently into his eyes, "do not reveal yourself to these demons. They must know not the true power of your abilities or who we are, for they will surely destroy us."

"I know mother, don't be the perfect or the best in class or athletic competitions, or it will bring too much attention to myself."

"You must go forth and redeem our world - promise me!" She held his head between her hands and stared into his eyes.

"I promise," Trueman replied.

"Neither fill your mind with fear of these demons," she said.

"Mother, it is possible to tolerate the monsters for the sake of an angel like you," he replied, stroking her cheek. "I love you."

"And I you," she replied.

"The light overcomes the darkness, the promise is true," she said.

"The promise is true!" he repeated confidently.

"And know this also," Faith said as she lay her hand over his heart, "the hope of the promise lives within you now!"

She, being at peace now with her duty to raise her son in The Way fulfilled, said, "Come quickly, we have duties to fulfill ... and I sense a malevolent spirit about this place."

Chapter 20

Spirits in the Material World

"Go to the tabernacle in spirit
when you are not able to do so physically!"

~Padre Pio

Prince Bodhidharma sat in the lotus position in front of his three apprentices: Trueman Dyer son of Faith Dyer, the expatriate, Menelik, the tall Ethiopian descended from the offspring of King Solomon and the Queen of Sheba, and Vimmul, the most faithful son of Bodhidharma.

These three were especially picked to learn the secret knowledge Bodhidharma had gathered. The training was in preparation to lead cohorts to Earth, not as mercenaries, but now as free peoples undoing the chaos created by the Mantis.

"You have all excelled at the physical training you will need to command cohorts on missions," the Prince said. "Now I will teach you spiritual mysteries that very few humans possess, shown to me by a messenger of God. This knowledge will give you an edge over others in the physical realm." Bodhidharma stared at Trueman when he mentioned the spiritual being.

The Sentinel, mother would say, Trueman thought. *Does he know that I know?*

"You have been chosen out of all the rest to embark on this journey with me," Bodhidharma said. "I have lived a long time by techniques passed on to me by those I have encountered along the way. Some places I traveled to because I wanted to go there. Other places I went because I was forced to go under compulsion of death to my loved ones by the hated insect Mantis if I did not go. You will have similar journeys but not under compulsion, but rather by your free will. Starting today I will give you a unique ability only few possess, the gift of spirit travel," he said with a conspiratorial tone.

"Spirit travel is dangerous if the techniques are not well learned. Pay attention or you could return to a dead corpse and not be able to reenter it!" he said with emphasis.

"The spirit leads the mind, which leads the body, and thus you are protected. Most spirits that dwell in the heavenly places in their truest form are pure, unpolluted by the ways of the material realms, but not all. We are certainly not pure, and thus lies much danger when we enter the realms of the spirits. When the mind and its selfish desires lead, the spirit can be trapped, abandoning the body.

"The last key to your survival is to never leave your body unattended. It must be carefully guarded, or your enemies will have their way with you in the physical realm as I learned the hard way," he said with sadness.

"Assume the lotus position now and begin meditation. The spirit will travel from your physical body only when you have reached the 7th and final level of meditation. It may come slowly or quickly depending on your skill level. Based on your previous training, I know the three of you possess this ability or I would not have chosen you."

Trueman started slowly deep breathing and exhaling, slowing the pace of his heart as he approached each meditation level. When he reached level seven his heart and breath by any outside observer was essentially stopped. He trusted Bodhi, the name his beloved mother called the Prince in their private moments. Trueman was also allowed to use the name but he usually added Uncle to his mother's nickname, even though he knew they were only engaged to be married. Bodhidharma was really like a father to him now, taking a keen interest in his upbringing and training.

Trueman's physical body was experiencing the sensation of slowly becoming fluid, like a liquid substance beginning to flow down a trough. He felt a slight pop as his spirit exited his body. He found himself on the ceiling looking down on the four meditating bodies below him in lotus position. He recognized himself in physical form and remembered Bodhidharma's stern instructions not to lose focus on the destination.

"The banyan tree, meet at the banyan tree!" *Focus... focus... focus...*

Bodhidharma was there waiting for Trueman. His spirit hovered, suspended in space under the branches of the large banyan tree in northern India, the birthplace of Buddhism. Stars speckled in the night sky.

"I knew you would be first," he said. "Do you know where we are?"

"Earth?" Trueman asked. The Prince had placed a large picture of the banyan tree mounted behind him on the wall of the training room and had spent an entire session on only one topic ... focusing on the destination. He also monitored their progress in the spiritual realm to ensure they were on track.

"The real true Earth, our ancestral home!" Bodhidharma replied.

Trueman stared at his hands, then at the oddly surreal landscape. Everything was so crisp and clear. The colors shined and there was a sharpness to the edges of all the objects. The branches, leaves, and grass took on a life of their own, no longer appearing as inanimate objects. He felt the wind moving through the banyan tree blowing across his face. The numerous stars shining above were bright and sparkling silver in the night sky. He was not just in the landscape; he was part of the landscape.

"How is it possible to travel so far in such a short time?" Trueman asked in bewilderment.

"Almost any destination is possible by traveling in the spiritual realms as long as you don't lose focus. We can travel great distances, but unfortunately, have a limited ability to interact with the physical world while in this condition. Also, there is always the danger to your physical body if it is not well protected or if you stay out too long. That is how my enemies were able to kill me ... the body I left behind was not fully protected."

It was not often that Bodhi spoke that frankly about his past, especially about such a moment as his death. Trueman listened carefully.

"I have been to Earth many times over the centuries when the rifts open," Bodhidharma said slowly. "After my capture and subjugation by the Mantis, I was sent back to foster diverse religions. The insects wanted to make sure that no central core religion was adopted by all the inhabitants of Earth to further fragment and divide them."

"It feels like a dream," Trueman said slowly, turning his hands over in front of his eyes.

"The first few times you spirit travel it feels like a dream until you get used to it. Eventually you begin to understand how to manipulate the journey, then you realize it is just as real as any other plane of existence.

"I planted the memory of this place in your minds before we began. The others should be showing up soon. You have to have a destination and a purpose in mind before you make any journey or you will just float in space, a complete waste of time and putting yourself in danger for nothing."

Just then Vimmul appeared, followed shortly by Menelik. Bodhidharma waited for them to get acclimated to their new surroundings, then began the advanced instructions on spirit travel. The importance of a pure spirit and staying with established protocols were critical since there were other realms existing in the spiritual dimensions that fed off negative energy. Being trapped there could prevent one from returning to their physical bodies resulting in certain death. Each were asked questions about their desires. Where did they want to go, who did they want to see?

When it came to Trueman's turn to respond to the questions, he said, "I have always been curious about what it was like during the time of Jesus."

"Those times were chaotic as is the case over most of Earth's violent history." Bodhidharma said. "I met Jesus only once during one of my assignments to survey the Roman Empire for the Mantis. I was in the city of Jerusalem during a feast day when I felt a strong spiritual presence and was drawn to it out of curiosity.

"I found Jesus walking by the pool of Bethesda and followed him from a distance. It was said that when the pool water rippled from an unseen source it was because an angel was present. The first person to enter the water was healed of their disease. I watched as Jesus spoke to an elderly man crippled since birth. He told the man to get up and walk, which he surprisingly did, rejoicing as he went. This increased my curiosity even more and I moved in closer. He must have felt my presence and turned to observe me.

"'Greetings Rabbi, I am Bodhidharma,' I said.

"'Are you an evil spirit?' Jesus asked. I assumed he must have sensed my alien enhancements as evil or being used in an evil way.

"'I am neither good nor evil,' I replied.

"'He that gathers not with me scatters abroad,' Jesus said as he turned to leave. His appearance as he walked away was transfigured, a surreal bright light enveloped him - for protection no doubt. No truer words were ever said about me since my whole mission on Earth at the time was to divide, not to unite people. The purpose was to keep them in darkness so their exploitation by the Mantis could go on undetected."

"What happened then?" Trueman asked.

"His rebuke was like a physical slap across my face, even though he had not raised a hand to me. I determined at that moment that there are some people and places better left alone. From then on, I did not try to spread any religion or influence near where his spirit was working.

Jesus, friend of sinners, Bodhidharma mused. "In my early travels on Earth I was a nomad, learning the ways of the many people groups spread around the world. Unfortunately, we cannot go back to change anything we have done, either physically or spiritually. We can only now move forward to try and make it better. If we are going to unite the Earth, we will need to learn many languages and customs."

Chapter 21

Do Insects Sleep

Deep inside the secure Nepali Embassy, a diplomatic compound in Resurrection City, a new phase in the relationship between Prince Bodhidharma and the Quaker mystic Faith Dyer began.

"I trust you and Trueman are comfortable in your new apartment," Bodhidharma asked as he and Faith sat at the kitchen table drinking tea. The apartment was modest in size but well-appointed and in the most secure area of the compound.

"I am. Thank you so much for being so attentive to our needs," Faith replied.

"Now that our engagement to be married has become public and Trueman has begun training to be a leader, extra security measures become necessary. My enemies will try to get to me through you and your son. I hope you understand."

"I am concerned that the guards will restrict my movements about the city, and I will be unable to complete my mission to be a voice to the people here," Faith replied.

"You will barely know they are there," Bodhidharma explained. "I have assigned the same Gurkha guards who protected you during the battle for the Citadel. You saw them again when I came to the cafeteria to ask for your hand in marriage and you blessed them. They will be dressed in Valerian clothing and will keep their distance. You will be able to recognize them but the people around you will not know they are your guards. There will be no interference with your movements unless they see danger approaching."

"That will be an acceptable arrangement. Perhaps I can persuade them to become followers of the Way as well," she said as she squeezed Bodhidharma's hand, teasing him. Trueman had already retired for the evening, and they made their way to the living room to catch up on the latest news and spend some quality time together.

Do insects sleep? Trueman thought as he lay in bed wondering about the Mantis menace, the curiosity sprang on him out of nowhere. Perhaps it was his experience with spirit traveling, opening up so many possibilities that were closed to him before. He could go almost anywhere and see for himself without being observed. *Do insects sleep?*

Faith and Trueman were connected in strange ways that had no earthly explanation and they kept nothing from each other. Trueman knew Bodhidharma's secret, the indwelling angel, critical to his survival. He also knew the revelations brought to Bodhidharma by the angel including the fact that at least one other planet existed where the Mantis carried out

129

their evil schemes directed at the exploitation of Earth. That planet was called Novaya Zemlya (New Earth). It was near Gannicus by cosmic standards and Trueman was itching to explore!

He assumed the lotus position on the floor, slowed his heartbeat and breathing, moving slowly through the meditation levels. His spirit popped out of his body soon after achieving level seven as he concentrated on Novaya Zemlya and its location. He began to panic when he found himself floating in space above Gannicus and not at his destination.

He redoubled his efforts, concentrating with focused intensity visualizing Mantis insects on the surface of Novaya Zemlya. He repeated the name of the planet until he was instantly hovering over a massive structure that he knew must be a Mantis compound. He watched from above as tall scaly insects moved about on four legs.

Trueman glided through a closed door, then down the hall and into a classroom that was in session. Four dimensional diagrams, drawings, and designs floated in the air in front of instructors as they described their meaning.

The Mantis operated in shifts with each group spending about fifteen minutes beside each 4-D display, then they moved to the next station. It was strange being so close to the monsters that had tortured his mother and were partially responsible for his creation - at least the alien parts. He reached out to touch one and his hand went right through the serrated forearm of the nearest Mantis. He shivered.

Trueman found that in the spirit state he could understand the intricate, subtle meanings in their language. After following behind one group for several sessions, he was able to comprehend each display and their purpose. His mind was like a fax machine. Each document passing through and being imprinted there.

Trueman inherited the ability to instantly recall written documents from his mother but this was far beyond anything he had ever experienced before in the material world. There was something about the spirit realm that propelled the mind into an advanced state of understanding. He hoped he would remember it all and understand it when he returned to his body.

The night wore on, and slowly, each group retired to other rooms where ropes were hanging from the ceiling. They would leap up to grab a rope with their mouth. Once secure with clamped jaws, their arms and legs folded up into their chest and abdomen and they closed their eyes, entering a state of torpor or dazed sleep.

Trueman began to feel a need to return to his home on Gannicus as well and just as he thought of it, he was back in his body. He opened his eyes and looked around the familiar bedroom. He was quite elated, celebrating in his mind, when he found that he remembered everything … the designs, the diagrams and their purpose. His heart raced as he thought of where this could take him in the future.

One night each week he spirited away to Novaya Zemlya and returned, learning and storing the knowledge about astronomy, space travel, rifts, the multiverse, anti-gravity devises, and other spacefaring civilizations. He also recorded the tragic information he was able to put together regarding the horrible treatment of Russian and Chinese expatriates kidnapped from Earth to Novaya Zemlya.

Apparently, the Roman revolt on Gannicus triggered a new flurry of mercenary activity by the Mantis, setting up yet another world for infiltrating Earth. The timing coincided with the rule of the Russian dictator Joseph Stalin and his Great Purge, resulting in the imprisonment of millions of people in the Gulag labor camps in Siberia.

Stalin setup show trials, consolidating his power by sending communist party leaders, army officers, and the intelligentsia to these death camps. Even peasants who expressed the least bit of opposition to his policies followed the Russian elite to the Gulags. This offered the Mantis a perfect opportunity for an unlimited supply of mercenaries with little concern for their disappearance from Earth. Most who entered the labor camps never returned to Russian society anyway. It was a death sentence.

Similarly, when communist dictator Mao Zedong consolidated his power in China, it presented another opportunity. The Mantis were particularly fascinated by the cultural revolution and the many re-education camps setup to purge the intelligentsia and opposition elements in China. Trueman could tell that these techniques were being repeated on Novaya Zemlya creating an endless supply of mercenaries. By the end of Mao's reign nearly 70 million Chinese died through starvation, forced labor, and executions or disappeared into the mercenary ranks of the Mantis Empire.

Trueman was crushed as he saw the brutality in the camps which operated on opposite sides of the planet. The Russians and Chinese were barely aware of each other's existence. The only way to survive the camps and live through this hell was to swear allegiance to the Mantis. At that point if deemed worthy, they were removed from the harsh Mantis operated Gulags and re-education camps to become trained mercenaries under the command of other well indoctrinated mercenaries. This also allowed them to marry and start families, to live a more tolerable life. However, their families were held hostage when they made their mercenary raids. Failure was not an option for them because it put their families at risk of being thrown back into the hell of the Gulags and re-education camps.

Trueman learned another valuable piece of intelligence - Mantis insects do sleep, but it pales in comparison to the vast knowledge he gained as a spirit traveler!

PART THREE

EARTHBOUND

Chapter 22

John Sator's War

United States Army Yuma Proving Ground
Yuma, Arizona, 2035 A.D.

John Sator lay on the crumbly ground of the Sonoran Desert, his body insulated from the cold by a half inch pad barely large enough to hold his body. The pad lay underneath his army issue sleeping bag. A light snow covered the landscape and his sleeping bag.

The cold was nothing compared to other deployments. Once, he almost froze to death in a Colorado snowstorm when a massive 'Siberian Express' cold front made an unexpected turn at the Canadian Yukon and roared straight down to the Midwest states.

He stared at the stars, always numerous and bright in the absence of light this far away from any town. He remembered camping trips he used to take with his Boy Scout Troop to Big Bend National Park as a youth; canoeing on the Rio Grande river through the Santa Elena canyon was like gliding through a medieval cathedral with all its many spires rising overhead.

John Sator mused over his 20 years of army service mostly testing high tech killing machines and protective gear at the Yuma Proving Ground, one of the largest military instillations in the world. He remembered them all as part of the army's Future Combat Systems Projects: *Reactive Armor for the tanks, Non-Line of Sight Cannon, Mine-Resistant Ambush Protected MRAP's for military vehicles. The Counter C-RAM System - hard to believe Gatling guns are still state of the art, 150 years after being invented - and now Railguns.* He was lead engineer on the Railgun Project dubbed the "Game Changer," the pinnacle of his career.

Originally developed by the Navy for at-sea ship-based applications, railguns use electrical energy to create a magnetic field around a metal shell propelling it by kinetic energy at Mach 8 toward a wide range of targets. Kinetic energy warheads do not use gunpowder or other explosive materials, which makes them safe to handle and fire compared to conventional weapons.

After creating and testing the 40-ton tracked vehicle railgun prototype, there was a major problem with the development of the most powerful single ground attack weapon ever created; the United States Army was giving up on it for lack of money. The Yuma Proving Grounds were being shut down to pay for the social net. To John Sator, it seemed everyone was part of the social net these days, getting what handouts they qualify for and complaining about the ones they don't.

The old saying his father used to tell him rolled over in his mind … *"When the people find they can vote themselves*

136

money, that will be the end of the Republic." He could picture his dad's weather worn face after years working cattle on the Texas rangeland. John didn't find out until later the quote was from Benjamin Franklin.

Not only was there not enough money to continue most military operations or live fire training for its dwindling military, support for allies around the world was now a thing of the past. Taiwan was absorbed by China. South Korea was fighting for its life, holding on to its bombed-out capitol and the southern half of the country. Israel was left out to dry, surrounded by jihadist led countries waiting for the right moment to attack.

The Russians had regained most of the old Soviet Union without firing a shot, starting with the Ukraine. All they did was turn off the natural gas pipeline to the European Union in the terrible winter of 2027 and not turn it back on until an "agreement" was reached.

Global catastrophes were happening almost daily now, reflecting the many fast-paced events running up to the start of World War II. A decision would be made tonight; would John Sator fade away as old soldiers are supposed to do or continue fighting and betray his country?

The sky slowly turned from black to blue in the Yuma desert as the fireball that is the sun moved up over the horizon into a cloudless sky. Bravo company awoke. They moved slowly through the usual rituals of visits to the latrine, opening of field rations, and cleanup.

"Fall in troops!" Colonel Sator shouted at the top of his lungs. He waited for the lines to form, shoulder to arm length, shoulder to arm length, then he yelled, "Attention!"

"This is how it is going to go today," he said. "This will be the last live fire exercise at the United States Army Yuma Proving Grounds. We are going to show professional soldiers from around the world what real soldiers are capable of. This will be a flawless demonstration of the largest, most effective offensive ground attack vehicle ever built!"

He waited a few minutes for that to sink in. "At ease and circle up," he said.

The company formed a semi-circle around the Game Changer while Sator proceeded to go over each soldier's duties, as if they had not heard it all a thousand times; you do what you train for.

All was ready when the dignitaries' vehicles began to arrive. Most were weapons officers from what was left of the free world's armies: England, France, Germany, Italy, and the beleaguered Poland, still holding out against the Russians. Israel and South Korea sent token representatives as well, hoping to lobby for much needed support for their militaries. It was an exercise in futility since the Railgun Project was being aborted and the U.S. was defunding its own military. Many came just for a chance to see what the weapon was capable of.

With everyone gathered around, the rear metal doors to the monstrosity called the Game Changer were swung open revealing the modular reactor, a smaller version of the nuclear reactors powering submarines. Several troops sat at control panels pumping up the reactor to supply electric power to the railgun. It had all the specs necessary to defeat any existing vehicle on the battlefield: greater muzzle velocity, increased firing ranges and terminal velocities.

A hum pierced the air, increasing in volume as the power supply pulsed through the machine. Well out in front of the Game Changer were about 30 large metal targets dispersed about the undulating landscape: old tanks and tracked troop vehicles, mostly burnt out hulks with several newer mothballed versions for show up close.

A loud thump sounded over the area as the first shell slid through the rails and slammed into the nearest tank, pulverizing it into a cloud of smoke and debris. The sound of the railgun picked up speed as its turret quickly turned - thump… thump… thump. Clouds of dirt and metal shards appeared over each target. Thirty vehicles quickly disappeared over the gunnery range in less than seven minutes! The test was flawless. The hum began to die down as the technicians dialed back the reactor. Applause and shouts of amazement sounded over the gunnery range.

As quickly as it started, the demonstration was over. Everyone gathered around the Game Changer with awe and praise. Colonel Sator shook hands and accepted the many well-deserved accolades without revealing his doubts about the future of the United States armed forces, or his country.

The Israeli liaison officer Major General Kovner lingered after the others left, pulling the Colonel over for a private conversation.

"Colonel Sator, have you come to a decision?"

"I have. I've asked the officers and non-coms who are single with no serious family ties and all being involuntarily retired from the military, to stay here … for a celebration of sorts. Everyone else is going back to base. Does our agreement still stand?" Sator asked.

"It does," Kovner replied. "Promotions for everyone who volunteers, and your own Battalion to command. The Game Changer will be built in Israel. We want this weapon!"

"We are all being honorably discharged so I suppose that makes us free to choose where we want to go. We choose to fight for Israel and the people of the Book!"

Chapter 23

In Hoc Signo Vinces

Golan Heights, Israel, 2037 A.D.

"Jewish blood comes with a high price now," Israel Defense Forces (IDF) General Kovner said. "No more lambs to the slaughter for us. We learned that lesson during the holocaust. My great grandfather and the partisan avengers struck fear into the hearts of the German SS murderers."

John Sator sat talking with Meir Kovner, his military contact in the United States and now his commanding officer in Israel. They were slowly drinking bourbon whiskey at a makeshift card table in an underground tunnel on the Golan Heights.

"When do you think the bloodletting will start?" Sator asked.

Kovner took a swig of whiskey and thought for a minute. "For us it happens every day, a stabbing here, a bus bomb next week over there, it comes in dribbles. Did you know that we eliminated almost all of the planners of the Munich Olympics massacre after they killed every one of our Israeli team athletes? It took years but that is the message we sent loud and clear to the world – you may kill us, but you will pay handsomely with your own blood!"

It was dark as Hades outside atop the Golan Heights this night. The two left their bunker to get fresh air, which was brisk and cold, as the wind blew up from the Syrian plains below. All the intelligence reports agreed, there were distant tank formations numbering nearly 4,000 by some estimates, massing in Syria to crush the Golan front of Israel.

The country was surrounded by Muslim powers intent on its destruction. There would be no pre-emptive strike by Israel like the one that started the Six Day War after a similar mobilization of Egyptian troops on Israel's Southern border in 1967.

Russian troops were now everywhere occupying front line positions imbedded with indigenous local military units with ground to air missiles. They would be used to protect their aircraft housed at airports in Damascus, the Syrian capital and Cairo, the Egyptian capital. One could only prepare and wait, hoping it was another bluff to gain diplomatic advantage over the weakened Western powers.

Major General Sator stared up at the distant stars above. They were as bright as the stars above Yuma Proving Ground. General Kovner had been true to his word. Sator was in command of a Brigade in the Israeli Army made up of mostly Christian recruits from many nations. As the official foreign governments support for Israel deteriorated, a call went out for help and many volunteered. Christians and Jews from around the world were flocking to the defense of Israel, many with past military experience of their own.

After the call went out to support Israel, almost overnight the country became more of an armed camp than usual. Kovner, being the architect of this outreach to the world and bringing the railgun technology to Israel, was put in charge of the motley groups of Americans, Italians, Australians, Swiss, Irish and the myriad other nationalities that made up the bulk of the Northern Army Group.

Sator's Brigade consisted of six brand new railgun Game Changers, each spearheading a company of twelve IDF Mark VI Merkava main battle tanks with 200 support troops, over fifteen hundred men in all. It seemed like a pitifully small force against so many tanks facing them in Syria, except for the accuracy and speed of fire of the game changers and the secrecy with which they were deployed. At night, tunnels were constructed deep into the side of the Golan Heights plateau, shielded by carefully laid-out camouflage which resembled the natural terrain at the entrance and firing exits of the tunnels.

Daytime activities showed the arrangement and support of the 72 main battle tanks dug in along the surface. It was hoped that foreign intelligence services were fooled into thinking this sector of the Israeli defenses was their weakest spot. So far, the element of surprise was holding, but it could still be Custer's last stand. There were few reserves since most of the rest of the Israeli Defense Forces were already deployed along the other main fronts of the country to save Jerusalem and Tel Aviv from a massive onslaught.

Sator insisted on choosing his own Brigade insignia which consisted of the sign that Emperor Constantine had used on the shields of his army - the Chi-Rho – by this sign you will conquer! Constantine faced a Roman army twice his size during the civil war of 312 AD. His victory came quickly, and he marched into Rome.

"Whether today, or tomorrow, or next year, we will be ready for them Meir, you can rest easy on that point," Sator said as they looked out over the Golan Heights.

"Of that I have no doubt," Kovner replied. "Their blood for ours!"

Chapter 24

Dare You to Move

News of the Mantis / Earth rift opening wide in space exploded across the airwaves in Resurrection City sending the community into an uproar.

The time for training was over. War gear was rapidly loaded onto torpedo-like transports. A large warehouse near the space port began to fill up with personnel.

Trueman sat in a briefing room with Menelik and Vimmul listening intently to Bodhidharma. He must have had his own spies in the concentration camps the Mantis maintained on the planet Novaya Zemlya; either that or he had done some spirit traveling himself, to have the in-depth kind of detail of the Mantis's plans that he was laying out for them.

"You will each be given individual instructions about the purpose and place of your missions. We will be traveling through our own secure rift and try to get ahead of the Mantis mercenaries. Should any one of you or your teams be captured and interrogated, you will know nothing about what the other teams are doing on Earth. Therefore, you cannot compromise anyone else.

"I would have preferred another year to prepare you, but the rift openings the Mantis use cannot be accurately predicted with that kind of precision. I am about to give you a gift that will heal you quickly if you are wounded and make you virtually immune to disease. There is one side effect however, it will extend your life beyond its normal lifespan."

Trueman, Vimmul and Menelik exchanged glances. Trueman, already aware of this technology shrugged and smiled, "Why not, we might as well join the family." The others smiled and nodded their heads in amused agreement.

Bodhidharma proceeded to explain. "This is the latest in Nano technology. The tiny micro-bots that I am going to introduce into your bodies induces pluripotent stem cell regeneration that will act as an internal repair system for the body. These micro-machines will gear-up the replacement of old dying cells and can maintain the normal turnover of regenerative organs, blood, and skin virtually indefinitely. However, you can die if you are hurt badly enough, or as I found out, when you are oxygen deprived. This technology is what has kept me alive all these years. You are the first to receive this legacy … you are like sons to me!"

Trueman pondered that last comment … *are we really or figuratively his sons? Is he being sentimental with the prospect of our failure and death, or…?*

"Does anyone object to receiving this enhancement?" Bodhidharma waited a moment for each one to formally acknowledge consent, then reached into a medical bag and pulled out a blood aspirator/injector. He held it up to the carotid artery in his neck and aspirated his own blood, then

146

walked over to Vimmul, injecting it into his neck. He repeated this procedure twice more.

"What you now contain in your bloodstream is technology capable of quickly repairing any damaged tissue anywhere in your body. That does not mean that if you get your head blown off it will grow back. There are obvious limitations, so do not act like you are invincible. This will allow you to do more, suffer greater pain and stress, even be near death, and still recover. Let no one know that you have this ability or that it came from me. Do you understand?"

"Yes," the young men replied. They were separated at that point to receive their individual instructions.

"Trueman, your team will be inserted near a secret underground bunker at the Kennedy Space Center," Bodhidharma said. "The Mantis have a head start on us, so they may already have control of the facility.

"It's extremely important that we take control of this underground communications bunker. All hell is about to be unleashed on Earth, the start of a new world war. The Mantis mercenaries are instructed to hold the space port until relieved by their Chinese allies on Earth. You must not let that happen. Keep communication with the International Space Station open at all costs! Do you understand?"

"Of course!" Trueman replied. "You know you can count on me."

"Here is your team list," Bodhidharma said. "They will follow your orders."

"I understand." *More than you know*, Trueman thought. He reviewed the Roman insertion team list he would lead.

147

Trueman Dyer Team Cohort:

Seediq – 25 years old, 13th Legion Valerian leader

Luna – 23 years old, mate to Seediq, 13th Legion, Medic in field triage

Rem -24 years old, 13th Legion second to Seediq

Belk – 21 years old, 13th Legion

Moro – 21 years old, 13th Legion

Ben – 19 years old, 13th Legion

Mars – 25 years old, 9th Legion

Lumen – 22 years old, mate to Mars, 9th Legion, Medic in field triage

Mac – 24 years old, 9th Legion

Eben – 23 years old, 11th Legion

Mark – 22 years old, 11th Legion

Elb – 21 years old, 11th Legion

Trueman considered the list. He recognized some of the names as being part of Seediq's inner circle. "I have seen Ben around Resurrection City and he was badly injured during the war with the Mantis. Why is he going on this mission?" Trueman asked.

"True, he did lose an eye, but otherwise he is healthy and besides, he refused to be left behind. All these 13th Legionaries fought the Mantis alongside Seediq and will not let him or Luna go on this mission without them. They are bonded for life, Seediq's trusted inner bodyguard so to speak," Bodhidharma said.

"What of these choices from the 9th and 11th Legions?"

"Seediq refused to recruit anyone else from the 13th Legion just in case the mission was a disaster and they all lost their lives. He felt the 13th had suffered enough during the 100-years war and so recruited members from the other two legions he leads."

"That makes good sense," Trueman replied. "So, is this mission going to be a disaster?" he asked.

"Not if you follow directions. There is always some risk. If you get in and get out quickly, staying focused only on the assignment, there should be minimal danger compared to most assignments.

"Seediq is a capable military leader, listen to him. Do not get bogged down in Earth's problems. They are too large for us to solve right now with one engagement. We can nudge events, but we don't have the resources to be a major player yet, compared to what the Mantis have at their disposal," Bodhidharma said.

The Prince continued, "My intelligence sources tell me there is some animosity towards Seediq from a few of the 9th and 11th Legionaries. When they surfaced, they discovered that Nain was the last major underground battle of the 100-years war. It happened right before the battle for the Citadel where we drove the Mantis off the planet. These legionaries struggle with the loss of so many when the war ended immediately afterwards. Some blame Seediq for bringing the Mantis to them.

"The truth is their pride doomed them. If they had listened to his advice and moved further down river, the battle would never have taken place and they would all be alive today. It was the arrogance of their leaders that doomed Nain, not Seediq."

Bodhidharma led Trueman into the hall and to his table, already occupied by the Roman cohort. He noticed Menelik and Vimmul at the head of other tables with their cohorts.

The tables were widely separated and conversations between them was forbidden.

It was a hard life on Gannicus, Trueman thought as he looked over his cohort. All had scars of one kind or another, poorly treated with basic medical triage. Ben had a metal patch over one eye secured with what appeared to be a tiny screw embedded in the ocular circle of the skull. Scars protruded above and below the patch, giving him a somewhat sinister look.

"I am Trueman Dyer. I will be leading the cohort to Earth. Has Bodhidharma told you anything about our mission?" Trueman asked, directing the question to Seediq.

"He has," Seediq said. *Too young to lead*, he thought … *this boy will get us all killed.*

Truman waited, "… and those instructions were?"

"To protect you and follow your orders," he said as he scratched the scar on the side of his face.

"Nothing more?" Trueman asked, somewhat surprised by the lack of information given to them by Bodhidharma.

"He said that you hold the keys to the success or failure of the mission. Therefore, your life will be protected at all costs and your instructions followed to the letter. Have you ever led a mission before?" Seediq asked.

"I have been well trained, and have seen the Mantis off world," Trueman replied with confidence. "Did you know that the Mantis sleep by clamping their jaws onto ropes hanging from the ceiling?" The suspicious glances from the legionaries around the table proved he had not been very convincing.

"No matter," Seediq said, "the more injuries or deaths we sustain, the more money and resources our legions and families will receive. Prince Bodhidharma has been very generous to us for participating in this off-world adventure. Can you tell us what our mission is?" he asked.

"We are going back to our home world ... Earth, to make right the wrongs of the Mantis. Did he not explain that?"

"He did, but we know little of that, being underground for 100 years of fighting for our own survival," Seediq replied.

"How can we be from Earth?" Mars of the 9th legion asked. "It's a fairy tale to get us to agree to fight. It doesn't make any sense."

"You have lost your history because of the Mantis genocide. It will make sense to you someday, I promise!" Trueman said, with what he hoped was a confident manner.

"The mission we are going on is complicated and could change depending on the circumstances that develop once we are on the ground," Trueman was deliberately vague. He wanted to be able to maneuver quickly once on Earth with few questions from the cohort.

"Don't worry, keep me alive, follow my orders, and I'll get all of us back alive," Trueman promised.

"That is a promise I have made also and will expect you to keep!" Seediq said emphatically.

The heavily armed cohort made their way to the black torpedo-like rift flyer. This would be their first journey to an unknown world. They were told that this world was the place their ancestors were kidnaped from, but to the Romans, Earth was only a myth that would require a lot more evidence before the tale could be considered true.

Chapter 25

Slipstream

The transport carrying the Gannicun cohort was no more than a large torpedo knifing through the slipstream. To Seediq, it was like walking inside the smaller tunnels underground again - circular, with the apex not much taller than the average Roman legionary.

The sides were laced with straps of secured seating just above the floor. The cohort filed in and took their seats, strapping in securely. They sat stoically silent, waiting for whatever their fate brought them, not unlike their lives underground in the Karst tunnels.

There was a secret hitherto unused stable rift in the multiverse, discovered by the Sentinel angel and relayed to Bodhidharma, connecting this space with Earth in the remote solar system known as Epictetus. The journey there from Gannicus was fast and smooth, nearly traveling at the speed of light.

Once in the distant solar system, they slowed and entered the ice cloud of the 5th planet, the gas giant. A clear rift was open beneath layers of gaseous clouds. It could certainly not be detected from any other vantage point. This would have to be kept a well-hidden secret since the Mantis guarded their rift openings with warships. There was no way to pass through them undetected. This rift, undiscovered by the Mantis, would be their only way back home to Gannicus.

The ride was bumpy inside the slipstream rift. Their bodies were heaving against the seat straps, pushing and straining sometimes up, right, down, or left. The legionaries just stared ahead with little emotion. Sudden death or injury was no stranger to them. Trueman gauged the prevailing mood and adopted it, even though his heart was pounding, and he could tell his blood pressure was soaring. There was a certain exhilaration about it though … an adrenalin rush. All his senses were on the cutting edge trying to get out.

"Tell your cohort they are landing near a bunker hardened to withstand massive explosive blasts," Bodhidharma had said to Trueman before he left. "We are to take that bunker and hold it. Control of the base is essential to keep communications open with any orbiting platforms. This is our mission!"

Trueman relayed further in-flight instructions to Seediq and his cohort, preparing them for the assault. "Make sure you don't kill anyone from Earth. We will need them as hostages or allies, understand?" he asked. Seediq looked down the line of legionaries and nodded with a serious look on his face.

The spacecraft was piloted by two Gurkha warriors from Bodhidharma's palace guards. Their descent into Earth's space went undetected due to their antigravity wells serving two purposes: to bring them slowly down to the surface and to help mask their radar signature, a key element in cloaking technology. They maneuvered the vessel into a deep hollow behind a large coastal sand dune about a mile from the underground bunker they would be assaulting.

The Kennedy Space Center was deliberately constructed on an isolated part of the east coast of Florida called Cape Canaveral. At that point, the land juts out into the Atlantic Ocean separated from the mainland by natural intracoastal waterways. This location minimizes the danger of civilian deaths in case of a rocket malfunction, and for secrecy, far from prying eyes. There are many isolated natural undeveloped areas on the Cape.

When the spacecraft powered down Seediq called to Ben as the rest of the cohort exited the craft. "Ben, stay with Trueman and don't let him leave the vessel until we return."

"Yes Seediq, I will," Ben replied, flipping his knife out in his left hand.

Trueman began to protest but thought better of it. *They must think they are protecting me, keeping me safe here from harm*, he thought. *No need to upset the balance just yet.*

When the others left, Trueman questioned Ben.

"What was that all about Ben, why did Seediq leave us behind?"

Ben hesitated for a moment, collecting his thoughts, then reluctantly replied, "Bodhidharma pulled Seediq aside to speak with him before we left Gannicus and gave him strict instructions that if anything should happen to you, we better not return to Gannicus, or our lives would be forfeit."

"He would never follow through with that kind of a threat!" Trueman replied emphatically.

"Why not?" Ben asked. "It seems clear to us."

"My mother would never allow it, even if I was lost on this mission."

"Well, if everything goes as planned," Ben replied, "we won't have to worry about it since you are staying here in the ship, safe and sound." Ben began flipping the knife.

"It's not going to go as planned with me sitting here," Trueman said.

Frustrated, Trueman settled back in his seat and looked back down the aisle of the ship towards the rear of the vessel. Sitting in the last seat was a little girl dressed in a plain grey Quaker vest and bonnet, her skirt extending to her ankles. She was smiling at him. Trueman turned slowly to Ben.

"Do you see that little girl, sitting in the back?" he asked as he gestured to the rear of the vessel.

"What girl," Ben said with wariness in his voice as he leaned over and stared into the back compartment. "There is no one back there." He turned back to watch the front exit, wishing desperately for Seediq to return and relieve him of this unwanted duty. He did not like guarding Trueman, but he trusted Seediq, who had seen them through many skirmishes. Trueman was untested, unknown to them.

The little girl with an angel's face stood up and spoke, "You will find what you have lost."

"What did you say?" Truman asked. He rubbed his eyes to make sure he was not imagining things. "What have I lost?"

"You will see," the little girl said, motioning for him to come to her.

Trueman stood and slowly moved toward the rear of the vessel. Stopping in front of her, he leaned down to get a better look at the little Quaker girl. Her innocent face, framed by the simple wimple covering her head, angled up at him with loving eyes. She reached up with both hands and tenderly stroked his cheeks, then turned and her face suddenly shined like a ray of sunlight reflected on it.

"You will see," she whispered as she disappeared among the baggage in the rear of the craft.

Her touch brought on a revelation to Trueman. He was no longer surprised by her appearance since unusual events were becoming the norm for him lately. He sensed danger for the cohort outside and that realization compelled him to action. He immediately moved forward past Ben, who was startled and reached up to restrain him. Trueman grabbed his hand and twisted it, wrenching his tendons to near the breaking point and forcing Ben down to the floor.

"Ben," he said, "I respect your courage and your loyalty to Seediq, but we have bigger problems on our hands here than just keeping me alive. Your friends are in grave danger; follow me and learn, and maybe, just maybe, we might be able to save them."

Ben looked up, startled at Trueman's strength and ability to disable him so quickly. "Lead the way!" he reluctantly said. Trueman let go of his strong hold on Ben and quickly moved to the front of the space craft. Ben followed.

"Step aside," Trueman instructed the Gurkha pilots in their native tongue. "I will pilot the craft from here!" he said with emphasis. They exchanged glances but quickly got up and moved past Trueman, taking seats behind the main console. They were well aware of Trueman's lead role in the mission and his relationship to Prince Bodhidharma.

"Sit there in the co-pilot's seat and listen up, it may save all our lives," Trueman said.

As soon as Trueman hit the pilot's seat, a surge of adrenalin coursed through his body. *Train what you are to do and do what you train for...* Bodhidharma had been relentless in his training for the leaders of his cohorts. This was the real thing now, and for the first time, Trueman felt he was truly in his element; no more holding back, shielding his abilities from others.

He remembered vividly his earliest memory of being in one of these Mantis designed craft, sitting in his specially built seat between his mother and Bodhidharma when he was just a youngster. His instant recall memorized everything from an early age. The spirit travel he undertook to the other planet called Novaya Zemlya (New Earth) allowed him to learn everything there was to know about the rift flyers: from the sensors to the weapons array and the gravity wells.

There was no more hiding it now and he let all the knowledge bottled up in his consciousness unleash his mind, firing synapses to his muscles for action. He activated the control panel's sensors. What he saw spurred him even further to action, awakening the alien in him even as his physical world sped up.

Sure enough, his premonition triggered by the young Quaker girl was revealed as his instrument scans detected a band of warriors waiting in ambush ahead of Seediq's cohort as they made their way to the underground compound.

"Do you see those figures Ben?" Trueman pointed to the screen on the control panel where ghostly humanoid figures with weapons in hand were spread out in ambush formation fifty yards in front of the Gannicun cohort.

"Yes, is it one of the other cohorts from Gannicus?" he asked.

Trueman replied forcefully, "Most certainly not!"

"How do you know that?" Ben asked, turning to look at Trueman. "We don't know what the other cohorts were assigned to do"

"Because they came from a space craft piloted by two Mantis insects. Do you see that?" he asked, pointing to the craft on the sensor positioned behind the men waiting in ambush. "Those signatures in the pilot and co-pilot seats can only be from Mantis insects! Strap in, we need to move fast, or disaster awaits our friends," Trueman said.

Ben obeyed quickly and strapped himself securely in the co-pilots seat. He was surprised by the swift action as Trueman powered up the space craft and pulled back on the lifters, raising the craft up. He pushed the flyer forward quickly toward the waiting melee that was only moments away from becoming a death trap for their cohort.

Seediq and his men were startled when a rift flyer zoomed overhead and came swiftly to a halt 40 yards in front of them. A reddish-orange pulsing glow emanated outward from the vessel paralyzing those waiting in ambush and putting them into a coma. The beam then quickly coalesced on the cockpit of the alien craft, disabling the Mantis pilots as well.

Seediq and his men came running as Trueman settled the spacecraft down, powering off, and exited the craft.

"What have you done?" Seediq asked angrily.

Trueman said nothing, but Ben weighted in. "He just saved your lives!"

Seediq surveyed the scene, not recognizing any of the comatose soldiers who turned out to be Chinese mercenaries, from Novaya Zemlya. He instructed his men to collect their weapons.

"When was the last time you saw a Mantis soldier insect?" Trueman asked.

"It has been some years now," Seediq replied.

"Follow me." Trueman led Seediq to the alien craft with its insect occupants passed out in the pilot seats. "Tie the Mantis and the Chinese soldiers up securely. I will instruct the Gurkha pilots to guard them and get this craft back to Gannicus after we take over the bunker. How they knew we would be here should be discovered."

"We can interrogate them," Seediq said.

"We don't have much time," Trueman replied. "Best to let our Gurkha pilots handle it. Our ship sensors show an especially large hurricane offshore heading this way. We need to take over the bunker quickly and get indoors."

"Who is going to pilot our spacecraft home, if the pilots leave us?" Seediq asked.

"I will," Trueman replied. Seediq's eyes widened as he began to view Trueman with a new appreciation for his skills and forethought.

Chapter 26

The Bunker

"Hold your positions," Trueman said to Seediq after they had snuck up and concealed themselves near the bunker complex.

It was 3am and the approaching storm clouds looming overhead masked the light from the moon and stars. It was dark as Hades. They observed several men standing outside the bunker beach side entrance illuminated by a light above the door.

After several minutes watching and listening to their conversation, Trueman said to Seediq, "When I give you the signal, follow me in but remember, do not kill anyone. We will need these people to complete our mission. Is that understood!"

"We hear you, but do not understand," Seediq said.

"You will," Trueman reached out and clapped his hand on Seediq's shoulder. "You will brother!" There were familiar patterns running through Trueman's mind from the cultural and technological knowledge upgrades Bodhidharma had subjected him to before they left the warehouse on Gannicus.

The bunker structure, built during the cold war beneath ridges of dunes set back from the ocean, was designed to withstand a nuclear attack and still maintain communication with orbiting satellites ... and now, a post-cold war space station. The bunker was connected to the headquarters of NASA by a single long underground passage. The only other entry/exit point was here, the one leading out to the ocean side. Trueman figured with the approaching category 5 hurricane, this would be where the above ground command center would be moved to.

Trueman approached the two men smoking cigarettes not far from the door to the bunker. He was dressed in black military garb with a QBZ-95 assault rifle slung over his shoulder. The rifle was taken from one of the Chinese mercenaries.

"Hey fellows," Trueman called out, "this is not the night to be out patrolling. My radio communications are shot, must be the storm. Can you let me in, so I can report no activity on the beach side?"

"No problem," one of the technicians said. "Give us a minute to finish our cigarettes."

"Hey," his companion said, "isn't that a Chinese military rifle?"

Trueman let the comment resonate through his mental filter and an answer came front and center in his mind.

"Yes," Trueman said quickly, "they like us to train with these sometimes, so we are familiar with a range of potential enemy ordinance. I prefer the Israeli Tavor assault rifles myself, but we must follow orders."

"Understand that," the first technician said. "My father was in the military and used to take me to the gun range all the time."

"Come on in," the other technician said as he slid his badge through the door key lock mechanism. "We have coffee brewing."

"Perfect, thanks!" Trueman said as he raised his hand behind him, signaling Seediq to move in.

Seediq's cohort made swift work of it, safely rounding up a total of six NASA technicians who were in the process of managing the transition from topside communication to the underground bunker. They were placed under guard in a Quonset style chamber located off the main tunnel. It contained bunk beds, bathrooms, and a common area for recreation.

A quick pass through found no one else present. The bunker was quickly locked down with guards posted at the two entry/exit points: the tunnel door leading to the main complex and the beach side door. They knew it would only be a matter of time before the essential personnel monitoring the space station and other NASA assets in the above ground main communications center would seek shelter from the hurricane below in the bunker.

Seediq commenced a more thorough look at the facility. Several Quonset style rooms led off from the main corridor in addition to the one containing bunk beds. One contained metal canisters filled with C rations, dried food, and water. Another housed a kitchen and small cafeteria stocked with fresh food and refrigerated items.

The bunker command center lay at the end of the main corridor in the largest Quonset with a bank of computers and oversized screens. They had already been turned on and were receiving signals from many orbiting satellites and the international space station.

Trueman stood in front of this bank of computer consoles dialing up the schematics in his mind, like a large rolodex planted there by Bodhidharma's Earth history and technology upgrade. The images and language appeared in his mind's eye – Windows 19.5.

He went to the nearest desktop computer and accessed the internet's world wide web. Searching realtimeweather.org, the national weather service page opened. He clicked on hurricane tracking. The super storm covered a large swath of the Atlantic Ocean as it bore down on central Florida, with the center eye of the storm headed straight for Cape Canaveral. When Seediq returned to the communications hub he stood by Trueman dumbfounded, staring at the massive storm.

"We are going to be in for the ride of our life," Seediq said. "The Mantis knew we were coming. That puts the whole operation at risk - and now this storm!"

"More likely Bodhidharma knew what the Mantis were planning and placed us here to prevent it." Trueman said. "They must have arrived first, and when we came, they moved to ambush us. If we had arrived any later, they would have already taken over the bunker. Our mission would have been much more difficult to succeed with them inside and us outside with this hurricane about to strike. We should count our blessings!"

"What blessings?" Seediq asked.

"The ones you are going to thank the Creator for when this is all over. We are in a battle here, not only against flesh and blood, but against spiritual darkness." Trueman said.

Seediq gave him a puzzled look. "Spiritual darkness?" he asked.

"Just trust me on this!" Trueman said.

"I'm beginning to trust you," Seediq replied as he thought back on the events of the last few hours.

Chapter 27

Seediq's Upgrade

Bodhidharma was skeptical of Seediq's commitment to the Earth mission. Since Valeria lost its history during the genocidal war with the Mantis and only the very young survived, there was no experience beyond the tunnels and the need to live and fight, one day at a time.

The fact that they originated on Earth meant little to them now, only that they had survived the Mantis genocide. As a matter of fact, many surviving Valerians thought the Earth origin theory was a myth perpetrated by Bodhidharma to get their cooperation for an off-world military intervention.

The Romans only wanted peace and a chance to get their lives back to some semblance of normalcy. Knowing this, Bodhidharma indulged Seediq's curiosity about technology, informing him that the mission to Earth would reveal many exciting new technologies that he could use to help his people.

Bodhidharma did not want to upset the balance of power on Gannicus by introducing technology too fast on the

Valerian continent, which frustrated Seediq. Bodhidharma entrusted Trueman with the technology necessary to the success of the Earth mission and the decision about whether to share portions of that technology with Seediq.

In the bunker, Seediq and Trueman moved to a corner of the computer room and settled in to watch the screens. Trueman knew it was only a matter of time before the technicians in the above ground communications complex discovered that there was a problem in the underground bunker.

The remainder of the cohort, not on guard duty, had fanned out to look for loot, tech, or whatever else they could find of value. Seediq liked to be where the technology was, the more advanced the better, even though he didn't completely understand it all. He knew just being around the tech, he could pick up bits and pieces of it; sort of like learning a foreign language, the more you saturated yourself in it, the quicker you learned it.

Seediq believed technology was his people's ticket to continue to advance Valeria and protect it from the Mantis. He spent the years since coming to the surface of Gannicus learning everything he could from the English language to the technology that Bodhidharma showed him. However, he was not given free access or much detailed training in what he was seeing, and this bothered him. He did not completely trust Bodhidharma or Trueman because of this secrecy.

"So, tell me Trueman, what's in this for you?" Seediq asked.

Trueman thought for a moment, unsure how much Seediq knew about what was really happening on Gannicus, or the purpose of their mission here on Earth. He guessed if Seediq was willing to risk his own life and Luna's, as well as the lives of his people, that he was sufficiently committed to their cause for Trueman to open up to him about some aspects of his life.

"Did you know that my mother was born on Earth, then kidnapped when she was still a girl, and experimented on like a dog by the Mantis on Gannicus?" Trueman asked.

"I have heard rumors about the off-world goddess and her miracles but was unsure whether they were true, or a story Bodhidharma was promoting for his own purposes," Seediq replied.

"They are true enough, but she is no goddess. The correct term for her would be a prophetess, though she would not admit to that."

"A prophetess," Seediq replied. "I have heard of such on Gannicus before the war with the Mantis, thus and prophets were well known."

"They want her back ... the Mantis want my mother back!" Trueman blurted out. "And I will move heaven and earth to prevent that from happening, that is what's in it for me!"

Seediq remained silent, a clearer picture of Trueman emerging in his mind, *someone I can trust,* he thought.

Trueman continued, "Bodhidharma has captured several small groups of Russian mercenary infiltrators on Gannicus since you came to the surface, and that was their mission, to surveil and capture my mother," Trueman said slowly, with some sadness in his voice.

"I am here to end the Mantis tyranny on Earth and by doing that, securing my mother's safety on Gannicus. The

Mantis influence needs to decrease, while ours increases, that is the only way to keep our people safe!"

Our people, Seediq thought. *He must truly believe that we all came from Earth.*

"I understand and agree with you completely!" Seediq said. "Family is everything. If what we are doing here will protect our people on Gannicus, then count me in all the way!" He was seeing for the first time the true depth of Trueman's character. *This is no boy*, he thought.

"They used to be out for blood with us too, for a hundred years. Suddenly the fighting ended, thanks to Bodhidharma and the mysterious avenging angel," Seediq said. "I have seen him."

"Who?" Trueman asked, puzzled.

"The angel, of course," Seediq proudly replied. "It was he who invited us to the surface to meet Bodhidharma and your mother Faith. As I remember it, you were just a few years old at the time and now look at you! You grew so fast. Can you explain that to me?"

Trueman, shocked by the angel's revelation, remembered the day Seediq spoke of, the day his people emerged from their underground kingdom. He took a moment to consider his response. He needed allies and Seediq was a Gannicun leader who was resourceful and respected … *but how much to reveal?* He sensed a kindred spirit in Seediq.

"Do you want to know where angels come from? Do you want to know why the 13th legion was formed and its many legendary battles on Earth?"

"I want to know everything," Seediq replied. "All of it."

Trueman looked into the serious face of Seediq, *we shall see*, he thought hopefully.

"I will give you this knowledge and more, all the technology you can stand, but I do expect your trust and your loyalty to me and my family in return, including Bodhidharma."

"Is the Prince your father then?" Seediq asked.

Why did I automatically include Bodhi as part of my family? Trueman wondered. *Perhaps because he has always been there for me since my earliest recollections,* he thought to himself, *like a father.*

"He and my mother are engaged to be married; so yes, he will be my father."

Seeing Trueman's confused expression, Seediq seized the moment. "You will have my loyalty," Seediq replied to clear the air of doubt, "provided you do not ask me to betray my own people!"

"That, you will never have to worry about," Trueman said. "Your people are my people!"

Trueman slowly walked to his backpack and pulled out a visor front loaded on a helmet and a touch screen devise. Turning these on, a voice spoke.

"Language," the touch screen asked.

"English, Spanish, Russian and Chinese," Trueman answered.

"Geo-Political Region," the touch screen asked.

"Earth," Trueman replied.

"Subject and Time period," the screen asked.

History and Technology through the 21st century," Trueman replied.

"Now," Trueman said, "put this helmet on your head." Seediq obeyed.

"I want you to stare at the screen in front of you. Whatever you do, don't blink, don't close your eyes, and don't blink! The eyes are the only way for the information to be transmitted from the devise into your brain. The connection is through those nerves and synapses connecting your eyes to your brain. If you blink, you will sever the connection and you will have a gap in the flow of information."

"I understand," Seediq said. "Whatever happens, don't blink."

"This devise cost Bodhidharma dearly and it cannot be replicated. It is only for a one-time use. After I start this process, it will proceed to the end and then the information will be lost. It cannot be repeated. Do you understand?"

"Don't blink, I get it," Seediq replied.

"With this device, I can load you up with all the knowledge you can hold, but it will be painful, so hold on to your seat."

Seediq hesitated for a moment, gauging whether Trueman was serious or pulling a joke on him. "I'm in for all the tech I can get," Seediq said slowly.

"Pull the visor down. Keep your eyes open and focused on the screen no matter what you feel. You may get dizzy and disoriented, or even nauseous. You cannot absorb this much information on a conscious level, but you can in a subconscious stream. When it is over, your conscious mind will be able to retrieve the information when you need it. Are you ready?"

"Yes, ready."

"I am starting the sequence … now!"

Seediq concentrated on keeping his eyes wide open but felt nothing at first. Then a burning sensation surged and gorged through his brain, the nerve endings tingling wildly. He mentally shook it off without moving his head and began to feel a crispness in his thought processes, brain synapsis firing off, an eagerness for the information overtook him. He hunkered down in his chair with hands tightly wrapped around the arm handles. "It's intense," he said through clenched teeth.

"Hold on, it will be over soon," Trueman replied.

Suddenly Seediq bolted back in his seat but held his eyes steady, focusing every fiber of his body, jerking now and then with a few choice Gannicun curse words.

"Sores and Blisters!" Seediq gagged, keeping his eyes open.

"Two more minutes," Trueman said.

Seediq nearly threw up, but the knowledge he was gaining was immense. The lights of knowledge were coming on in Seediq's head. The device ran its course and began to power down.

"Damn." Seediq pulled the helmet off and threw up on the floor beside Trueman.

"The 13th legion was Julius Caesar's own legion," Seediq gasped. "We need to get this information back to my people on Gannicus!"

"We will," Truman replied with a smile, "in time. We must win here first!"

"Of course, thank you for giving me this gift," Seediq said exhausted. "I will be forever in your debt. It answers a lot of questions for me and my people."

"Our people," Trueman said, "the people of Earth. There are several Earth colonies setup on distant planets by the

Mantis. We're not alone and some of those colonies will be our enemies here unless we can convince them otherwise."

At that moment satellite feeds began to go silent on the computer screens in the communications bunker.

"It's time I went up there to see what is going on," Trueman said.

"Up where?" Seediq asked.

"Up there," Trueman said pointing toward the sky.

"I'll explain later. Send your most trusted inner circle of legionaries here and then go to the tunnel doorway leading to the surface. Don't let anyone in until I come back." The look on Trueman's face was serious.

I guess this is what he means by loyalty, Seediq thought. "Yes sir," he replied.

"Oh, and one more thing, if anything should happen to me, you are in command. Don't let this facility fall into the hands of the Mantis or their mercenaries. And try not to kill any of our potential allies waiting to get into the tunnel. This is their facility and they do not want to lose it either. Do you understand?"

"Now I do understand!" Seediq replied.

Seediq got up immediately and left the room, curious what Trueman had in mind to do now. Was he going to use the ship to reconnoiter the space above the planet? He returned with Luna, his mate, Rem, Belk, and Ben. They were armed and ready for any mission.

"Do exactly what Trueman orders you to do without hesitation!" Seediq commanded his legionaries. "He is completely in charge of this mission from now on." He then left the room to assume his watch at the locked tunnel entrance, the one with access to the facility from topside.

Seediq approached the massive door protecting the land side of the bunker. He was followed by the remaining mercenaries from Gannicus, armed and ready behind him. He looked up at a motion activated monitor. At least thirty people, men, and women, accompanied by half a dozen security guards with machine pistols were waiting anxiously to get in. Others could be seen behind the first group, moving down the tunnel toward their position. His recently acquired 21st Century language and customs upgrade kicked in as he picked up the microphone and announced to the crowd.

"This is a level one emergency!" Seediq said forcefully. "This bunker has been commandeered by United States Special Forces. We have been ordered to protect this facility against an imminent attack. Only civilians and unarmed security may enter this part of the compound."

This should give us some time until Trueman returns, he thought. *What is he up to?*

Seediq could see the crowd start to panic as an intense debate erupted between the security and the civilians over giving up their weapons. A tall man in camouflaged green and brown flecked uniform stepped through the crowd and picked up the microphone from the other side of the door. He appeared to be a senior officer in his mid-fifties. He keyed the mic.

"I am General Howard Clark, commander of the Florida National Guard. I order you to open this door!" His serious manner, square jaw, his whole countenance was of a man of authority.

Seediq let the sequence of military command structures scroll through his mind, *what would a soldier from Earth do?* he pondered. He could only go with what he had learned

173

from the technology upgrade, and hoped his response was correct.

"Listen carefully," he said, "this is a Federal facility and we are a United States Special Forces unit ordered to secure this location against attack, this is not subject to negotiation. When the hurricane has reached a level that is dangerous to above ground facilities, we will allow you to shelter here if you agree to place all your weapons in a container and turn them over to us. In the meantime, stay where you are."

This should buy some more time, Seediq thought.

General Clark turned toward the armed guards, made a frustrated gesture, and they all settled down to wait.

PART FOUR

BLOOD OF THE PROPHET

Chapter 28

The Good Wounds

"I am going to position myself in the middle of the room and I want each of you to take up places to the north, south, east, and west of me facing out towards the walls," Trueman said.

The others looked at each other puzzled. "Just do it," Ben said emphatically. They all moved to their positions without question.

"Whatever happens you must protect my body. I'm putting my life into your hands," Trueman said. They looked at each other with puzzled expressions on their faces.

He sat in the middle of the room facing the monitors and took up the lotus position. Closing his eyes, slowly moving through the meditation levels, his heartbeat and breathing slowed considerably. It was so quiet in the room you could hear a pin drop.

Luna, Rem, Belk, and Ben occasionally glanced back at Trueman, then each other, exchanging curious expressions. Focusing again on the walls in front of them, they wondered what could possibly come through those walls to attack Trueman.

Trueman's spirit slipped out of his body. He hovered near the ceiling taking in the room. The four Gannicuns were facing out from his position and the computer monitors were gray and static, receiving no signals. Focusing, he forced his awareness into overdrive.

Suddenly, outside the bunker, his spirit hovered over the beach watching the approaching hurricane which was just making landfall. An atomic blast was forming just offshore south of his location in the atmosphere above the ocean, lighting up the dark stormy night as if it was a bright sunny day. Trueman concentrated with renewed effort on the International Space Station, wondering if it was still there. Just as he began focusing on it, his spirit swiftly ascended into the stratosphere, higher and higher, until he was outside the space station.

"This can't be good," Ben said as he looked up at the monitors and felt a rumble move through the underground tunnel.

"What in this strange world is going on?" Luna asked. They had been hearing the increasing howling of the approaching storm for some time but now a loud boom shook the bunker as the shock wave of an atomic blast passed over it.

Trueman's spirit made a pass by the International Space Station and circled around it, stopping outside the cupola windows. Four pairs of eyes stared through him toward the Earth below. He turned and saw the vast circular hurricane clouds looming across the Atlantic, making landfall along the Florida coastline at the Cape, then noticed smaller mushroom clouds along the eastern North American continent.

Darn, he thought, *a full nuclear attack is under way. This is happening too fast*! When he looked back, only two people remained in the cupola.

"Something is taking out our satellites," he heard someone yell!

Just then, a flaming spear-like object flashed by behind him, almost slashing him in two, and crashed into the solar array, exploding on impact. Emergency and decompression alarms blared throughout the station!

He looked back in the direction the missile had come from and saw a distant space station approaching. He then scanned to survey the damage to the ISS infrastructure - debris was slowly floating away in all directions. Trueman entered the ISS through the thick bullet proof glass of the Cupola.

"Delay that order," Cheka Lysenko, the Russian crew member said pointing a pistol directly at Commander Foster's head. Alexei Sokolov floated behind him.

"I'm afraid we've made a secret security treaty with the Chinese" Lysenko said. "They are moving East, and we are moving West. In a very short period of time, there will only be two superpowers left."

"Hitler and the Japanese had the same idea when they started the second world war." Commander Foster reminded him. "It didn't turn out very well for them."

"Alexei, get on the Com and let our Chinese allies know that Russia is in control of the International Space Station and they may proceed to board us!"

Trueman began to panic, realizing his whole mission was about to be blown up in front of him. He remembered

Bodhidharma's instructions - *Take control of the under-ground communications bunker. All hell is about to be unleashed on Earth, the start of a new world war. Keep the communication with the International Space Station open!"*

He began to feel his spirit body heating up, beginning in the center, and moving out to his arms ... *the pistol, grab the pistol* ... he intuitively knew exactly what to do.

Trueman cupped his hands around the Glock pistol. At first, nothing happened, then Lysenko's face turned ugly and his body twisted and contorted as he suddenly threw the gun to the side with a scream. His hands were red as if he had held them over a fire for a few moments. Commander Foster and Franz Moser took the opportunity and quickly subdued the two Russian crew members.

"Suit up, and seal all the bulkheads," Foster announced over the intercom, "initiate decompression protocols."

"Franz, get this station out of range of those Chinese missiles ... Now!"

"Yes, sir!" Moser shouted back as he moved down the corridor.

Trueman was bewildered, unsure how he had interacted in the physical world, something Bodhidharma had never hinted was possible. However, he knew the Sentinel angel was capable of limited physical power to slow a physical blow, manage pain and improve healing. Perhaps the angel's energy flowing into Faith's body to resurrect her from the dead when she was pregnant with Trueman has been growing in him.

With the station back in friendly hands, Trueman exited the vessel and approached the other space station to investigate, entering near the center of the largest structure.

It was the control room. Compared to the ISS he had just left, which was patched up and old, this was state of the art and brand new. The crew were mostly Chinese with a few Russian advisors onboard.

He ranged through the entire ship and found what he was looking for, the armaments module. Long and spread out with air to air missiles and, *shocking*, what looked like tactical nuclear warheads. He realized his plan to liberate Earth from the Mantis threat could be over before it started with this kind of firepower roaming above them in space.

Exiting the Chinese space station, Trueman began moving back to Earth when he noticed a shimmer in space. It was as if sunlight was reflecting off an undulating seashore with waves crashing about. His curiosity got the best of him and he willed his spirit to move in to investigate. As he approached, he bounced up against an invisible barrier near the curious spectacle. He pushed harder, and again harder, until he popped through and found himself immersed in the shimmering, now darker reflection. As he did so, the shimmer began to fade and take form as spirits moving over each other.

Darkness enveloped him as he sank into the undulating frenzy. Flashes of evil faces careened by him and he began to feel heat, then pain, as the teeth of the faces scrapped over his spirit body. The pain became intense as more and more of the disembodied spirits moved around him, circling closer toward him. He could sense their need to devour him, and he felt the weight of their bodies pressing into him. He could not breathe, even though in his mind, he knew breathing was not necessary in the spirit. Nevertheless, the pressing against his body of so many oppressed souls was taking its toll. Life itself began to ebb out of him.

"He's not breathing," Rem said.

"Who's not breathing?" Luna asked, still staring forward at the empty wall in front of her.

"Trueman … I mean the Commander."

"Don't touch him, remember what he said, no matter what happens, let him be."

"He's starting to turn blue," replied Rem.

"What!" Luna exclaimed. She knew from her medical triage experience during the Mantis wars that blue lips and skin were not a good sign.

"Lay him on his back. We need to get some air into him!"

Trueman felt immersed in a quagmire, like dark quicksand, with every movement sinking him deeper into deaths' waiting arms. His life's essence was being sucked out of him and into the spurious spirits that were consuming him. It was when he was near certain death, that he saw a vision of his mother Faith, sitting on the garden bench on Gannicus, reaching out to touch his heart, *the hope of the promise is within you*, her words brought it all back into perspective and he screamed ...

"The Blood of Jesus, Save Me!" Feeling the crush of the bodies over, under, and on all sides squeezing the life out of him, he screamed again, "The Blood of Jesus, Save Me!"

"He's bleeding," Luna said. "Go get Seediq, Now!" Ben ran as fast as he could to the blocked entrance to the tunnel complex.

"Trueman is dying, Trueman is dying!" Ben yelled desperately. "He's bleeding all over!"

Seediq acted without hesitation, keying the microphone to the other side of the door.

"General Clark, do you have a doctor with you? We have a medical emergency."

"Yes," General Clark replied waving forward another officer with medical pins on his lapel. "What is it you need?"

Seediq turned to the other legionaries. "Quickly, go to the communications bay, but don't speak to anyone. They must not hear us speaking Latin. It is a dead language here, either Latin or your rough English accents will betray us. Let me do the talking."

The legionaries all moved quickly down the corridor. Seediq waited until he was the only one left in the tunnel.

"We have a medical emergency and need your help," Seediq said quickly and unlocked the door. He turned and quickly ran back to the communications bunker.

The doctor was the first through the door followed by General Clark and the security guards. The rest moved in behind them into the tunnel complex. All were perplexed that they were allowed in without giving up their weapons.

When the legionaries arrived in the communications bunker, Trueman was twisting and turning on the floor, clearly trying to get away from some unknown force.

General Clark cautiously led the way and instructed the civilians to stay behind them until they were able to ensure the safety of the compound as the doctor sprinted ahead.

When the doctor reached the communications bunker, blood was pouring from small cuts on Trueman's forehead and oozing from the pores of his skin. Round red spots on his hands were also bleeding.

The doctor began to remove his clothing, checking for any other wounds, noticing blood coming from his right side. The shoes came off revealing holes in his feet that were oozing blood. The doctor sat back on his heels, crossing himself, not believing his eyes.

"What are you doing," Seediq yelled. "Save him!"

The doctor hesitated, not knowing what to say or even believing his eyes. "He is not dying," the doctor declared. "He is in a lot of pain because he is showing symptoms of a condition called Stigmata, the wounds of Christ!"

Upon that declaration, some of the National Guardsmen went to their knees and crossed themselves. Among the cohort of Gannicuns, wary glances were exchanged and a few who could remember similar reverent expressions from their deceased parents, went to their knees as well.

Knowing as they did the reputation of Trueman's mother as a prophetess, this unexpected revelation from their erstwhile allies, confirmed that he must be a prophet as well. Their eyes were opened to the possibility that they could have some kinship with these people from Earth … common ancestors.

Trueman, still trapped in the quagmire in space above the Earth, felt an immediate relief after calling out for help. The weight on his chest and body lifted just as a light appeared filling the visible space around him. The disembodied souls began flying off in all directions like banshees. The light began to coalesce into a near human form with wings stretching out behind it. Then slowly, a huge figure emerged from the light. It was a tall muscular man dressed in the military gear of ancient middle eastern Earth history.

"You should be more careful where you go in the spirit here, Trueman Dyer. The atomics you witnessed below have made the walls of hell weak in this part of space."

"How is it you know my name?" Trueman asked.

"Because you're the grandson of a martyr. Now go, return to your bodily form!" the angel ordered.

Trueman's physical body on Earth suddenly surged upwards with a great gasp. Everyone stepped back as if moved by an invisible force. Trueman's eyes cracked open, slowly scanning the room, and taking in the countenance and stance of those present around him, assessing the situation quickly.

Signaling Seediq over to him, he whispered to him. "Have the Gurkha pilots move the rift flyer up to the outside doors of the bunker, shielding the hurricane's wind, and take the Earth commander out. Show him the prisoners waiting in the transport. Make sure he sees and touches the Mantis insects, then instruct the Gurkha pilots to go – have them leave immediately for Gannicus."

At that point, the tremendous pain he had been unknowingly masking suddenly entered his body and he passed out on the floor.

Chapter 29

Martial Law

Trueman was carried to a bunk in the sleeping quarters. Luna stayed and cared for him, wiping the blood from his wounds. As she washed the blood off his forehead, she saw to her astonishment, that the wounds there had disappeared.

The deeper wounds on his hands, feet, and side stopped oozing blood and began to heal in front of her startled eyes. She looked around to see if anyone had noticed and decided to keep this to herself for now. She covered him with a blanket.

The rest of the National Guard soldiers along with the Roman legionaries filtered into the barracks, keeping an uncomfortable distance from each other until their leaders returned. The legionaries circled near Trueman's bunk seeking an update on his condition.

Seediq and General Clark returned from outside. They sat down on either side of an all-purpose table at the front of the underground barracks. Their troops, each holding their weapons in the down position, moved to stand behind their respective leaders.

"Ok, you have my attention son, now who are you, and what are you doing here?" General Clark asked.

"As I said before, this is a Federal facility and we are United States Special Forces troops ordered here to secure this location against attack. You have seen the prisoners we have taken. We have accomplished that task and can now turn the facility back over to you. We will be on our way to return to other duties."

"I have served for over 25 years at all levels of the military including being imbedded in foreign military units and I can tell you that you are not U.S. Special Forces!" General Clark said sternly. "Let me tell you why I know you are not one of us. You are armed with an assortment of Israeli and Chinese assault rifles … and one weapon I have never seen before. What do you call that?" Clark pointed at the unusual looking Lorsgun lying on the table in front of Seediq.

"It's called a Lorsgun, especially designed for close-in tunnel fighting, similar to where we are now." Seediq's expression began to change from business like to that of someone expecting trouble. He laid his arm over the weapon, hand near the trigger. "This weapon killed several Mantis insects at once some years ago when all the barrels fired at the same time."

General Clark was beginning to see this group as having as much of a potential threat to himself as the Chinese and Mantis prisoners he had just viewed outside.

"Dr. Poteete," he asked, "how would you describe the wound on that fellow's face over there," pointing to the crudely stitched up slash on Ben's face. The medical knowledge in the tunnel fighting on Gannicus was rudimentary. Ben's face was slashed by the barbed forearm of a Mantis soldier, taking out the eye with it. They were only capable of pulling the two flaps of skin together and stitching them tight resulting in an ugly scar. It was partially covered with a crude metal patch.

"It appears to be a wound treated in the field with no medical follow up. I have read of similar treatments for ancient Greek warriors who were slashed across the face with sword or spear, losing the eye, very rudimentary medicine. Certainly, atypical of the medical treatment available to United States Special Forces troops today sir."

"I want you to give up your weapons and stand down," General Clark said to Seediq as he stood up. "I am placing you all under arrest until we can figure out who you are and where you come from."

With that, the National Guard troops behind him raised their weapons to the ready. The legionaries, not all understanding English, looked confused. Some raised their weapons, while others looked to Seediq for instructions. Seediq stood, his hand now on the trigger of the Lorsgun, pointing directly at General Clark.

"We are Roman Legionaries and we do not surrender. *Omnes In*," Seediq shouted in Latin, the words for *All In*, the well understood signal from their tunnel fighting days. With this word, the rest of the legionaries brought their weapons to bear on the National Guardsmen, understanding completely what was at stake! The tension in the room was explosive. Any unexpected move was certain death.

Seediq, Trueman spoke into his mind, *we cannot leave Earth yet!* Seediq slowly turned back to where he knew Trueman lay in his bunk, but he could not see him.

"What did you say?" he asked.

I'm speaking directly into your mind, don't speak out loud, just think your response. Your upgrade allows us to communicate telepathically. These people are our allies. If you want technology, the place to find it is here on Earth, not Gannicus. We must convince them. Let me take the lead on this!

Go ahead, Seediq replied in his head. This strange exchange did not go unnoticed around the room. Seediq was looking back to no one in particular, seeming to communicate without speaking.

Moments later a path opened up among the legionaries and Trueman slowly walked to the table. Seediq followed him with his gaze, amazed that he could even stand much less walk after what he had been through. Trueman sat down in Seediq's place and Seediq took up a position behind him. Ben also stepped up and they both eyed General Clark with Lorsguns at the ready.

"Who we are is not important General Clark, but why we are here is," Trueman began with emphasis, gesturing with his outstretched arms for him to sit down again. General Clark, now somewhat overwhelmed by the recent series of unexplainable revelations he had witnessed the last few hours, slowly sat down to listen to what Trueman had to say.

"We are part of a group that has been successfully fighting these alien creatures you saw in the ship outside. We call them Mantis, a powerful space faring insect species that has been manipulating Earth's history for generations." This statement got the attention of the National Guard troops who were rolling their eyes and exchanging mirthful smiles, snide comments, and laughter.

"Shut up and listen," General Clark said to his men. "You didn't see what I saw. These creatures do exist, so I have no reason to doubt what this man says - for now. There were two Mantis insects along with Chinese prisoners. I touched the creatures with my own hands. They are real. They were tied up in what appears to be a spacecraft. I saw it slowly rise off the ground and disappear. I don't know what this is, but I do know this is no joke!"

Trueman waited until the commotion settled down and continued. "Their purpose here is to create chaos and disunity, so they can exploit our resources without being challenged. They do this by inserting human mercenaries, now mostly Chinese and Russians, into the highest levels of government and other powerful groups. They do best in organizations whose leadership resides in the hands of a few people or groups like dictatorships, communist, or Islamist countries, places where there is little tolerance for self-expression or independent thought," he said.

"A perfect example of this was the worldwide chaos that ensued during World Wars I and II. We suspect that a repeat of those times is here again. We see the beginnings of it with the Chinese mercenaries the Mantis brought here to take over this facility. We had foreknowledge of this event and were sent here to intercept them. Our immediate mission was to make sure they do not succeed in acquiring this facility, but we may consider staying to help out further if you request it. However, we are under our own orders and could leave at any time if called to do so by our superior."

Some of the legionaries who spoke better English than their fellows were translating in Latin to them. The National Guard doctor noticed and moved closer to listen. He had a good grasp of Latin from his Catholic religious and medical training.

"Why are your men speaking Latin," he asked Trueman. "Are you a religious order or something?"

"We are not a holy order as you know it, but our success against these evil forces is in large part due to divine intervention," Trueman replied, thinking of his mother's journey; the Sentinel angel who accompanied her and now resides in Bodhidharma – becoming the avenging angel.

"Without going into too much detail for now, let's just say that we are an international group not affiliated with any of your governments and with the same goals as you, to stop this chaos and keep your society intact and in control of its state, national, and especially its space faring capabilities. We will help you as allies or depart as friends. Those are your choices, but as Seediq said, surrender is and never will be an option for us."

"I can't understand everything I have seen here the last few hours," General Clark said, "but this chaos you are describing is worse than you know and quickly unfolding as we speak. The Florida National Guard was activated statewide two days ago. This was in response to a report that the Chinese military has taken over the Panama Canal. A large fleet of warships has been spotted in the Pacific, making a beeline to the Isthmus of Panama. That is why we are here," he said.

"There are only a limited number of ports in Florida capable of accommodating warships and Port Canaveral is one of them. However, based on the reported size of the fleet that is approaching, the deep-water Port of Tampa is the most logical place if Florida is their destination. It is the only port large and deep enough to accommodate warships of that size and number. So, unless they split up, or go north up the eastern seaboard, I suspect that is where they will disembark and cut a swath across Florida, isolating the southern half of the state.

"Just before you let us into the underground tunnel complex, we got word that atomic bombs were falling on the United States and by the earliest reports, have destroyed Washington, D.C., and most of the military installations that house our air forces. That tells me that the Chinese are not coming with air superiority and this will largely be a ground war. We have lost communication with most of our satellites and the International Space Station, which is most likely why they have so far left this facility untouched. They want to take it over and control our space assets from here!"

"That is not good news," Trueman said. "I'm afraid I have worse news though. The Chinese space station has been taking out your satellites. Their station is militarized and has on board about 25 tactical nuclear warheads. So, they may not need air superiority if they start using those."

"How do you know this?" the General asked surprised.

"We have our sources," Trueman replied. "We need to band together as allies if we are going to stop this takeover. We know things, and you have the people and resources to turn that knowledge to advantage."

The General considered that for a moment. "Agreed!" he said. "I am going to recommend to the Governor to declare martial law. With the hurricane, the atomic weapons, and

191

now it seems, no foreseeable federal response to assist us, there is going to be complete chaos here.

"A Florida National Guard Special Forces unit will be here as soon as the hurricane passes. Unfortunately, there are only twelve of them. I want you to join forces with them and go directly to Tampa which will give us some much-needed intelligence on the ground there to assess the Chinese strength and capabilities. As soon as we know what we are dealing with, we can bring resources to bear to fight them. If Tampa Bay is the target, I will move my headquarters to the Central Florida Fairgrounds in Orlando in order to be centrally located and coordinate the fight.

"We will join your special forces on this expedition to Tampa!" Trueman said as he stood up and shook hands with General Clark across the table.

Chapter 30

Dancing in the Minefields

"I am assigning you to lead a group of mercenaries, or whatever they call themselves, to help us reconnoiter the arrival of a Chinese naval fleet at Tampa Bay harbor. They originally claimed to be special forces – black ops – working out of DC but they do not appear to be part of any military organization I am familiar with. However, they know things, which makes them valuable to us!" General Clark said emphatically.

"What things?" Captain Alex Connor, the commanding officer of the Special Forces unit asked, puzzled.

"They knew about the Chinese and Russian attacks before we did, and they knew the Chinese were taking out our orbiting satellites. They appear to be on our side, but they speak Latin which leads me to believe it is more likely they are working secretly for the European Union or possibly NATO."

"Latin, I thought that was a dead language. Can they be trusted?" Captain Connor asked.

"That is for you to find out on this mission," General Clark replied. "Consider them to be allies at this point unless you have some reason to believe otherwise. Their leader is a man named Seediq, no last name, but they all defer to a young man named Trueman Dyer. He apparently has special knowledge about what is going on. I can't go into details at this point, just keep your eyes and ears open and be careful. They could be very useful, or a danger to us, that has yet to be determined!"

The column of Humvees rolled out of Cape Canaveral at the crack of dawn headed for Tampa Bay to reconnoiter the expected arrival and strength of the Chinese invasion of central Florida. A 12-foot alligator lumbered up and over the raised highway slipping into the swampy conservation area on the other side of the road.

"What in God's creation is that? It looks like a dragon," Trueman asked Captain Conner.

The captain stared at him astonished for a moment before answering. "Haven't you ever seen an alligator?" *Curious,* he thought.

Since his recent out of body experience resulting in the stigmata wounds, Trueman was having strange shivers of his consciousness which included sometimes visualizing the auras around living creatures. The alligator had a reddish glow as it went up and over the highway, perhaps rushing after prey or a mate, heightening its aura signature.

Trueman hesitated, trying not to give away his shock. Of course, his environmental tutorial upgrade had described and pictured alligators, but seeing one so large, up close ... and red, was a surprise. *Have to be more careful hiding these new abilities,* he urged himself. "Never seen one alive before."

He stared with fascination at the lush sub-tropical landscape and the many birds in the conservation area. The experience with his heightened awareness was like watching an HD TV on steroids. The Valerian continent on Gannicus, where he spent most of his young life, was a bone-dry landscape with few animals scratching out a tenuous existence.

The recon column pulled out of the Cape's conservation area onto highway 528 heading west for Orlando just as the sun broke free from the Atlantic Ocean. It shone bright behind them lighting up the highway.

The hurricane had rolled northeast across central Florida and the Gulf of Mexico slamming into Mobile, Alabama. The devastation was reported to be worse than hurricane Katrina's. There was some speculation that the atomic bomb exploding in the air had somehow mixed up the circulation patterns enough to increase the hurricanes strength and speed. As is usual after a hurricane clears out, dragging the clouds and rough weather with it, the sky above their route was unusually calm. The surreal sky had a bright blue turquoise cast with few clouds.

"General Clark was not very clear about your military unit designation. He just said it was an opportunity to imbed our two forces to enhance our mission objectives. So, I'm assuming you are an international or United Nations force. Apparently, you have some intelligence sources he deems worthy or we wouldn't be on this mission together."

"I couldn't have explained it better," Trueman said crisply, not wanting to give up too much information.

The column was made up of seven Humvees each mounted with the old reliable 50 caliber machine gun on the roof with gun shield turrets surrounding it. The Special Forces unit consisted of twelve soldiers. Coincidentally, there were also twelve Roman legionaries as well. The Humvees were packed with ammunition, food, and water, enough to last 24 soldiers for three weeks. Trueman sat behind Captain Conner who occupied the passenger seat in the lead vehicle while Seediq shared a similar place at the back of the column behind Conner's second in command, Lieutenant Ulysses Moreno.

Crossing over the St. John's River was spectacular for Trueman's enhanced senses. The early morning foggy mist, illuminated by the sun, gave the whole wet landscape a serene dreamy visual effect. The river moved north in a slow, almost imperceptible flow through oxbows and switchbacks. To the uninitiated eye, it looked like another swamp filled with wildlife of all kinds, rather than a river.

Once past the river crossing, they reached the first toll booth and found it deserted. It was not unusual for the turnpike authority to allow free, no toll days before, during and after a hurricane, but this was different. The place was without any apparent electricity, no green lights over the lanes, no police presence. Windows were broken from flying debris during the hurricane. It was abandoned.

Not a good sign of things to come, Conner thought. He turned the radio on and dialed to WDBO, a popular talk show station in the area. The announcer was interviewing local emergency personnel and the news was not good. After almost a week of preparing for the hurricane and several days of severe weather as the enormous category 5 hurricane approached, passed over, then departed, most gas stations and grocery stores were closed for lack of supplies.

Residents were in a near panic and being encouraged to remain indoors. Many first responders had simply packed up their families and moved out of Florida to avoid the hurricane and then didn't return after the outbreak of the nuclear war.

A local agricultural Extension Agent soon entered the conversation on the radio with an assessment of food supplies and why they were so desperately low. Apparently, government planners had long ignored calls for encouraging more local food production. Instead, they favored continued residential and commercial development, much of it focusing on the tourism, technology, and health care sectors.

The result of this short-sighted policy was that only a thirty-day supply of food was available in the warehouses and grocery stores in central Florida. No one considered that trucks and planes, which daily brought food to the area, would suddenly stop coming. The lack of a Federal response and the multiple disasters taking place in other parts of the country contributed to the diminishing supplies and the uncertain future availability of food.

The Extension Agent then discussed the good news; the largest cow calf operation east of the Mississippi River was a one-hour drive southeast of Orlando - the Deseret Ranch. Contacts were being made to get a cattle drive moving to Orlando soon, which would help alleviate shortages. In the meantime, residents were encouraged to ration what food they had left.

The 528-highway approach to Orlando brought the team up the southeast side of the city, along the northern border of the Orlando International Airport. There were no planes in sight except for overturned Cessna aircraft on a side runway. Most air carriers flew their large passenger aircraft to safer locations before the storm.

Captain Conner noticed considerable activity up ahead around an approaching toll booth and slowed to a stop. Florida Highway Patrol, Orange County Sheriff, and City of Orlando police were keeping traffic, which had backed up, from approaching the tool booth. Conner keyed his com to the other Humvees.

"Heads up to police activity ahead," he said, "get frosty and ready in case there is trouble. Remember, our mission is in Tampa. We can't stop for every dog that barks if we expect to get there and do our job. Assume your positions and await orders."

The machine gun operators stepped up into their turrets and everyone brought their weapons to ready positions. To avoid the backed-up traffic, the convoy slowly moved off the road and continued forward in the pullover lane normally used by emergency vehicles.

A lone Highway Patrol car made its way towards them with emergency lights flashing. Captain Conner announced a stop to the convoy and stepped out of the Humvee as did Trueman. As soon as Trueman excited the vehicle, Seediq got out and moved quickly forward followed by the Legionaries in short order. This panicked the remaining Special Forces reservist who opened their doors to use as shields and ready their weapons. The Highway Patrol car stopped and called for backup. Conner moved quickly to stop the escalation.

"Everyone remain where you are and don't fire unless fired upon. I'm going to move forward unarmed and get what information we can and will return shortly."

He turned to Trueman and said rather sarcastically, "Since your men don't seem to have much discipline, moving wherever you go, stay here or you are going to get people killed for no reason."

"My men are sworn to protect me! If that offends you, then I am sorry. It's just the way it is with us."

"I'll remember that, and we'll talk about this later," Conner said as he walked off.

This is no Special Forces unit, it's something completely different, he thought, and wondered how he ended up in command of such a ragtag group. *Not unlike the irregulars I worked with behind enemy lines in the Middle Eastern proxy wars, protecting their warlord chieftains from assassination by rival groups.* Conner returned after a lengthy heated conversation with the local police.

"Apparently, the Latin Kings gang has taken over the toll booths and are extorting money from anyone passing by. The police say we can go through if we help them disperse the gang away from the toll booths."

Captain Connor instructed the patrolman to have all the police vehicles put their sirens on as a distraction. Their emergency lights were already flashing as the line of Humvees moved quickly up the emergency lane of the highway and up a side embankment parallel to the toll booths.

There was considerable panic among the gang members since they now had the police in front of them and military vehicles flanking them. Some ran to their cars parked to block traffic between the toll booths, but many remained where they were. There was an empty 57 Chevy parked to the side facing the Humvee column.

"Everyone remain where you are and don't fire unless fired upon," Connor repeated into his shoulder radio, mostly for Trueman's benefit.

"On my command, I want each 50-caliber machine gun to open fire on that unoccupied '57 Chevy in a 5 second burst starting with the 1st Humvee and cycling to the last. Understood?"

"Yes sir," each machine gun operator replied.

"Open fire."

The loud rapid-fire staccato commenced, and the gang members tumbled out of the toll booths and into their cars like rats leaving a burning warehouse. A few attempted to return fire but to little effect. The '57 Chevy was reduced to a mangled metal pile of rubbish.

When it was over, the patrol cars started pursuing the fleeing gang members and Captain Connor ordered the convoy back on the road past the toll booths toward Tampa.

Trueman was impressed that no one was injured and respected Connor for his coolness in a stressful moment. *His Special Forces unit is well trained,* he thought.

"Are the police going to be on our side when the fight with the Chinese commences?" Trueman asked Connor.

"Yes, of course, we can count on them."

"How about the Latin Kings' gang members, will they be with us or against us?"

"Most likely," Conner replied slowly, "with food, jobs, and money being in short supply, they will side with whoever can offer them the most goodies."

"If what General Clark has told me is true," Trueman said, "we will need all the allies we can get."

The city of Tampa is considered old by Florida standards. It was established around Fort Brooke on Tampa Bay for protection against Seminole Indians in 1824. The civilian population was only about 1,000 in the 1850 census.

Today, Tampa Bay houses the largest deep-water port in Florida and is one of the most active commercial ports in North America. It is the logical place to make landfall for a large Chinese naval force carrying 250,000 troops and equipment, rivaling the Normandy invasion of Europe by the allied forces during World War II. Nazi Germany had three years to prepare defenses to repel the Normandy invasion. The Florida National Guard had less than three weeks.

The location offers a quick route across central Florida via Interstate 4 and the 528 East/West Expressway to the Kennedy Space Center. Isolating south Florida opens three smaller deep-water ports: Port Canaveral, Ft. Lauderdale, and Miami. Taking the space center would effectively end the US presence in space and ensure China's world dominance.

The stakes are high, and because of the sneak attack on Washington and the major east coast military bases being severely damaged, little help could be expected from Federal sources. The Florida National Guard, Army Reserve units in Florida, and whatever civilian militias that could be mobilized quickly, were the only thing standing in the way of a quick Chinese victory.

Chapter 31

Scuttle Buttin

The blessed right reverend Joseph Peale was a former professional wrestler. He came late to the Lord.

At 35 years old, he had a mid-life crisis, was born again, and used his wrestling earnings to put himself through seminary college. His voluptuous fan wife Barbara took her wedding vows seriously and with their daughter Natalie, reluctantly followed Joseph on his journey.

Pastor Peale's first church assignment was the Emmaus United Methodist Church in Seminole Heights, an older neighborhood in Tampa, Florida, near Lowry Park. Most of the parishioners were elderly and the church appeared to be on its last legs. Such assignments were not uncommon for new pastors with enthusiastic recent conversions.

Joseph was known as "Pahokee Joe" in wrestling circles. He grew up in a sleepy muck farm town on the shores of Lake Okeechobee in the Everglades Agricultural Area.

Barbara was a devoted young wrestling fan when she first met Joe. He was new to professional wrestling and was tearing up the circuit with his quick moves. He developed a large following of young fans.

One night, Pahokee Joe was wrestling the Iranian Bomb, a 350-pound wrestler who was a former Olympic champion weightlifter from his native Iran. The older wrestler became uncontrollably mad as the fans cheered Joe's spectacular moves thwarting the big man at every turn.

As the wrestlers were maneuvering for the final stage of the match, the Bomb unexpectedly changed the rehearsed ending to an MMA submission move called the Calf Crusher. He slammed Joe face down on the mat and leaned back on his opponent's contorted right leg. Joe slapped the mat repeatedly indicating he was submitting to defeat. This did not stop the Bomb however, who leaned back further, wrenching Joe's knee out of place.

The referee became frantic trying to stop the Bomb, but the wrestler kept up the potentially career ending torture. At that moment, Barbara entered the ring with a metal folding chair and quickly ended the match by bashing the Iranian over the head with it. Barbara became an overnight sensation as the video of her quick response to end her hero's wrenching torture went viral on social media.

She spent the next six weeks helping nurse Joe back to health at a rehabilitation center. All the wrestling fan magazines and tabloid news outlets carried their love story as they courted and were married six months later. After that, she cheered Joe from ringside, always with a metal folding chair close at hand in case the opposing wrestler decided to deviate from the scripted match.

The duo, Pahokee Joe and Cinnamon Girl, staged famous tag team matches consisting of wrestlers and their significant others with social media views in the millions. They called themselves Double Trouble and entered the arenas playing the opening rifts of Stevie Ray Vaughn's Texas blues song 'Scuttle Buttin.' The music, the fanfare, and the smoke machines churning low hanging clouds swirling around the wrestler's feet as they entered the arena was a sight to see!

Pastor Joe, as he was now affectionately known, also served as a volunteer grief counselor at St. Joseph's Hospital, an acute care facility in Tampa near the neighborhood church. And that is how he met the President of the Tampa chapter of the Outlaws Motorcycle Club. The biker gang president's brother Justin was in a coma at St. Joseph's Hospital after a confrontation with rival gang members – the Pagans.

He first came to pray for comatose Justin at the request of Justin's wife Marsha. There was little hope as the doctors predicted he would not recover. Joe supported the family's decision to start a feeding tube and continue intravenous solutions to keep Justin alive.

Seven days later Justin came out of the coma amid great celebration until everyone realized he would never be the same. He had reverted to an earlier stage in life, where the cares of an adult were not present. He was a child again.

Joseph brought Barbara to the hospital and introduced her to Marsha. They became fast friends. Their daughter Natalie started babysitting Marsha's two young children so that she could spend more time at the hospital with her husband. Justin learned to walk again even though his movements were slow and required a cane. There was always a smile on his face, nothing fazed him.

It was during this traumatic experience that Pastor Joe first noticed the many souped up Harley Davidson motorcycles that were parked here and there about the Seminole Heights neighborhood he served. His enquiries found that many Outlaws MC members and their families lived in the area. He decided to embark on a new mission to revitalize the church; he bought a Harley Davidson motorcycle. Barbara was thrilled!

Natalie, Barbara's daughter, was pretty, athletic, and given the genes handed down to her from her father and mother, was a rather sexy, tomboyish teenager. She took to the outdoor motorcycle lifestyle with ease under the strict supervision of one or the other of her parents. However, she was only allowed to ride a dirt bike, not a souped-up Harley Davidson.

Barbara was a natural mentor to these new Seminole Heights church congregants and related well with the women and children. However, except for Justin, the men did not attend church.

Pastor Joe, Barbara, and Natalie attended their first public gathering of the motorcycle club at a natural lands park outside the city. The park boundary ran for several miles bordering the Hillsborough River. It was an afternoon event. Justin had just been released from the rehabilitation center and was attending with his family.

Barbara and Natalie spent their time with Justin, Marsha, and their children as Joe began introducing himself around. He was tolerated for the sake of Justin but his status as a Methodist preacher did not sit well with some members of the gang.

Several hours into the event and many beers later, the biggest Outlaw in the group, nicknamed Bear, could be seen walking slowly toward Pastor Joe with an entourage following him. Fights were not uncommon when gang members came together with their ladies to party, especially late in the day when the booze was flowing freely.

Bear walked straight up to face Pastor Joe. His body language was very clear; this was going to end in a fight or Joe was going to back down and leave the park.

"So, are you the preacher today, or the wrestler?" Bear asked, leaning directly into the face of Joe. The news of this encounter quickly passed through the crowd at the park, and shortly, everyone was surrounding the two large men.

"I will always be the preacher and the wrestler," Pastor Joe replied. He was not intimidated by a one on one fight, even with a man the size of Bear at 6 feet 6 inches tall and weighing nearly 400 pounds. A young Joe Peale had won the prestigious Florida State College's heavyweight wrestling championship for two years in a row before entering professional wrestling. Weighing nearly 250 pounds, he bench pressed 600 pounds during the heyday of his career. There were few men alive who could beat him in a fair fight. But Outlaw bikers rarely fought fair.

They stared at each other, head to head and toe to toe. By this time, Barbara and Natalie were frantic on the outskirts of the crowd trying to push in and find out what was happening.

"You're not welcome here," Bear finally bellowed.

"We were invited here by Justin who is a member of the Outlaws," Joe replied calmly.

At this point, Bear's entourage began egging him on to finish it. "Tear him up … send him back to his pulpit … get it over with," they yelled.

Pastor Joe had been in confrontations like this in his life and many were averted by just standing firm and saying few words. Either way, he always let the other man throw the first punch. He would watch their midsection to gauge which fisted hand would come up at him first, then immediately deflect the blow and come straight up with a hard blow to the lower jaw from underneath; but with Bear, the strategy didn't work.

The giant man merely shook his head to clear the shock of the blow to his jaw and grabbed Joe in a huge bear hug. Two men quickly stepped up and took hold of Joe's arms. Bear reared back and struck Pastor Joe in the face. Joe, expecting the blow, angled his head down so the fist landed on his forehead, not the fleshy part of his face. Bear wrenched back holding his hand where the knuckle bones had cracked. Joe's field of vision went dark for a moment as the blow jolted his head back. When he regained his sight, he saw another Outlaw step up and land a painful punch to his midsection.

Barbara was frantic! She grabbed Natalie by the arm and pulled her away, making a beeline for the nearest beer cooler surrounded by metal folding chairs. She quickly closed two and gave one to Natalie.

"Follow me and do exactly as I do, or your father will end up in the hospital tonight!"

They ran back, pushing their way through the crowd, arriving just as another Outlaw was lining up to deliver a punch. Barbara reared back with all her strength and brought the metal chair in an overhead arc, landing it on top of the head of the would-be assailant. His knees buckled under him as he went to the ground, his hands covering his head. She and Natalie went straight for the two Outlaws holding their beloved Joe and began pummeling them with blows from their metal chairs. The two quickly released Joe and backed off. Barbara and Natalie stood on either side of Joe with their metal chairs at the ready.

Eric Malinowsky, the President of the Outlaws club stepped forward facing them. He slowly began clapping his hands, looking around and smiling at the crowd around him. "Welcome to the club, Double Trouble!"

Pastor Joseph Peale stood tall, a little unsteady on his feet, and put his arms around his wife and daughter. Blood was dripping from a cut on his forehead and several ribs were bruised, but otherwise, nothing was broken.

"Triple Threat," someone from the crowd yelled out to praise Natalie for her bravery!

Eric addressed the crowd. "Joe Peale is now an ex-officio member of the Outlaws Motorcycle Club, Tampa Chapter!"

The crowd cheered, erupting in applause, as much for Joe, as for Barbara and Natalie. Then everyone started laughing and moved up to give them hugs and accolades. Unknown to the Peale family, the unusual ritual, the club initiation ceremony was now complete!

Joseph became the club's trusted counselor, helping where he could, never judging. After several years, the surprise Chinese attack on the United States came and changed everything.

The Outlaws were camped out at Tampa's Lowry Park for their annual get together of the Florida clubs when the first atomic bombs fell. Taking advantage of the ensuing chaos, the Outlaws took over Lowry Park Zoo as their headquarters. The park's zoo complex sported large very secure fencing to keep the animals from getting out, which also made the zoo easy to defend from within, since there were limited access points through the impenetrable fences.

There was total confusion in the city as police forces were only half manned and many times personal interests overruled job security. Groups with the largest membership and weapons to back up their territory began to exert their influence, superseding local governments. The zoo ensured the gang a steady supply of meat. Most of the city's population were unsure where their next meal would come from. The widespread nature of the disaster combined with the uncertainty of a new world war, had everyone hording supplies, less willing to help their neighbors, much less those in another state.

It was only natural when Eric, the long time and respected club president of the Outlaws, invited the pastor and his family to stay at the secure park. Joseph considered it an opportunity for him to continue to minister to his flock, in and out of the church, with spiritual guidance and food.

The usual wild antics associated with motorcycle gangs was tempered somewhat by the presence of the Methodist preacher and his family. He, Barbara, and now 17-year-old Natalie made frequent trips to the elderly in the neighborhood, ensuring they had enough to eat. They brought along the only meat available, although somewhat exotic in origin at times, there being no cows at the Lowry Park Zoo.

Chapter 32

Outlaws in Lowry Park

The news of the Florida Governor's declaration of martial law had been circulating among the populous for several days now. The Special Forces convoy of Humvees mounted with 50 caliber machine guns made its way north on Interstate 275 through the city of Tampa, moving slowly to avoid abandoned cars.

They attracted considerable attention from groups of people on foot and an occasional police car or motorist passing by, but no one dared stop them. The machine guns were manned with soldiers standing in their turrets just in case there was any trouble.

The convoy of Humvees took the Sleigh Avenue exit and turned west towards their destination – Lowry Park. The Park bordered the Hillsborough River and housed a large boat ramp making it an ideal embarkation point to reconnoiter Tampa Bay which was several miles downriver; easy access to surveil the strength of the incoming fleet of Chinese warships and troop transports. Arrangements had been made for a Long-Range Interceptor 35-foot Coast Guard boat to meet them. Other naval assets were being moved north, out of Tampa Bay to other gulf ports in anticipation of the arrival of the enemy fleet.

As the lead elements of the Special Forces convoy turned into the entrance of Lowry Park, they were met with a half dozen Outlaw Motorcycle Club bikers standing in their way with AR-15 assault rifles at the ready. The Outlaws became agitated as more machine gun mounted Humvees began pulling up into position around and on either side of Captain Connor and Trueman's lead vehicle.

One of the gang members set off a loud horn blasting a warning to everyone inside that they were under attack. With that, the loud waffling sound of Harley Davidson motorcycle engines could be heard revving up from inside the zoo fence. When the front gates of the zoo opened, fifty motorcycles poured out of the entrance, barreling down to confront their would-be attackers.

"Lock and load," Captain Connor loudly announced to the convoy over his lapel mic.

For Trueman in the lead vehicle, time began to slow down. He heard the high-pitched whine of a motorcycle coming from behind him. It moved past his right door window. He turned to look at a woman wearing a heavily blacked out helmet covering her whole head. Her long brown hair was billowing out from below the helmet.

She turned to look at him as her dirt bike passed the Humvee, but her expression was not discernable under the shaded sun glass shield that covered her face. She pulled directly in between the two factions facing off against each other and slid her bike down to the ground, dust and dirt flying up. She stepped off the motorcycle leaving it where it lay and quickly pulled her helmet off. She held both arms up, one toward the Outlaws and the other toward the Special Forces soldiers.

"Hold your fire," Natalie yelled, standing her ground. "Hold your fire!" she screamed.

At that moment in time, Trueman felt an uncontrollable pull and automatically shifted to his third eye, revealing the true nature of the spirit side of the young woman standing in front of him. She looked exactly like a picture he had seen during his Earth history upgrade … a picture of Joan of Arc. There was a sword in her right upraised hand, and she held a tall white banner on a pole in her left hand. Unlike the historical picture though, Natalie had long brunette hair flowing down the back of her silver armor.

Her whole countenance, from her face to the polished protective armor suit, showed a bright silver aura around her, made brighter by the sun's reflecting rays. Trueman immediately stepped out of the Humvee and walked straight up to the girl and stood beside her. He quickly raised one arm up to the Humvee force, which Seediq acknowledged with a nod of his head, and the other arm toward the larger Outlaw force beginning to coalesce around the entrance to Lowry Park.

"Hold your fire," Trueman yelled. "Hold your fire!"

Trueman was facing Natalie and could sense a shift in her sight away from the physical … *can she see my true self,* he wondered. An unseen force was pulling their spiritual selves toward each other … *can she feel this*? Natalie's face changed from fear of the coming confrontation to a look of bewilderment by what she saw around Trueman - a large bluish silver aura and white wings opening behind him reaching up to the sky.

And so, the erupting confrontation between the Outlaws motorcycle gang and the Florida National Guard Special Forces unit slowly merged into a standoff.

"This is our park and we have the numbers and weapons necessary to defend it. We don't want anyone else here!" Eric Malinowsky said as they started the negotiations around a conference room table in the zoo administrative wing. Eric was backed up by Bear and several other intimidating Outlaws bikers standing behind him.

Captain Connor was backed up by his second in command Lieutenant Moreno, a stern decorated veteran of middle east conflicts and Sergeant Major Freeman, a large muscular black non-com who taught hand to hand combat techniques.

Trueman had Seediq and Ben behind him, both with Lorsguns and bandoliers of shotgun shells crossing their chests. The multi-barreled shotgun was lethal in small spaces like tunnels – or conference rooms. And then there was Pastor Joe, the negotiator for this meeting with Natalie and Barbara standing behind him. And so, the four sides of the conference table were fully represented.

"Captain Connor, why don't you tell us why you need this site and cannot move to another location," Pastor Joe asked.

"Our orders cannot be changed!" he said. "We are to meet a Coast Guard vessel at the boat dock at Lowery Park in the city of Tampa tomorrow for the purpose of reconnoitering a naval Chinese invasion of Tampa Bay," Captain Connor said.

The Outlaws bikers burst into laughter at this revelation.

Connor waited a moment for the mirth to subside. "I have no way of getting in touch with this boat or its crew to move them to another location. I will remind you that Florida is under Martial Law and we could force you to move."

"Force me to move?" Eric bristled at that. "We don't recognize the authority of the government. Why do you think we became Outlaws?" he said derisively. "Besides, the idea that China is going to invade the United States is ridiculous."

"Look around you," Trueman said. "With everything that is going on here, you don't think we are ripe for a successful invasion. We can't even keep from fighting each other!"

"Alright," Pastor Joe said, holding up his hands to calm the tensions down. "I know the area pretty well. Eric, you are mostly holed up in and around the zoo compound, especially at night. The boat ramp is a considerable distance away from here with a road separating the zoo property from the camping area around the river's boat ramp. Why don't you take everything west of that north/south road and Captain Connor can take everything east of the road? Neither one of you should have to interact with each other since the road has its own exit out of the park. Besides, I'm sure once Connor has the information he needs, he will be moving out of the park. Is that right, Captain?"

"You are correct, we have much bigger fish to fry than fighting with a motorcycle gang. We can agree to those terms," Captain Connor replied. All eyes turned to Eric.

"Alright, even though we could easily send this pack of rats down the road, we will also agree with this time limited arrangement." Eric said reluctantly.

Chapter 33

The First Shots Fired

The next morning marked the arrival of the Coast Guard Long-Range Interceptor on schedule. Captain Connor took three Special Forces soldiers with him to reconnoiter Tampa Bay and left the others to guard the Humvees and boat ramp.

He left no instructions for Trueman or his legionaries since Trueman's soldiers appeared to him "a rag tag group subject to unpredictable independent action in the face of danger." Captain Conner was not used to having his orders questioned by anyone, especially in a firefight. He now considered them unreliable allies.

"What's a zoo?" Mars asked as the legionaries sat around their campfire after breakfast. They had bivouacked in the campground beside the boat ramp parking area.

"That's where they keep all kinds of animals behind cages for people to look at," Seediq replied.

"How would you know? You grew up in the underground caves and tunnels on Gannicus just like the rest of us," Mars said derisively.

Seediq thought for a moment, then answered, "Trueman told me about them. His mother is from Earth." He actually knew about it because of the strange Earth knowledge upgrade Trueman had given him, so technically he was telling the truth.

"Let's go see the animals then," Mars said.

"Yes, let's go see the animals. I understand that none of those animals exist on Gannicus and we may never get the opportunity to see anything like them again," Mark said.

Just at that moment, Natalie was traveling down the road intersecting the boat ramp area from the zoo complex on her dirt bike. Trueman sensed an opportunity. He stood and waved, flagging Natalie down. She slowed and turned back to their bivouac.

"Natalie, I trust you are doing well today?" Trueman asked formally.

"I am, thank you very much Trueman," she replied with some reserve, remembering the strange day before when she saw a silver blue aura encircling him … *and wings?*

"We would all like to go visit the zoo but need an invitation to be welcomed in there. Would you be willing to use your influence to help us?"

"Sure, why not," she replied, "but I don't know what the Outlaws will make of it. Are you willing to leave your weapons behind?"

Trueman looked at the legionaries lounging around the campfire and each nodded their willingness to disarm in order to see the strange creatures from Earth.

Trueman turned back to Natalie and asked, "We would be willing to disarm but can these Outlaws be trusted? I don't want to put my people at risk."

"I wouldn't trust them further than I could throw them, which is not far," Natalie said, which caused a stir among the legionaries. "But they all do exactly what Eric, their president, tells them - on pain of death," she replied. "So, if he agrees, you should not have any problems."

"Well, with your assurances that we would surely be safe," Trueman said, "please make the request." He could not explain it, but he trusted Natalie with his life.

Eric led the way, flanked by Trueman and Natalie at his side. The other Gannicuns followed, their mouths dropping with each new and unusual caged animal they passed: warthogs, gazelles, giraffes. They had left their weapons in the care of the Special Forces soldiers guarding the boat ramp.

"So why do you want Seediq to accompany you on a mission to scope out the Chinese naval fleet?" Trueman asked Eric, the Outlaw leader.

"Because I don't trust Captain Connor and Seediq will be my hostage while I'm away from the zoo. If you or his men try anything, you forfeit his life - understood?"

"I will leave that choice up to Seediq," Trueman replied as he turned to look at his second in command.

"I want to see this large Chinese naval force myself," Seediq said. "I'll gladly go with Eric and see if the invasion is real or not!"

Eric smiled and thought to himself … *I knew this one had balls. He's been around the block a few times,* he thought, as he stared at the scar on Seediq's face.

Eric, Seediq, Bear and about a dozen Outlaw bikers armed to the teeth loaded their Harley Davidson motorcycles with all kinds of explosive ordinance.

"Where's this Seediq guy going to ride?" Bear asked Eric derisively.

"Give him a 'Prospect' jacket, he can pile on behind me," Eric replied.

Seediq put on the jacket and slung his Lorsgun over his back. Stepping behind Eric on the Harley was awkward but not nearly as embarrassing as almost falling off as the bikers shifted into gear and roared out of the zoo compound. They exited Lowry Park onto Sleigh avenue. The entrance to Interstate 275 was near and they all sped up moving south to St. Petersburg all the while swerving back and forth to avoid abandoned cars.

They approached the Sunshine Skyway Bridge which spans four miles over the Tampa Bay inlet entrance to the deep-water harbor. The peak of the bridge allows 175 feet of clearance for ships to enter the bay.

The entrance to the bridge was blocked by two police cars with lights flashing. Eric slowed the group, moved over to the side pullover lane, and kept going at a steady pace. At first the four police officers manning the blocked highway scrambled to get behind their vehicles. Several pulled their guns, but when the officer in charge saw the AR-15s strapped to the backs of the bikers being slung forward at the ready, he motioned for the other officers to stand down. Eric gave a wave to the officers as he drove by them and proceeded up the bridge.

They had not gone far when the group came to a sudden stop with each one staring out into the Gulf of Mexico with unbelieving looks on their faces. Ships - large naval vessels, hundreds of them - could be seen stretched out to the horizon, all heading straight to the Skyway Bridge entrance to Tampa Bay. Eric threw his Harley into gear and roared up to the top of the bridge. They parked on the lane next to the four feet concrete barrier separating the southbound and northbound lanes of traffic. It was eerily quiet on top of the bridge except for the steady sea breeze swirling past them.

They slowly walked over to the four feet high concrete barrier facing the gulf. Ships were already moving under them and they could easily make out the faces of seamen scurrying about. The officers bridge, near the highest point on the ships was even closer and they generated a lot of scrutiny from that vantage point as the ships steadily moved under them.

Then they noticed the mega-ship, the People's Liberation Army Navy Surface Force vessel named the 'Liaoning,' a 67,500-ton refitted ex-Soviet Kuznetsov class aircraft carrier with planes and helicopters lining the deck.

"I've always wanted to do that," Eric said to his group of bikers staring at the ship.

"Do what?" Bear asked.

"Blow up something that big," Eric replied.

They all laughed heartily!

"How are you going to do that?" Seediq asked, not understanding along with everyone else, how Eric could accomplish such an impossible task.

"Follow me," Eric said as he moved back to the parked Harleys in the middle of the bridge. He unstrapped two satchel bags from his motorcycle, placing them on the ground, and proceeded to open them up revealing the contents. The first was a C-4 demolition explosives pack consisting of eight rectangular blocks wired together. The second was full of hand grenades.

"This is how it will go down," he said as he pushed LPD detonators into the soft ends of the C-4 blocks.

"I'll wait until the bow of the carrier has passed the bridge, then I'll activate the detonators and throw the C-4 satchel bag onto the midship deck of the aircraft carrier. The C-4 will explode in about ten seconds which should give the midship enough time to clear the bridge, so it doesn't blow up underneath us. We'll stay hunkered down here in the middle of the bridge until the blast subsides, then run over to the bay side railing and toss all our hand grenades into the hole the C-4 has blown in the deck of the ship. This should create enough havoc below decks to allow us to get the hell out of here, and I mean out of here," he said with emphasis, "as fast as we can, back to Lowry Park!"

Eric looked around at the incredulous smiles on the faces surrounding him. "This is not a joke!" he shouted. "No one is going to invade the United States of America and waltz in without a shot being fired!"

Everyone sobered up and put their game faces on. They knew when Eric made up his mind there was no changing it, regardless of the outcome. He started tossing hand grenades to each biker and hesitated when he got around to Seediq.

"I'm game," Seediq said. "I'd love to blow up something big!" *If this is the technology Trueman said we could access by staying on Earth a while longer, count me in*, he thought.

Everyone burst out laughing. "He's a bigger fool than you Eric!" Bear bellowed.

"Fool or not, we are doing this," Eric said. "Stay down behind the concrete barrier."

Eric proceeded to walk slowly over to the bay side railing with the C-4 filled satchel slung over his back. He positioned himself as if he were about to throw a disc, wound up, and slung the satchel up and out past the bridge. It fell onto the deck as Eric sprinted back to the waiting bikers. It was not long in coming as a huge detonation exploded with hot air and fire bellowing up above the bridge. Debris flung into the air and began to fall around them.

As the blast began to subside, Eric leaped over the center concrete barrier carrying the remainder of the hand grenades. He leaned over to get his bearings, locating the gaping hole in the flight deck, then pulled the pins and began tossing the hand grenades one by one into the gaping hole. The bikers followed suit and a great cacophony of explosions could be heard below decks.

By the time Seediq was ready to copy the biker's movements, pulling the pin and tossing his grenade, the vessel had moved far enough along that the grenade landed short of the hole. It rolled back down the deck underneath the bridge and exploded right under one of the parked airplanes. The topside explosion set off a chain reaction down the deck of parked planes with each bursting into flames and shooting explosive bursts up into the underbelly of the bridge, which began to sway underneath them.

"Let's get the hell out of here," Eric shouted as he sprinted to his parked Harley with Seediq right behind him. They roared back down the Skyway bridge as small arms and anti-aircraft fire from support ships in front of and behind the exploding aircraft carrier began to pepper the road around them.

The historic first shots fired during the communist Chinese invasion of the United States of America was met not by the armed forces of the United States but rather by the Outlaws Motorcycle Club, Tampa Chapter, led by its President Eric Malinowski, a veteran of foreign wars, and his fellow bikers. They were accompanied by a strange Special Forces soldier named Seediq (no last name) that no one knew what country, *or planet*, he hailed from!

Chapter 34

The Battle of the Green Swamp

"All war is based on deception!"

-Sun Tzu

The tremendous explosions heard around Tampa Bay coming from the Liaoning aircraft carrier signaled the beginning of a massive panicked evacuation away from the Chinese invasion forces.

Those that could find transportation fled north or south on Interstate 75 since the Florida National Guard was blocking Interstate 4 heading east. Others traveled by foot through the countryside, adding to the chaos.

The southeastern edge of the Green Swamp in central Florida was the perfect place to brunt the advance of the large Chinese army with their massive resources of men and equipment. The swamp extends about 30 miles along the North side of the I-4 corridor about halfway between Tampa and Orlando. Occasional smoke fires started by lightning strikes on the damp cypress forest and undergrowth vegetation have closed the interstate highway many times over the years when smoke from northerly winds reduced visibility to near zero. This route is the quickest way across central Florida, and if taken, would ensure that southern Florida was lost to Chinese control.

General Clark planned to combine smoke fires artificially started by the Florida Forest Service and phosphorescent mortar shells to confuse, disorient, and slow down the advancing Chinese forces. He would then bring all batteries to bear on their leading units at the sprawling North/South Highway 27 cloverleaf intersection with I-4.

This interchange is ideally suited for a surprise attack with a triangle formation killing zone that military planners dream of. The highway makes a slow turn several miles east of the swamp's end. Ample trees cover both sides of the road and throughout the median within 300 yards of the interchange, making forward visibility limited for those troops following behind the lead elements. The interstate highway dips down as it approaches the interchange with residential houses and mobile homes on both sides overlooking the highway. Mortar squads and machine gun nests can be positioned there, hidden out of sight above the highway.

A large swale sunk 15 feet deep in the middle of the cloverleaf on-ramp, designed to collect runoff during heavy rains, but otherwise bone dry, will conceal tanks, gun mounted halftracks, mortars, and machine gun units. It's only a short move up to the edges of the highway where prepared firing positions allow a range of direct forward fire. Other units on the highway 27 bridge will also have clear lines of fire down into the approaching force. The Chinese army would be unaware of the true strength of the National

Guard's positions or their disposition of forces until they were almost on top of them.

Due to the chaos caused by the atomic bomb attacks on the east coast and the aftermath of the hurricane, General Clark was only able to muster about 3,000 soldiers hastily collected from various understrength weekend warrior units. These were supported by an assortment of outdated armored vehicle mounted guns, tanks and tracked mortars recycled and handed down from active duty army units to the National Guard and Army Reserve over the years. They would need every element of surprise and focused firepower they could muster to be successful.

As with many battles, the battle of the Green Swamp began with small units skirmishing for position and advantage.

A motley group of marauders pulled off the Old Grade Road onto a dirt logging road that made its way east through the green swamp. The raised road ran parallel and several hundred yards north of the interstate highway. It made a perfect vantage point to lob phosphorescent mortar shells into the damp thickets of the swamp adjacent to the highway.

Eric Malinowsky led a mobile auxiliary of Outlaws who were willing to serve the cause of driving the Chinese out of Florida. Thirty-three Outlaw skirmishers took the lead position in the small convoy with their automatic rifles slung across their backs. The usual loud noises from their Harley Davidson motorcycles were muffled with extra baffling.

The Outlaws were followed by two M1064 tracked mortar carriers from the Polk County National Guard. Similar looking to tanks, the mortar carriers had their tops removed and large mortar pods bolted down in the middle of them.

The Forest Service fire starters were next. Although counter-intuitive, the Forest Service employs a well-trained cadre of firefighters who protect forests by periodically intentionally starting forest fires called prescribed burns. They help prevent forest fires by systematically burning ground debris and canopy fuels that build up over time underneath tree canopies in forest lands.

Captain Connor's Florida National Guard Special Forces unit with their Gannicun allies brought up the rear of the column with their 50-caliber mounted Humvees. Their machine guns pointed back west, the way they had come, for rear force protection.

The speed of the entire convoy was based on how fast the tracked vehicles could move from one location to the next, get setup, then range about a half dozen 120 mm mortar shells in a near 45-degree arc toward the tree line north of the interstate. This process required lowering their four metal braces, securing the vehicle from the tremendous downward thrust when the large mortars fired. The two-man crews worked like clockwork, first arming the mortar bombs, then delicately lifting and dropping them onto the firing pin at the base of the mortar tube.

Sergeant Goldweber was the senior mortarman for each mortar's two-man crew. He was a marine veteran of the desert wars who joined the Florida National Guard to be near his extended family in central Florida. He worked out the firing solutions at a portable table he set up between tracked vehicles. Out of curiosity about the technology, Seediq stayed close to the experienced mortarman.

"What are those instruments used for?" Seediq asked as he looked around the table.

"In order for the mortar to strike the ground precisely where you want it when you don't have line of sight, you need these instruments to set the elevation and traversing mechanisms on the mortars to match the map coordinates," Goldweber explained, as he demonstrated how each was used.

He stepped back and Seediq followed him as he critiqued the crews and set the mortars. Seediq maintained a spot between the tracked mortar carriers so that he could get a closer look at the mortar crews when they were firing. Each time the tracked vehicles moved forward and repositioned, the vehicles rear ramp was lowered and leveled to make a sturdy platform to prepare the rounds that would be fired, giving Seediq a clear line of sight to inspect their operations.

The mortars were similar to what had been used to destroy the Roman defenders of the underground village of Nain, one of the signature moments in Seediq's life. Subsequently, he wanted to know everything he could about this unusual technology.

The crews were young men who had joined the National Guard right out of high school; six months of army training, three in basic and three in advanced training, before arriving at the real thing – live firing mortars in warfare!

They were nearing the end of this exhausting operation, so far proceeding like clockwork, when the unexpected happened. An immense explosion shattered the leading mortar carrier. The ground trembled; hot flames and shrapnel shot up into the sky and out in every direction. This was real combat, where friendly fire can often result in up to 30% of the casualties in the field.

"Run!" Sergeant Goldweber yelled just before he was thrown back into Seediq, knocking him down and shielding him from the worst of the shockwave. The searing heat spreading out from the mortar track was another matter. Goldweber was killed instantly and his clothes were burning. Several mortar shells engulfed in the flames started popping off, exploding spontaneously from the heat.

"Everyone get back and move yourselves and your equipment away from the burning wreak," Captain Connor yelled as he ran up from his position. Three mortarmen were dead and Seediq lay face down, his clothes smoking and his skin beginning to turn a white ash color in the heat … but he was still alive.

Sprinting to help Seediq, Trueman ignored the shouts of Captain Connor warning him off. His eyes teared up from the smoke and heat around him. He dropped to the ground as the heat began searing his skin and heating his clothes to the point of ignition. He almost lost consciousness when he felt a golden glow emanating out from his body and forming around him. It shielded the heat and he took advantage of the respite to reach out, grabbing Seediq's body under the armpits and dragging him out and away from the inferno.

At this point in the operation, they were very close to the highway 27/Interstate 4 interchange where ambulances from hospitals in Orlando were waiting to take wounded out of the coming battle. Seediq was the first wounded casualty since the others could not be saved.

Luna insisted that she and Trueman ride in the ambulance with Seediq back to Florida Hospital in downtown Orlando. Captain Connor called off further operations since they were near Highway 27. Conner's Special Force's unit took the lead position, followed by the ambulance and the mobile auxiliary as they turned south toward the coming battle lines. On the way, Connor received an urgent message from General Clark.

"Return to the Kennedy Space Center immediately and bring Seediq's black-ops group with you. Make sure Trueman Dyer is with you!"

Chapter 35

Best Laid Plans

The ambulance made it quickly to the I-4 interchange where traffic slowed to a crawl as armored vehicles, machine gun crews and mortarmen moved into positions in front of them on top of the Highway 27 overpass bridge.

Both heavy and light tanks, self-propelled howitzers, armored personnel carriers and 50 cal. mounted Humvees snaked out of the cloverleaf swales taking up firing positions across I-4. The forward elements of the Chinese army and their mechanized mobile armor could just be seen emerging from the smoke-filled skies about 300 yards to the west.

The Outlaws, led by Eric, swarmed around and forward of the ambulance on their motorcycles in an effort to get the column moving forward again. Eric had developed a fond relationship with Seediq and wanted his friend to survive and live to see another day.

The presence of the motorcycle gang with AR-15 rifles at the ready first confused the officers trying to organize the ranks on top of the bridge. Captain Connor, running up to the front on foot, also added his weight to the request to move the column forward.

It was at that moment that enemy fire began to pepper the bridge sending chunks of concrete flying in all directions. Someone gave the order to return fire and the combined roar of main battle tanks and howitzers spewing canister rounds, heavy machine guns throwing sheets of lead, mortars popping off 120 mm rounds created a roar, an avalanche of sound that deafened the hearing and senses. Nothing exposed to that initial overwhelming arc of firepower could have been left untouched.

Considering all the other patchwork of disparate units that had been brought to bear in this battle, it was not a stretch of the imagination on the part of the officers to assume that these odd units around the ambulance were friendly. And so, the troops holding up the convoy, anxious to find cover from the in-coming fire, waved the ambulance forward and onto the I-4 eastbound on-ramp.

Just as the column began speeding up toward Orlando and the Florida Hospital emergency room, Trueman was startled by Luna.

"Trueman," Luna shouted, "do something!"

She and Trueman had been sitting helplessly watching the emergency ambulance medic as he worked to establish an intravenous (IV) solution that would replenish Seediq's much needed body fluids. His frustration was obvious after his sixth attempt failed. Seediq's blood pressure was near zero - survival was in doubt.

Luna got on her knees at Trueman's feet and pleaded with him. "We know you are the son of the Prophetess and I saw the golden dome that protected you when you pulled Seediq out of the fire. You must not let him die!"

Trueman had been thinking the same thing. He could not let his friend and brother die here before him. But Bodhidharma's instructions were perfectly clear … protect the technology he had given him to heal and extend his life. Once that became known, it would change everything, and people would fight and kill each other to obtain it.

The medic sat back exhausted from his failed attempts. "All I can do at this point is use a scalpel and cut an opening to his femoral artery and insert the IV there … it's risky. We'll be at the hospital soon. Better to wait for the emergency room doctors. Either way, he could die."

Seediq began to stir, moaning and thrashing in obvious pain from the third degree burns to 75 % of his body.

"Let me try something," Trueman said, as he stood and shifted to the head of the gurney, placing his hands over Seediq's head.

The medic rose to force him to sit down but Trueman's cold, focused stare stopped him in his tracks. Trueman focused back on his patient and closed his eyes. He began messaging Seediq's head and the moans slowly subsided; the squirming stopped almost immediately.

Without looking up, Trueman said, "Both of you go to the front of the ambulance and close the curtains. No one is to come back here!"

The medic looked confused and reluctant to leave, seeing the results of Trueman's touch, until Luna grabbed his arm and began pulling him forward.

"Let the Prophet do his work!" she said with emphasis on the word Prophet.

Under normal circumstances the brawny medic would have refused, but after watching Trueman calming the pain with only his touch, he reluctantly allowed himself to be escorted away from the gurney. The curtain separating the driver's cab from the back of the ambulance was pulled closed.

Am I realizing a new healing gift? Trueman wondered as he refocused on Seediq's recovery instead of just calming his pain. After a few minutes of concentration, *apparently not*, he determined, disappointed. Seediq lay completely calm, still breathing, but with no apparent improvement in the burned areas of his body.

Trueman allowed the medical knowledge infused into him during his upgrade to filter through his mind. He settled on what to do and looked into the drawers adjacent to the gurney where he found what he needed - a needle and syringe.

He rolled up his sleeve and very carefully began withdrawing blood from his arm. When the syringe was full, he laid it aside.

Moving back to Seediq's side, he adjusted his patient's head so that the right carotid artery in the neck was fully extended. He felt for a pulse but found none. *Not good*, he thought, and quickly slipped into viewing Seediq's neck through his third eye. His vision focused down through the layers of skin and tissue to the carotid artery. It was nearly flat with a small stream of blood moving through it. He reached up and grabbed the IV tubing and slowly inserted the needle through Seediq's skin and into the artery itself, securing it with tape.

He turned the saline solution on and grabbed onto the IV port located in the tubing just below the saline solution bottle. He inserted the syringe's needle into the port, slowly injecting his own blood into the tube. He watched as it mixed with the clear solution on its way into Seediq's body. He repeated this procedure twice more and each time he noticed an improvement in the condition of Seediq's burned skin.

Luna, overwhelmed with concern for Seediq, could not resist the urge to look, and gently cracked a small wrinkle in the edge of the curtain wide enough for her to see through. She watched as Trueman withdrew his blood and injected it into the IV port for the third time. She could see the burned skin on the top of Seediq's head begin to turn pink and the beginning of hair growth. She backed away from the curtain in surprised awe. *It's the blood,* she thought, *the power is in the Prophet's blood!*

There was quite a scene at the patient drop off area of the Orlando Florida Hospital emergency room. Trueman would not allow the emergency personnel to remove Seediq from the ambulance.

The Gannicuns stood their ground alongside Trueman, brandishing their automatic weapons and Lorsguns. Luna tried to explain to Eric, Captain Connor, and the local police, that Seediq had recovered sufficiently to accompany them to the Kennedy Space Center. They were allowed to peek into the rear of the ambulance and see and speak with Seediq. He was weak, but able to sit up on the gurney, and his skin had a pink glow to it.

"I'm alright thanks to Trueman. He rescued me in time from the explosion and I don't want to be admitted to the hospital," he explained. Trueman had already briefed Luna and Seediq on what to say to avoid being admitted, since he did not want any blood drawn and analyzed revealing the Nano-bots, the secret truth of Seediq's recovery.

"That's good enough for me," Eric said after seeing and talking to Seediq. *Strange, I've seen enough war wounds to know this one could easily have been fatal,* he thought. *The rumors are true then, about Trueman being special, so no sense in looking a gift horse in the mouth.* "Let's get this show on the road!" he yelled.

The ambulance was unceremoniously commandeered by the Outlaws and Gannicuns to allow more time for Seediq to rest and recuperate in a medically safe and secure environment on their way to Cape Canaveral.

Chapter 36

Blood for Blood

Six mobile tracked carriers housing the new rail guns and their crews called the Game Changers moved forward in their underground tunnels as the camouflage covers were removed from the face of the Golan plateau. There was no doubt now that war was upon them with Syrian artillery shells raining down on their positions.

Two soldiers sat at the control panels adjusting dials to pump up the reactor, similar to those used on nuclear submarines. This was the only way to provide enough power to send the metal projectiles at speeds approaching Mach 8 from the electromagnetic launchers. The kinetic energy weapon contains no toxic explosive materials. The mass and speed of the projectile provides the explosive force when it hits the target.

The Game Changer's long barrels emerged from the underground bunkers into the night air. A hum pierced the air, increasing in volume as the current of the power supply pulsed through the machines.

"Game Changers are ready," General John Sator said.

"Commence Fire!" The order from Israel Defense Forces General Meir Kovner could be heard over the earphones of the tankmen manning the Golan Heights. Seventy-two Mark VI Merkava main battle tanks dug in on top of the Golan Heights opened fire as one. The resulting booms echoed along the heights like jets just breaking the sound barrier. The massive tank attack coming up from the Syrian plain below, launched at 4 am, was illuminated nearly as clear as daytime by multiple flares periodically launched from the Israeli side.

The flashes from the barrels of the IDF tank ordinance could be easily seen but not the almost soundless thump of the rail guns in the Game Changers as they fired from their previously hidden underground bunkers in the side of the plateau. The approaching mass of 4,000 Muslim battle tanks was taking a brutally unexpected beating due to the damage being inflicted by the Israeli tanks and rail guns.

The Syrian artillery, which had begun bombarding the heights thirty minutes before the start of the tank assault, was ineffective in clearing the way for their tank corp. Badly needed air support was quickly called in from other fronts to try and minimize the losses that were quickly piling up as one tank after another was pulverized by the withering fire.

The combined firepower of the Muslim artillery and tanks with the ground support fighter jets began to take its toll on the Merkava tanks atop the Golan. Flashes from their gun barrels began to subside. However, the Muslim tanks were still experiencing withering losses from the rapid-fire accuracy of the rail guns. The attack was finally called off and a full retreat authorized. The Game Changers had won their first battle, but with terrible losses on both sides.

John Sator exited the rear door of his carrier and walked to the mouth of the underground bunker just as the sun began to rise over the battlefield. He slowly scanned the scene below with his binoculars. There was a frenzied effort to remove wounded from the battlefield. *Are they afraid that we will fire on them*, he wondered, *certainly not that, but what?*

His instincts began to nag at him. The reports of the nuclear attacks and the Chinese army disembarking on the mainland United States had only recently filtered through the ranks of the Israel Defense Forces. *We're facing Muslim and Russian forces. Both Iran and Russia are nuclear capable ... and are allied with China!*

Sator quickly returned to his carrier and keyed his radio microphone; "this is General Sator, all top side surface battalion tank forces and support troops move back to our second line of defense and brace for a nuclear attack! Game Changers move back into the middle of your bunkers and seal all hatches."

The crew of the Chinese Space Station readied a tactical nuclear weapon for launch targeting the Golan Heights. The weapon has a TNT equivalent slightly less than the nuclear bomb used at Hiroshima, Japan, during World War II. Tactical nuclear weapons are designed to be used on battlefields where stubborn resistance or choke points prevent the advance of offensive forces. The friendly forces can withdraw and wait nearby for the detonation blast to subside. As long as they move quickly through the area and don't linger there, they can safely get to their objective without any harm to themselves from the radiation.

The topside Israeli forces had cleared the area when the nuclear detonation occurred 500 yards above ground. The tremendous downward force of the explosion collapsed the underground tunnels on top of the Game Changers, but the sturdy metal infrastructure of the tracked carriers protected their crews. However, ventilation systems filled with grainy dust from the collapsed dirt.

The northeastern wall of the Golan defenses was now quickly breached as the Muslim forces and their Russian allies sped through the nuclear blast zone on the way to the heart of Israel - Jerusalem!

Twenty-four hours later, General Sator and the crew of his command Game Changer were standing hunched over in the crew compartment of the rail gun with wet t-shirts tied around their faces waiting for the soil borne dust to settle on the metal floor.

Each time they started up the nuclear power source and engaged the tracks, attempting to move out of the collapsed tunnel, soil and dust particles would begin swirling through the ventilation system into the crew compartment and they would have to shut it down. They were nearly out of water for drinking and for keeping their makeshift facial air filters wet. With tons of dirt on top and on all sides of the vehicle, the carrier could move only a few inches before the air became unbreathable, forcing them to shut down. They were exhausted.

Hovering above the Golan battlefield, three black cigar shaped Gannicun rift flyers scanned the terrain. One was piloted by Bodhidharma and the others by Vimmul and

Menelik. Each contained a cohort of Gurkha warriors and Roman legionaries. They all wore blue/black camouflage uniforms with space insignia patches and were armed with Israeli Tavor assault rifles. The scanning instruments were able to pick up the buried signatures of the Game Changers. Bodhidharma gave instructions to Vimmul and Menelik.

"Hover directly over the tanks and use your maneuvering jets to start a vortex, removing the topsoil until you see some metal exposed. Then move down over it and expand your gravity well's signature until it includes the hull of the Game Changer. Lift it up and out of the tunnel. We must be quick to get this done before we are all exposed to a lethal dose of radiation!"

Sator's Game Changer began to rumble, lifting the foot of soil borne dust up and down at their feet. Then, everything not tied down in the crew compartment began to slowly float up, as did the Game Changer itself. With the rail gun safely out of the tunnel and moved over solid ground, the gravity wells encircling the tracked carrier suddenly turned off and the heavy metal hulk slammed into the ground on top of the Golan plateau. The metal rear door of the vehicle suddenly swung open depositing dirty coughing soldiers, thankful to be alive, onto solid ground.

The six Game Changers were lined up facing south. Bodhidharma ordered his cohorts to assist the soldiers out of their suffocating quarters and quickly begin removing the soil from the interior of the tanks, getting them ready to move out.

"Who is your commanding officer?" Bodhidharma asked the nearest soldier.

"General Sator, over there," he motioned.

Sator was leaning on the open rear metal door of a Game Changer scratching with his bare hands to try and remove packed earth from the interior of the rail gun compartment as Bodhidharma approached him.

"That one must have had its door open when the nuclear blast detonated. The soil packed in so tight we don't have time to remove it without exposing ourselves to the radiation around here. There are no survivors. General Sator, I am Commander Bodhidharma." Sator seemed in a dazed state as he turned and stood erect.

"That is a naval designation, isn't it?" he asked.

"Usually, but in this case, it refers to a Commander of a United Nations Air Force unit … a Space Force unit to be exact," Bodhidharma said.

"Space Force? You pulled us out of the ground using those - spaceships?" Sator asked astonished.

"We did," Bodhidharma replied.

"You saved our lives then, most of our lives. We had less than a day's oxygen left and were nearly suffocating underground," Sator said. "I didn't know the United Nations had a presence in space."

"Very few people do and most of them are probably dead!" *Since it does not exist, I might as well plant the seed and hope no one calls my bluff,* Bodhidharma thought. "The surprise nuclear attacks destroyed the white house and the congress in Washington, D.C. as well as the United Nations General Assembly in New York while they both were in session. The leadership of the free world no longer exists."

"Promise me you will recover this Game Changer from the battlefield and see that the dead are returned to their families. We can't let the enemy find this technology," Sator said.

"I promise, but now we need to get you up and out of here quickly or the radiation exposure here will kill us all!" Bodhidharma warned.

"Your assistance is appreciated," Sator replied, eyeing the three torpedo-like craft parked near his Game Changers. Fifty of Bodhidharma's troops were scrambling to get Sator's Game Changers cleaned up and ready for combat while the rest were providing water, coffee, tea, and honey covered biscuits to his dust covered troops. Sator himself was a bit unstable on his feet and Bodhidharma assisted him over to one of the portable chairs set up for his troops.

"What you have done so far to brunt the attack is commendable, but you must push on. The battle still rages not far from Jerusalem," Bodhidharma said as Sator finished eating several biscuits and drained a large cup of coffee.

General Sator stood and quickly assessed the condition of his men. The short rest and nourishment helped restore their vigor. He conducted a quick inspection of the equipment in his five remaining Game Changers before ordering the advance and quickly moving off toward Jerusalem. *With luck, we'll catch the Muslim forces between us and the third line of defense before they reach the holy city*, he thought with confidence the battle could still be won!

Chapter 37

Space Invaders

"We are not going to die Claire!" Edward Foster, the International Space Station Commander said, trying to calm Claire McAlpin. The crew and the two vacationers, minus the two Russian Federal Space Agency crewmembers, were crammed into the hotel module with the hatches firmly and electronically locked.

"Your space station reality show will top all records for viewership after this gets out," Foster said to lighten the mood. "You're going to be the most famous actress on the planet!"

"I doubt with World War III waging, that this episode will get more than a mention on the nightly news ... assuming they're still having the nightly news."

"You may be right," Franz Moser, the European Union Space Agency crew member lamented. "If only we had not run out of maneuvering propulsion,"

"It would not have mattered," Jamila Smith-Owens, the NASA engineer replied. "All the Chinese space station prototypes had a rocket propulsion engine so there is no reason to believe this final version, secret as it was when it was launched, did not have one too. They would have caught up to us eventually, even with our maneuvering jets operating at full capacity."

"So why didn't they just blow us out of the sky?" Dolph Bjelke, the Danish engineering student asked. "They most certainly have enough firepower to do it."

"Well, for one thing, they had their two Russian spies on board the ISS," Tokugawa Shikibu, the Japan Aerospace Agency crew member replied.

"And for another," Commander Foster said, "we still have a lot of state-of-the-art technology on the International Space Station and they will keep us all alive until they have squeezed every bit of intelligence out of us they can. After that, it's anyone's guess what will happen to us."

"So, what's our next move?" Claire asked.

"These quarters are so cramped," Foster replied, "we wait until they unlock and open the hatch, then overpower whoever comes in first. The hatches are not designed for more than one person to move through them at a time."

"That just might work," Moser chimed in.

At that moment there was a rumbling sound throughout the space station and the hotel module went totally dark, startling everyone. The generators powering lights and life support systems were down. All was quiet, visibility zero.

Bodhidharma slowly maneuvered his rift flyer up from behind the satellite debris they were hiding in and activated an electromagnetic pulse directly focused on the distant interlocked International and Chinese space stations.

Trueman sat in the co-pilots seat and Seediq watched from a standing position behind the pilot's console.

"Blasting them with a sustained electromagnetic pulse will permanently blind their sensors and allow us to move directly up and dock with the space station undetected. Any instrument that is turned on when the pulse hits will be fried and useless, which includes the environmental life support controls. Once docked with the ISS, we'll move through it to the Chinese space station, and take it by surprise," Bodhidharma said.

"How long will it be before the lack of life support ends up killing the astronaut crews?" Trueman asked.

"There'll be enough oxygen for 24-hours at least but the cold temperatures will freeze them to death before that." Bodhidharma replied. "It's difficult to tell how quickly the cold will set in. It depends on the amount of insulation in the station's walls."

Trueman and Seediq's cohort were strapped in and waiting to begin the assault, each with a small cross bow designed for commandeering space craft since the short arrows could not penetrate the space station walls like projectile firearms or other sophisticated disruptors could. A contingent of well-trained technicians from the Kennedy Space Center waited in the flyer with duffle bags full of replacement parts and equipment needed to rapidly get life support and propulsion back on-line once the takeover was completed.

The prisoners waited in silence on the ISS, each in their own deep thoughts about their chances of surviving this life-threatening ordeal. Under normal conditions, even with lights out, there are numerous electronics operating in all the modules allowing one to make out dim light sources indicating systems are operating normally, but this was a total blackout. You could not see one inch in front of your face. Pale red emergency battery backup lighting slowly flickered on creating a surreal other worldly atmosphere in the module.

"What's going on?" Claire finally asked the question on everyone's mind.

"There is only one explanation for this," Jamila said from her sitting position next to Claire, "an electromagnetic pulse. It could be nuclear in origin or an especially powerful solar flare with a very direct path to our location."

"That's absolutely correct," Moser said. "I'm thinking solar flare, since a nuclear blast with an electromagnetic pulse that strong would have to be close, and we didn't feel a strong shock wave when the pulse hit. It must be solar in origin, but I've never heard of one that strong in the history of the space program."

"There's a first time for everything," Commander Foster said. "Is anyone thinking what I'm thinking?"

"The electronic locking systems on the hatches are disabled," Dolph said.

"Give the brilliant young man an A+!" Tokugawa said enthusiastically.

"Everyone grab something you can use as a weapon," Foster said as he held up a heavy-duty flashlight. "These work great as a club and could come in handy if the emergency lights begin to fail us."

"What's the plan?" Claire asked as she climbed into her bunk compartment looking for her flashlight. Waiting scared her but doing something about it gave her a new since of purpose!

"Crew members come with me and you and Dolph stay here and manually block the hatches from the inside!"

"We are all at risk here and I for one am not staying behind!" Claire said with a stern expression.

"Me neither!" Dolph chimed in.

"All right," Foster conceded, "but stay close in a single file as we move through the modules. Moser and I will take the lead. Dolph, you and Claire bring up the rear. If there is any trouble developing ahead of you, find cover fast or retreat to the hotel module!"

Suddenly, a rumble could be heard and felt throughout the space station coming from the direction of the ISS emergency escape vehicle.

"Well, there goes three less adversaries we have to worry about. Someone just launched our only escape vehicle," Moser said sarcastically.

"You are such an optimist," Foster said, mimicking Moser's sarcasm.

"I thought all the electronics were fried by the pulse," Dolph said.

"The escape vehicle was designed to be the most shielded part of the International Space Station for just such occasions," Jamila said. "I wonder to what extent the Chinese have prepared for this; how many astronauts can escape from their space station?"

"Whatever we are going to do, we better do quickly," Tokugawa said, "or we will end up stranded here with no life support and we'll freeze to death."

"Let's move out," Foster said, and they began slithering quickly through the modules as if swimming through a deep ocean shipwreck towards the Chinese docking station with the ISS. When they arrived, they bunched up around the closed portal.

"With electronics down, everything will have to be manually operated. This will be the trickiest part of the whole operation since any noise could alert the Chinese to our presence. Moser and I will very slowly unlock the ISS hatch, then Tokugawa, you and Dolph will move forward and unlock the Chinese station hatch. While you are doing that, I want Jamila and Claire to get on either side of me and prepare to swing me into the Chinese compartment as soon as their door swings open."

Claire and Jamila looked at him with puzzled looks on their faces, then turned their heads towards each other. "What?" they whispered in unison.

"I will position myself floating and headfirst at a 90-degree angle in front of the door. You each position yourselves on opposite sides of me and grab my arm and leg. As soon as the door opens fully, you sling my body through it. The micro-gravity will allow me to continue forward and I will overpower the first person I come near. Then do the same for Moser. Tokugawa and Dolph can then pull in behind us on their own power. Jamila, you and Claire could follow us, assuming we are not all dead, in which case, I would recommend you both go back to the hotel module. Pretend you were not a party to this foolish venture."

The operation proceeded with few surprises. The first hatch was well oiled and silently slid open. The hatch attached to the Chinese Space Station was another matter. It appeared frozen. They all waited nervously while Moser went to fetch a large wrench. As they pulled hard on the first turn, the noisy squeaks from the hatch were drowned out by a loud rumble coming from the CSS.

"What's that?" Tokugawa whispered from his position by the hatch.

"It sounds like an escape pod launch," Jamila said. "Are they abandoning the ship?"

As she said this, another rumble sounded. "Quickly, turn the wrench," Foster ordered. And so, the hatch was opened masked by the noise from the occasional launch of small escape pods from the CSS.

As the door swung open, Claire and Jamila flung Foster through it and turned to Moser next. Tokugawa and Dolph then disappeared through the hatch. Claire leaned in and peered through the hatch opening where a chaotic scene was unfolding. There was total pandemonium on the Chinese Space Station as the fight for control of the craft was intense.

Claire turned to Jamila and smiled, raising her heavy flashlight, and said, "Let's join the party!" They both swung into the CSS.

The Gannicun space craft was able to dock with the International Space Station thanks to modifications made at the Kennedy Space Center. Seediq and his legionaries, used to fighting in the close quarters of the underground tunnels on Gannicus, led the way into the ISS followed by Bodhidharma and Trueman. They had been given a quick lesson on what to expect but moving in the very low gravity of the ISS was something that they could not train for. They heard the noise of fighting and followed it quickly to the entrance of the Chinese Space Station.

249

Seediq turned back to his legionaries and gave them the same look he had back in the breach tunnel so many years before. "*All in*," he yelled. They roared into the CSS, screaming and yelling at the top of their lungs and over-powered the remaining Chinese space crew members in a matter of minutes.

The NASA space technicians subsequently moved in and were able to quickly replace the essential elements of life support and propulsion to the stations and the whole tenor and direction of the war on the Earth changed at that moment.

Bodhidharma's United Nations Space Forces were now in control of an orbiting platform of atomic weapons that could strike at any battlefield around the globe. This was enough to quickly enforce a cease fire among the warring parties, followed by the withdrawal of all armed forces back to their countries' boundaries before the hostilities began.

Chapter 38

Hope Springs

Faith Dyer sat strapped into her secured side wall seat on the torpedo like space transport vessel Valerian. She is finally returning to Earth in December in the year of our Lord 2037, exactly 377 years after she left unconscious and frozen in a cryogen tube.

The journey to the stable rift in the multiverse, discovered by the Sentinel angel in the remote solar system known as Epictetus was fast and smooth, nearly traveling at the speed of light from Gannicus. Once in the distant solar system, they slowed and entered the ice cloud of the 5th planet. A clear rift was open beneath layers of gaseous clouds.

Faith gripped the hand of Rambahadur, the head of her Gurkha personal guard, as they entered the rough and tumble turbulence of the rift tunnel. Their seat straps strained up, down and sideways. Rambahadur had been protecting her since she first awoke in the Mantis Citadel.

"Do not fear my lady," Rambahadur said, "Trueman, Seediq, and Bodhidharma have all successfully made this journey before us with no loss of life. Bodhidharma would never risk losing you. He has made that very clear to me many times!"

"Thank you Rambahadur," Faith replied. "I always feel safe with you and your Gurkha cohort protecting me."

They exited the slipstream outside Earth's solar system and the path smoothed again. Several hours later the flyer approached the Kennedy Space Center and circled, eventually coming to rest next to the other four torpedo-like Gannicun space vessels already parked there.

A huge crowd had gathered near the flyers in anticipation of the arrival of this new spaceship. It was made public that the craft was coming with a delegation from a distant galaxy. It was as if they were expecting aliens with bulbous heads to exit the spaceship.

Bodhidharma, Trueman, and General Clark stood together at the head of two columns: the Gannicun Gurkha and Roman cohorts and the Florida National Guard Special Forces unit. The warriors stood at attention with their rifles held in front. They formed lines to the flyer exit door in preparation for a formal welcome of Faith Dyer. They all wore patchy blue/black camouflage uniforms.

The leadership of the western powers were almost entirely obliterated by the surprise Russian and Chinese nuclear attacks, including Washington, New York, London, and the European Union headquarters in Brussels. Bodhidharma was able to convince what remained of the regional leaders of the western powers that there had indeed been a secret United Nations Space Force and that this space force should be put in control of Earth's space to prevent any further wars. Secret preparations for the colonization of the moon and application for protection status with the Guild was already underway with the assistance of the Sentinel angel.

General Clark was one of the few military leaders who knew what was truly going on with the Mantis infiltration of Earth. He had touched the large scaly insects. After being briefed by Bodhidharma and watching his swift action to take over the Chinese space station and end the war, Clark was onboard with his plan to maintain the peace.

Bodhidharma planted rumors that an alliance had been made with the distant planet and a delegation was arriving. He was deliberately vague about their origins, other than that they were human. Introducing a potential war with the Mantis Empire along with Romans, Gurkhas, and a several thousand-year-old life span was certainly too much for the people of Earth to fathom, at least until the protective status with the Guild was assured.

The exit door to the flyer rose and Faith Dyer stood in the entrance dressed simply but formally in a traditional Quaker style dark blue blouse, jacket, and gray skirt. Instead of a headscarf, a formal white whittle covered her head, but she still allowed her thick braided red hair to fall down her back to her waist.

The crowd murmured loudly as she stepped off the flyer onto a red carpet. She was followed by her Gurkha guards in full regalia including the long-curved Gurkha knife secured in a red waist sash. The cohort sported state of the art Mantis space rifles held at the ready close to their chest. The rifles used electromagnetic and sound wave pulses to disrupt the space around an enemy either disabling them or killing them depending on the rifle settings. A multicolored baffle set the weapon apart from anything seen on Earth.

As Faith reached the end of the red carpet, Bodhidharma leaned forward for a formal embrace with only cheeks touching. "There is much to bring you up to date on, so we must be careful not to reveal too much about ourselves now."

"Faithful Bodhidharma, I will bridle my tongue until you declare what news these times reveal to us. Have no fear - my future husband!" Faith responded. She nodded affectionately to Trueman and winked, then shook hands with Seediq.

Bodhidharma smiled warmly and turned, raising his arm to show her the way to their accommodations.

A great crowd gathered at the Kennedy Space Center to celebrate the victories won in Florida and around the world. They had pushed back the overreach of the Russian and Chinese alliance which would have divided up the Earth into godless, mind-controlled command economies with no civil rights, democracy, or interest in the weakest among us. The Mantis were the actual puppeteers orchestrating the play, tragic scenes creating worldwide chaos, which only benefited the Mantis Empire in the long run.

Trueman, Seediq, General Clark, General Sator, and recently promoted Colonel Conner watched from the ranks of the many military groups assembled. Governors from various southeastern states, which had sent National Guard and Army Reserve units to Florida to brunt the Chinese attack, spoke of their hopes for the future.

The Chinese invaders had outflanked the initial Florida National Guard defenders at the I-4 interchange forcing them to retreat back to positions east of the St. John's River. They blew up the bridges across the river, temporarily halting the Chinese advance. It was at that point that reinforcements arrived from the nearest southern states: Georgia, South Carolina, Alabama, and Mississippi. This trapped the Chinese in the sparsely populated area between the river and Orlando.

A stalemate ensured and the general leading the Chinese invasion force was given an ultimatum, unconditional surrender or annihilation with tactical nuclear weapons from the Space Station. When their intelligence confirmed the takeover of the space station by the UN Space Forces, the Chinese stood down and surrendered. Once disarmed, they were forced back to their ships in Tampa Bay for a quick departure to their homeland.

Chapter 39

Echoes of Boston Common

With the ceremonies over, a much anticipated and secret surprise journey took front and center in the minds of Bodhidharma and the Sentinel angel.

The rift flyer descended onto Boston Common and landed hidden behind a row of elm trees near Beacon Street. A foggy shadowy dawn reduced visibility as the overcast sky and cold winds swirled.

"Come with me now Faith and I will show you the surprise I have been keeping." *We have been keeping*, the Sentinel angel spoke into Bodhidharma's mind. "We have been keeping," Bodhidharma corrected himself with a wry smile which Faith knowing returned.

I wonder the gist of that conversation, Faith thought. She looked out over the landscape, barely able to make out the Freedom Trail on the other side of the stand of elm trees which showed the way to the Massachusetts state capitol building. They walked the short distance flanked by an unseen cohort of bodyguards.

Crossing the mostly empty, deserted Beacon Street, Bodhidharma led Faith over to the east side of the capital building and there it was - the statue of Mary Dyer, her martyred mother. It sat on a large square stone block with the following inscriptions chipped into its face:

MARY DYER

QUAKER

WITNESS FOR RELIGIOUS FREEDOM

HANGED ON BOSTON COMMON 1660

"MY LIFE NOT AVAILETH ME IN COMPARISON TO THE LIBERTY OF THE TRUTH"

"The people remember her after all these years," Faith said with tears in her eyes.

"They do," Bodhidharma replied as he held her in his arms. "They remember her, your mother, and she inspires new generations," he whispered.

Through her tear-filled eyes, Faith caught a glimpse of a little girl peering around the stone block base of the statue. She wore a plain gray head covering like the ones Faith used to wear as a child, as was the dress which fell to the ground, a simple Quaker style. She seemed very familiar.

Faith turned, bent down, and said to her, "Sweetheart, are you lost child?" Bodhidharma stood staring ahead as if in an unhearing trance. The little girl disappeared around the back

257

of the stone block without an answer to her question and Faith followed her. She was concerned the little girl was a lost homeless orphan, a common occurrence during the colonial times Faith grew up in.

Bodhidharma strained against the force holding him. His vision was blurred as if he was looking through a thick murky glass window. *What is happening*, he spoke into his mind at the Sentinel angel.

Be calm, the Sentinel responded, *the holy spirit is here and working, there is nothing to fear.*

"Are you lost child?" Faith asked again after catching up to the little girl behind the stone block.

"No, I am found, among the elect, as are you!" her smile was angelic, as she looked up at Faith. She placed her palm against the stone and a door opened. A bright, nearly blinding light shown out of a room revealed inside the stone platform.

"Come and see where I live," the child said as she stepped into the room.

Faith followed her. She could not tell where the light came from, it was just part of the room, illuminating everything. She recognized the place as the room she grew up in, the simple room she and her sisters shared in the 17th century Rhode Island colony.

The little girl reached into a pocket sown into her skirt and pulled out three gold coins holding them up in the palm of her hand for Faith to take.

"Here, have these gold coins, for you and the road ahead."

Faith reached out, curious, and took the mysterious coins and suddenly found herself kneeling in front of her mother Mary.

She felt her mother's calming hand as she stroked her head. "Stand child," she said softly.

Faith stood facing her mother, staring into her brown eyes. She was just as she remembered her on the day of her return from England, a Quaker missionary, full of energy and vision, ready for the arduous journey ahead. They stared into each other's eyes, relishing the moment. Each reached out at the same time, slowly and gently touching the other's cheek.

"You have acquitted yourself well, my daughter," Mary finally said.

"I have tried to be faithful to you and the Way," Faith replied.

"You have discovered many triumphs as it often is with the young and faithful. The road ahead will be perilous. You must endeavor to persevere. Take this gift of the gold coins and place them in this medallion."

Mary opened a box sitting on a side table and pulled out a beautiful silver medallion attached to a long chain. Faith studied it for a moment and marveled at the intricate design.

"It's called the Seed of Life medallion." Mary pulled the chain over Faith's head and turned the medallion over on its back side. "The coins go into the medallion thus." She assisted Faith with the placement of the three coins into three recesses behind the medallion. "Wear this at all times when going forth. It is tuned to you for your protection. You will learn how to use it."

Faith, holding the medallion, noticed the geometric form of the Seed of Life begin to move, then warm in her hands. She began tingling from the energy emanating from it.

Faith awoke to Bodhidharma's alarming call, "Faith, Faith, where are you!"

"Here," she yelled from the rear of the statue, coming back to her earthly senses. She looked around and saw no special lighted room or Quaker child, just the back of the stone block in front of her.

"I'm here!" She placed the strange medallion with its Seed of Life insignia underneath her clothing, out of sight, unsure whether to be comforted by it, or alarmed by its presence. The gift from her martyred mother was warm against her bosom.

"I must send you back to Gannicus!" Bodhidharma said as he and Faith stood beside the black rift flyer at the Kennedy Space Center.

"I had looked forward to our marriage now that Trueman is full grown, but the guild has refused to grant protectorate status to Earth because the Mantis are not actively involving themselves here but are using human surrogates. I must quickly establish permanent colonies on the moon and Mars so that we can apply for protection as a Secondary space faring species."

"I would much rather stay here with you and Trueman," Faith pleaded.

"I can't guarantee your safety here. I don't know how long this truce will hold. There are too many unknown factions working. Besides, Trueman, Seediq, and I will be off world in space most of the time."

"I understand," Faith said as she reached up and touched Bodhi's cheek. "We can delay our bonding for a while longer." For just a moment, the coal black eyes of Bodhidharma shifted to the sky-blue color of the Sentinel's eyes and then back. They kissed and held each other close, unsure when they would be able to marry and settle down.

"The Lord has hidden from me what lyeth ahead for us, and so, for better or worse, we strive to do His will," Faith said sadly and turned to enter the rift flyer.

"Farewell my love," Bodhidharma said. "I will see you back on Gannicus as soon as we have established our bases in space and secured the peace here on Earth!

Chapter 40

The Prophetess

Resurrection City, Gannicus 2038 A.D.

Mary Dyer stood under the huge white oak tree on Shelter Island in the colony of Rhode Island. Native Manhanset Indians, who were indentured by their chiefs, and black slaves imported from the island of Barbados to work the tobacco fields, sat in a circle around her. Thirteen-year old Faith Dyer knelt beside her mother lovingly clutching her skirt. She looked up, as her mother raised her hands to the heavens and spoke.

"In the beginning was the Word, and the Word was with God, and the Word was God. The same was in the beginning with God. In Him was life and the light shineth in darkness - and the darkness comprehended it not."

The group fell silent to absorb and contemplate the revelation, as was the Quaker custom, listening for the voice and inspiration of the Creator. Little Faith sensed movement in the distance. She raised her small frame to see over the seated worshipers, just making out a band of soldiers

262

approaching with muskets and halberds through the woods.
She threw her arms around her mother's waist pulling her
tight just as a hangman's rope quickly descended from the
tree. The noose secured itself around Mary's neck, swift as
the strike of a coiled snake, and she was jerked out of Faith's
grasp, disappearing into the cavernous leafy branches of the
oak tree!

Faith screamed, "Take me with you mother, don't leave
me!" She suddenly awoke in a sweat, her sheets twisted
around her in her narrow bed on Gannicus. The dream,
terrible nightmare that it was, finally convinced her of what
she must do. She lay still, taking in the silence, the quiet …
letting it slowly calm her.

She knew that a storm was coming, one that only the
spirit could see her through. This would be a different storm
from the one that raised her up into the metal spaceship. The
question remained whether she would live through this one
or die the martyr's death like her mother. She savored the
silence, the calm before the storm she knew was coming.

Faith stepped boldly, head upright, and made her way to the
Allsop tree. She was followed by her two companions,
women from Earth, sisters who had ascended into the metal
trap with her and had survived the Mantis experiments.
They were now devoted followers of the Way.

Faith stood facing South in front of the tall lone tree atop
a small hill at the center of the Commons in Resurrection
City. The tree was the oldest living thing on Gannicus. It
represented perseverance. It had a circumference of 30 feet
and a trunk that twisted as it rose, with a bark that looked as
old and worn as the tree itself. A few leaves could be seen

sprouting from the ends of its short stocky branches, indicating that it was still alive after nearly a thousand years. To the people, it was a sacred tree.

The survivors of the genocidal war the Mantis waged against the Roman population on Gannicus gravitated to the park at the end of the day to relax and take in the last rays of the sun, something they were unable to do living under-ground for so many years. The park was near full of people in small groups scattered about.

Faith raised her hands to the heavens and shouted in the language of Gannicus, "I am the daughter of a martyr!"

Silence for a moment, then "hear hear," could be heard from those closest to her. Roman Gannicuns were no strangers to martyrdom since their ancestors, elders, parents, brothers, and sisters during the 100-year's war, all gave themselves up to keep their civilization alive. All had sacrificed to keep the young among them alive to continue the fight. Even so, they lost their history and their spiritual leaders as fewer and fewer were left with the knowledge to pass on their traditions. The massive destruction of most of the Valerian continent's surface left few known records.

Faith turned and stepped 45 degrees and stood in front of the tree facing West. "I am the daughter of a martyr. I would have followed my mother to the grave if she had not forbidden it!"

Again, more shouts of "Hear Hear," as some stood and moved closer. They recognized her as the famous foreign woman everyone was talking about. Curiosity pulled them closer to the sacred tree.

"My mother crossed the ocean to discover the truth and returned to a foreign land to reveal it, but she was hung from a tree like this one because she would not be silent."

"Hear Hear, Hear Hear," the shouts increased as the crowds grew closer. The other Christian women who had followed Faith to the Commons picked up the chorus with their own shouts of "Praise God" and "Hallelujah," in their own language. This brought even more curious stares and the crowd swelled until several hundred stood around the tree.

Faith moved another 45 degrees to face North, raising her hands once again. "I am the daughter of a martyr," she paused, "my mother passed the truth to me and I have crossed the universe to bring this knowledge of truth to you, even if I am to be martyred for it."

More, even louder shouts continued, interspersed with hallelujahs splitting the air. She moved slowly to face the East. All of those on the Commons that day were following her every move now.

"I am the daughter of a martyr. You will know the truth, and the truth will set you free!"

The roar from the crowd rose with shouts of praise and encouragement. As it began to subside, one loud voice shouted, "The Prophetess!" All went silent as it sank in.

Gannicus had many prophets during their Renaissance before the genocidal war with the insects. This was well known - but none survived - nor did their knowledge. A yearning among the people rose and shouts of "Reveal, Reveal," could be heard among them.

Faith fell silent for the inspiration which was not long in coming. She started at the beginning. "God created the heavens and Gannicus ..."

The spirit moved among the people, beginning with the weeping of the foreign women who were more sensitive to its voice. The wave of light spread to the Gannicuns, who had not wept for so long due to the needs of their stoic battle with the insects.

"God created humankind in his image, in this image of the Eternal Being he created them. Know this, the spark of his light is inside every one of us!" She waited to let that sink in, then continued, "and the Creator saw everything he had made, and behold, it was good."

More shouts of acclimation could be heard as several hundred were added to the faithful that day. A tradition was born as the sunlight dimmed under the Allsop tree, on the Commons of Resurrection City. A prophetess had returned to Gannicus!

In a second story building adjacent to the Commons, two Russian mercenary intelligence agents watched closely and meticulously recorded these events. They followed with keen interest Faith's every move as she left the Commons and moved back into the busy city proper. Ground operatives stood calmly inconspicuous as they monitored the dusty road entrances waiting for Intel instructions.

"She walked past Oglethorpe Avenue and is taking the side street called Carfax Close," a field operative reported to Intel.

"Everyone come together at the intersection of Carfax Close and Sharpe Street. Commence engagement there!" barked the Intel agent.

Faith moved slowly through the thick crowd surrounded by her faithful expatriates and a half cohort of Gurkha guards disguised in long robes as followers of the Way. Their weapons were hidden under their robes but close at hand in case of trouble. The medallion hanging near her heart beneath her robe began to heat up. She clutched it with both hands as she continued to move forward.

A strong sense of evil, strands of death coming together and coalescing at the intersection ahead of her, began to overwhelm her senses. On the outside it appeared she was in an attitude of prayer, head bowed slightly as she tried to fathom the meaning of the sudden coming to life of her mother's gift, the medallion, and the knowledge of imminent danger ahead. She felt the intensity of the moment heighten as they approached the Sharpe Street intersection. She looked up ahead but saw nothing unusual except the mingling crowds increasing significantly as the two roads intersected.

I fear not death, for I was there once before, she reasoned, *but I cannot abide harm to those around me!*

She motioned with her hand at her side, waving it back and forth, a secret signal to Rambahadur, the head of her Gurkha personal guard, to move up next to her. He slowly moved up beside her and as he did, she reached up and placed her hand on his shoulder.

"Deliverance!" she shouted, clutching the medallion tightly, as she and the Russian mercenaries arrived at the intersection at the same time.

The metal casing of the medallion seemed to fuse with her body as she and Rambahadur were taken up in a swirl of wind and light, disappearing out of sight, and reappearing moments later far away and high above Resurrection City in a rocky mountain meadow. Several small herds of sheep and goats grazed undisturbed around them in a sparsely grassed field. She looked down at the distant city below with lights turning on to forestall the twilight gloom. Faith relaxed as her medallion began cooling off.

"She seems to have disappeared into the crowd. We cannot locate her," a field operative nervously reported to Intel.

"Keep looking for her, she can't have gone far," Intel replied.

Even though Resurrection City was covered in twilight, Faith could still see the sun on the far horizon from her position on the sloping high mountain meadow. The sun's rays were beaming, stretching above and behind her.

She turned, and her eyes fell on the distant snow-capped mountains. Some were high enough to be hidden by colorful cloud covers reflecting red, yellow and bright purple hues interspersed with smoky greys in shadow. The exposed rocky mountainsides, interspersed with patches of stunted bristlecone pine trees, glowed reddish gold in the direct sun light.

Somehow through her medallion's pull, she felt drawn up into those mountains. She pulled out the medallion and looked on it. The Seed of Life symbol was swirling, moving within itself.

She turned to Rambahadur and brushed back the hood of her robe. He did the same to his hood. They stood silent for a few moments on the quiet mountainside meadow looking down on Resurrection City. Rambahadur, protecting and looking after Faith as the head of her personal guard since she was resurrected from the dead at the Citadel, was becoming used to these silent moments that she reveled in.

Faith did not want a personal bodyguard, much less a half cohort, but Bodhidharma insisted on it, explaining it this way; *"My enemies will try to get to me by bringing terror and blackmail to you. I could not live with myself if I allowed that to happen!"*

"Rambahadur," she finally said, "I want you to return to Resurrection City and get a message to Bodhidharma and Trueman on Earth that I am safe and will return soon."

Rambahadur nodded his understanding. "Royal Highness, please don't be gone long. Your people will mourn your loss and Bodhidharma will surely punish me for letting you go."

Faith slowly turned, lifting her eyes, and fixing them on the majestic mountains in front of her. As she did so, a deep tree lined ravine opened between the giant rocky crags. It was lit up in the same bright colors she had seen when she died, and her spirit left her body at the Mantis's Citadel - the colors of heaven.

"Do you see that tree lined entrance to heaven up ahead Rambahadur?"

"Yes, I see it my lady, but I don't believe my eyes!"

"Tell Bodhidharma what has happened today and what you have clearly witnessed in Resurrection City and on this mountain. Tell him the life he promised to help me achieve has begun: to carry on my mother's legacy, to stand up in assembly and to be a bold witness to the people. Like Enoch of old Earth, I am being invited into heaven, not to die but to live more fully. I will return and bring my witness back to Gannicus, to Earth, and to wherever humankind dwells!"

269

"May you walk with the Creator and return to us quickly!" Rambahadur replied, clearly concerned.

"I will count on Bodhidharma's blessings for my friends, especially for you Rambahadur, the leader of my cohort!"

Faith, focusing now on the brightly lit ravine, slowly and deliberately walked toward it. Just as she entered the heavenly space she whispered, *"By the grace of God, go I,"* and the ravine closed on itself. The sun set below the horizon and the rays of light disappeared from the mountainside.

Rambahadur, watching in silence from the grassy meadow with tears in his eyes, turned and began the long journey back to Resurrection City.

Faith heard the sound of wind swirling behind her as the heavenly portal closed, but her eyes were fixed on the vivid, pristine, natural landscape in front of her.

An emerald, green meadow dotted with clumps of multicolored wildflowers seemed to flow in front of her, undulating down to a shiny blue lake. The lake water was like a mirror reflecting the blue sky above it. On the far side of the lake she saw a high cliff with a beautiful waterfall cascading down its sheer rock walls.

Above the waterfall a ball of bright light began to form, expanding as it came over the lake toward Faith. The light was so intense it appeared to reflect off the lake and the sky at the same time. There was no fear in her, only anticipation, as she watched the bright ball approaching. The light began to coalesce, taking form as it settled on the meadow, transforming into a large angel wearing a white tunic. The angel's hair was like Jason's golden fleece at Colchis, sparkling as it flowed down the back of his tunic.

"Welcome to Eden, Faith Dyer!" the angel announced.

Epilogue

The veil lifted and I see clearly now! All of creation opened to me, to the state Adam was in before he fell. I was shown how all things have their names, according to their nature and purpose. Wonderful depths lay open to me beyond what I can describe by words - to know the mystery of faith and the hidden unity in the Eternal Being. My soul now breaths for the pure effects of the light of God seeded in my heart and experiencing the growth and spreading of it!

The Journal of Faith Dyer

Author's Notes

It's hard to imagine the level of persecution taking place during the Reformation, the religious revolution that took place in the Western Christian church in the 16th century. Many examples are memorialized in Foxe's Book of Martyrs. However, the persecution of the early Quaker movement (also called the Society of Friends) that arose in the mid-17th century by the political establishment and their protestant allies was severe and not as widely known.

Early Quakerism rejected not only the Catholic but also many of the Protestant theological interpretations. They rejected the need for priests and pastors alike given the belief that every human being has the inner light of God within them. Anyone could stand up and speak in meeting assemblies when prompted by God, including women, who made up 45% of the early Quaker movement. All were considered spiritually equal and part of the "the priesthood of all believers." By 1680, Quaker numbers rose to about 80,000 in England and the American colonies with limited fixed leadership or spiritual hierarchy. Quakers met to worship almost anywhere, often in barns, along the roadside or in open fields or orchards with local groups making decisions for themselves.

It was this movement that Mary Dyer joined and trained in England under George Fox and other well-known Quaker preachers, then returned to America as a Quaker missionary and eventual martyrdom at the hands of the Puritan leaders of the Massachusetts Bay Colony.

Mary Dyer is a real historic figure and a true heroine!
She is memorialized at the Massachusetts state capitol,
24 Beacon St., Boston, MA

Photo credit: Peter H. Dreyer slide collection #9800.007
City of Boston Archives, Boston

Unfortunately, persecution of Christians and other religious
groups around the world is on the rise in the 21st Century.
The mission of the Voice of the Martyrs offers practical and
spiritual help to persecuted Christians and their families.

Thanks so much for reading Book I, Earth Below Us! Please post a book review -it helps- on the Amazon book page: earthbelowus.com

Book II of the Spirit Life Series, Heaven Above Us, continues the adventure of Faith Dyer, her family, fellow compatriots, and new allies to assist her!

Regards,
Richard
earthbelowus2@gmail.com

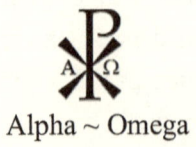

Alpha ~ Omega

www.ingramcontent.com/pod-product-compliance
Lightning Source LLC
Chambersburg PA
CBHW021952170626
46808CB00001B/129